“It’ll j
darling…

… *Morcheck said, trying to hold back his own tears. But he knew—as well as she knew—that she was really sick.*

—from “The Perfect Woman.”

ABOUT ROBERT SHECKLEY…

Born in Brooklyn New York 1928 Robert Sheckley hitchhiked across America to California shortly after his High School Graduation. After a myriad of menial jobs and an Army stint in Korea he sold his first story to “Imagination.” He gained quick notoriety as writer, publisher and screenwriter in the 50’s and 60’s, often writing satiric columns for the newly established “Playboy.” He continued writing and publishing until he passed away in 2005. Presented here in paperback is a small sample of his fine works…

TABLE OF CONTENTS

MASTERS OF SCIENCE FICTION

Volume 3

ROBERT SHECKLEY: "THE PERFECT WOMAN" and other stories

ARMCHAIR FICTION & MUSIC
PO Box 4369, Medford, Oregon 97504

The original text of these stories first appeared in *Imagination, Science Fiction Adventures, Future Science Fiction, Galaxy, Fantastic, Space Science Fiction and Amazing Stories.*

Cover suggests a scene from *The Perfect Woman*

For more information about Armchair Books and products, visit our website at…

www.armchairfiction.com

Or email us at…

armchairfiction@yahoo.com

Seventh Victim

The most dangerous game, said one writer, is Man. But there is another still more deadly.

STANTON Frelaine sat at his desk, trying to look as busy as an executive should at nine-thirty in the morning. It was impossible. He couldn't concentrate on the advertisement he had written the previous night, couldn't think about business. All he could do was wait until the mail came.

He had been waiting for his notification for two weeks now. The government was behind schedule, as usual.

The glass door of his office was marked *Morger and Frelaine, Clothiers.* It opened, and E. J. Morger walked in, limping slightly from his old gunshot wound. His shoulders were bent; but at the age of seventy-three, he wasn't worrying too much about his posture.

"Well, Stan?" Morger asked. "What about that ad?"

Frelaine had joined Morger sixteen years ago, when he was twenty-seven. Together they had built Protec-Clothes into a million-dollar concern.

"I suppose you can run it," Frelaine said, handing the slip of, paper to Morger. If only the mail would come earlier, he thought.

"'Do you own a Protec-Suit?'" Morger read aloud, holding the paper close to his eyes. "'The finest tailoring in the world has gone into Morger and Frelaine's Protec-Suit, to make it the leader in men's fashions.'"

Morger cleared his throat and glanced at Frelaine. He smiled and read on.

"'Protec-Suit is the safest as well as the smartest. Every Protec-Suit comes with special built-in gun pocket, guaranteed not to bulge. No one will know you are carrying a gun—except you. The gun pocket is exceptionally easy to get at, permitting fast, unhindered draw. Choice of hip or breast pocket.' Very nice," Morger commented.

Frelaine nodded morosely.

"'The Protec-Suit Special has the fling-out gun pocket, the greatest modern advance in personal protection. A touch of the concealed button throws the gun into your hand, cocked, safeties off. Why not drop into the Protec-Store nearest you? Why not be *safe*?'"

"That's fine," Morger said. "That's a very nice, dignified ad." He thought for a moment, fingering his white mustache. "Shouldn't you mention that Protec-Suits come in a variety of styles, single and double-breasted, one and two button rolls, deep and shallow flares?"

"Right. I forgot."

FRELAINE took back the sheet and jotted a note on the edge of it. Then he stood up, smoothing his jacket over his prominent stomach. Frelaine was forty-three, a little overweight, a little bald on top. He was an amiable-looking man with cold eyes.

"Relax," Morger said. "It'll come in today's mail."

Frelaine forced himself to smile. He felt like pacing the floor, but instead sat on the edge of the desk.

"You'd think it was my first kill," he said, with a deprecating smile.

"I know how it is," Morger said. "Before I hung up my gun, I couldn't sleep for a month, waiting for a notification. I know."

The two men waited. Just as the silence was becoming unbearable, the door opened. A clerk walked in and deposited the mail on Frelaine's desk.

Frelaine swung around and gathered up the letters. He thumbed through them rapidly and found what he had been waiting for—the long white envelope from ECB, with the official government seal on it.

"That's it!" Frelaine said, and broke into a grin. "That's the baby!"

"Fine." Morger eyed the envelope with interest, but didn't ask Frelaine to open it. It would be a breach of etiquette, as well as a violation in the eyes of the law. No one was supposed to know a Victim's name except his Hunter. "Have a good hunt."

"I expect to," Frelaine replied confidently. His desk was in order—had been for a week. He picked up his briefcase.

"A good kill will do you a world of good," Morger said, putting his hand lightly on Frelaine's padded shoulder. "You've been keyed up."

"I know." Frelaine grinned again and shook Morger's hand.

"Wish I was a kid again," Morger said, glancing down

at his crippled leg with wryly-humorous eyes. "Makes me want to pick up a gun again."

The old man had been quite a Hunter in his day. Ten successful hunts had qualified him for the exclusive Tens Club. And, of course, for each hunt Morger had had to act as Victim, so he had twenty kills to his credit.

"I sure hope my Victim isn't anyone like you," Frelaine said, half in jest.

"Don't worry about it. What number will this be?"

"The seventh."

"Lucky seven. Go to it," Morger said. "We'll get you into the Tens yet."

Frelaine waved his hand and started out the door.

"Just don't get careless," warned Morger. "All it takes is a single slip and I'll need a new partner. If you don't mind, I like the one I've got now."

"I'll be careful," Frelaine promised.

INSTEAD of taking a bus, Frelaine walked to his apartment. He wanted time to cool off. There was no sense in acting like a kid on his first kill.

As he walked, Frelaine kept his eyes strictly to the front. Staring at anyone was practically asking for a bullet, if the man happened to be serving as Victim. Some Victims shot if you just glanced at them. Nervous fellows. Frelaine prudently looked above the heads of the people he passed.

Ahead of him was a huge billboard, offering J. F. O'Donovan's services to the public.

"Victims!" the sign proclaimed in huge red letters. "Why take chances? Use an O'Donovan accredited Spotter. Let us locate your assigned killer. Pay *after* you get him!"

The sign reminded Frelaine. He would call Morrow as soon as he reached his apartment.

He crossed the street, quickening his stride. He could hardly wait to get home now, to open the envelope and discover who his victim was. Would he be clever or stupid? Rich, like Frelaine's fourth Victim, or poor, like the first and second? Would he have an organized Spotter service, or try to go it on his own?

The excitement of the chase was wonderful; coursing through his veins, quickening his heartbeat. From a block or so away, he heard gunfire. Two quick shots, and then a final one.

Somebody got his man, Frelaine thought. Good for him.

It was a superb feeling, he told himself. He was *alive* again.

AT his one-room apartment, the first thing Frelaine did was call Ed Morrow, his spotter. The man worked as a garage attendant between calls.

"Hello, Ed? Frelaine."

"Oh, hi, Mr. Frelaine." He could see the man's thin, grease stained face, grinning flat-lipped at the telephone.

"I'm going out on one, Ed."

"Good luck, Mr. Frelaine," Ed Morrow said. "I suppose you'll want me to stand by?"

"That's right. I don't expect to be gone more than a week or two. I'll probably get my notification of Victim Status within three months of the kill."

"I'll be standing by. Good hunting, Mr. Frelaine."

"Thanks. So long." He hung up. It was a wise safety

measure to reserve a first-class spotter. After his kill, it would be Frelaine's turn as Victim. Then, once again, Ed Morrow would be his life insurance.

And what a marvelous spotter Morrow was! Uneducated—stupid, really. But what an eye for people! Morrow was a natural. His pale eyes could tell an out-of-towner at a glance. He was diabolically clever at rigging an ambush. An indispensable man.

Frelaine took out the envelope, chuckling to himself, remembering some of the tricks Morrow had turned for the Hunters. Still smiling, he glanced at the data inside the envelope.

Janet-Marie Patzig.

His Victim was a female!

Frelaine stood up and paced for a few moments. Then he read the letter again. Janet-Marie Patzig. No mistake. A girl. Three photographs were enclosed, her address, and the usual descriptive data.

Frelaine frowned. He had never killed a female.

He hesitated for a moment, then picked up the telephone and dialed.

"Emotional Catharsis Bureau, Information Section," a man's voice answered.

"Say, look," Frelaine said. "I just got my notification and I pulled a girl. Is that in order?" He gave the clerk the girl's name.

"It's all in order, sir," the clerk replied after a minute of checking micro-files. "The girl registered with the board under her own free will. The law says she has the same rights and privileges as a man."

"Could you tell me how many kills she has?"

"I'm sorry, sir. The only information you're allowed

is the victim's legal status and the descriptive data you have received."

"I see." Frelaine paused. "Could I draw another?"

"You can refuse the hunt, of course. That is your legal right. But you will not be allowed another Victim until you have served. Do you wish to refuse?"

"Oh, no," Frelaine said hastily. "I was just wondering. Thank you."

HE hung up and sat down in his largest armchair, loosening his belt. This required some thought.

Damn women, he grumbled to himself, always trying to horn in on a man's game. Why can't they stay home?

But they were free citizens, he reminded himself. Still, it just didn't seem *feminine*.

He knew that, historically speaking, the Emotional Catharsis Board had been established for men and men only. The board had been formed at the end of the fourth world war—or sixth, as some historians counted it.

At that time there had been a driving need for permanent, lasting peace. The reason was practical, as were the men who engineered it.

Simply—annihilation was just around the corner.

In the world wars, weapons increased in magnitude, efficiency and exterminating power. Soldiers became accustomed to them, less and less reluctant to use them.

But the saturation point had been reached. Another war would truly be the war to end all wars. There would be no one left to start another.

So this peace *had* to last for all time, but the men who engineered it were practical. They recognized the tensions and dislocations still present, the cauldrons in which wars are brewed. They asked themselves why peace had never lasted in the past.

"Because men like to fight," was their answer.

"Oh, no!" screamed the idealists.

But the men who engineered the peace were forced to postulate, regretfully, the presence of a need for violence in a large percentage of mankind.

Men aren't angels. They aren't fiends, either. They are just very human beings, with a high degree of combativeness.

With the scientific knowledge and the power they had at that moment, the practical men could have gone a long way toward breeding this trait out of the race. Many thought this was the answer.

The practical men didn't. They recognized the validity of competition, love of battle, strength in the face of overwhelming odds. These, they felt, were admirable traits for a race, and insurance toward its perpetuity. Without them, the race would be bound to retrogress.

The tendency toward violence, they found, was inextricably linked with ingenuity, flexibility, drive.

The problem, then: To arrange a peace that would last after they were gone. To stop the race from destroying itself, without removing the responsible traits.

The way to do this, they decided, was to rechannel Man's violence.

Provide him with an outlet, an expression.

The first big step was the legalization of gladiatorial events, complete with blood and thunder. But more was needed. Sublimations worked only up to a point. Then people demanded the real thing.

There is no substitute for murder.

So murder was legalized, on a strictly individual basis, and only for those who wanted it. The governments were directed to create Emotional Catharsis Boards.

After a period of experimentation, uniform rules were adopted.

Anyone who wanted to murder could sign up at the ECB. Giving certain data and assurances, he would be granted a Victim.

Anyone who signed up to murder, under the government rules, had to take his turn a few months later as Victim—if he survived.

That, in essence, was the setup. The individual could commit as many murders as he wanted. But between each, he had to be a Victim. If he successfully killed his Hunter, he could stop, or sign up for another murder.

At the end of ten years: an estimated third of the world's civilized population had applied for at least one murder. The number slid to a fourth, and stayed there.

Philosophers shook their heads, but the practical men were satisfied. War was where it belonged—in the hands of the individual.

Of course, there were ramifications to the game, and elaborations. Once its existence had been accepted it became big business. There were services for Victim and Hunter alike.

The Emotional Catharsis Board picked the Victims names at random. A Hunter was allowed six months in which to make his kill… This had to be done by his own ingenuity, unaided. He was given the name of his

Victim, address and description, and allowed to use a standard caliber pistol. He could wear no armor of any sort.

The Victim was notified a week before the Hunter. He was told only that he was a Victim. He did not know the name of his Hunter. He was allowed his choice of armor, however. He could hire spotters. A spotter couldn't kill; only Victim and Hunter could do that. But he could detect a stranger in town, or ferret out a nervous gunman.

The Victim could arrange any kind of ambush in his power to kill the Hunter.

There were stiff penalties for killing or wounding the wrong man, for no other murder was allowed. Grudge killings and gain killings were punishable by death.

The beauty of the system was that the people who wanted to kill could do so. Those who didn't—the bulk of the population—didn't have to.

At least, there weren't any more big wars. Not even the imminence of one.

Just hundreds of thousands of small ones.

FRELAINE didn't especially like the idea of killing a woman; but she had signed up. It wasn't his fault. And he wasn't going to lose out on his seventh hunt.

He spent the rest of the morning memorizing the data on his Victim, then filed the letter.

Janet Patzig lived in New York. That was good. He enjoyed hunting in a big city, and he had always wanted to see New York. Her age wasn't given, but to judge from her photographs, she was in her early twenties.

Frelaine phoned for jet reservations to New York,

then took a shower. He dressed with care in a new Protec-Suit Special made for the occasion. From his collection he selected a gun, cleaned and oiled it, and fitted it into the fling out pocket of the suit. Then he packed his suitcase.

A pulse of excitement was pounding in his veins. Strange, he thought, how each killing was a new excitement. It was something you just didn't tire of, the way you did of French pastry or women or drinking or anything else. It was always new and different.

Finally, he looked over his books to see which he would take.

His library contained all the good books on the subject. He wouldn't need any of his Victim books, like L. Fred Tracy's *Tactics for the Victim*, with its insistence on a rigidly, controlled environment, or Dr. Frisch's *Don't Think Like a Victim*!

He would be very interested in those in a few months, when he was a Victim again. Now he wanted hunting books.

Tactics for Hunting Humans was the standard and definitive work, but he had it almost memorized. *Development of the Ambush* was not adapted to his present needs.

He chose *Hunting in Cities*, by Mitwell and Clark, *Spotting the Spotter*, by Algreen, and *The Victim's Ingroup*, by the same author.

Everything was in order. He left a note for the milkman, locked his apartment and took a cab to the airport.

IN New York, he checked into a hotel in the

midtown area, not too far from his Victim's address. The clerks were smiling and attentive, which bothered Frelaine. He didn't like to be recognized so easily as an out-of-town killer.

The first thing he saw in his room was a pamphlet on his bed-table, *How to Get the Most out of your Emotional Catharsis,* it was called, with the compliments of the management. Frelaine smiled and thumbed through it.

Since it was his first visit to New York, Frelaine spent the afternoon just walking the streets in his Victim's neighborhood. After that, he wandered through a few stores.

Martinson and Black was a fascinating place. He went through their Hunter-Hunted room. There were lightweight bulletproof vests for Victims, and Richard Arlington hats, with bulletproof crowns.

On one side was a large display of a new .38 caliber sidearm.

"Use the Malvern Strait-shot!" the ad proclaimed. "ECB-approved. Carries a load of twelve shots. Tested deviation less than .001 inch per 1000 feet. Don't miss your Victim! Don't risk your life without the best! Be safe with Malvern!"

Frelaine smiled. The ad was good, and the small black weapon looked ultimately efficient. But he was satisfied with the one he had.

There was a special sale on trick canes, with concealed four-shot magazine, promising safety and concealment. As a young man, Frelaine had gone in heavily for novelties. But now he knew that the old-fashioned ways were usually the best.

Outside the store, four men from the Department of

Sanitation were carting away a freshly killed corpse. Frelaine regretted missing the kill.

He ate dinner in a good restaurant and went to bed early.

Tomorrow he had a lot to do.

The next day, with the face of his Victim before him, Frelaine walked through her neighborhood. He didn't look closely at anyone. Instead, he moved rapidly, as though he were really going somewhere, the way an old Hunter should walk.

He passed several bars and dropped into one for a drink. Then he went on, down a side street off Lexington Avenue.

There was a pleasant sidewalk cafe there. Frelaine walked past it.

And there she was! He could never mistake the face. It was Janet Patzig, seated at a table, staring into a drink. She didn't look up as he passed.

FRELAINE walked to the end of the block. He turned the corner and stopped, hands trembling.

Was the girl crazy, exposing herself in the open? Did she think she had a charmed life?

He hailed a taxi and had the man drive around the block. Sure enough, she was just sitting there. Frelaine took a careful look.

She seemed younger than her pictures, but he couldn't be sure. He would guess her to be not much over twenty. Her dark hair was parted in the middle and combed above her ears, giving her a nunlike appearance. Her expression, as far as Frelaine could tell, was one of resigned sadness.

Wasn't she even going to make an attempt to defend herself?

Frelaine paid the driver and hurried to a drugstore. Finding a vacant telephone booth, he called ECB.

"Are you sure that a Victim named Janet-Marie Patzig has been notified?"

"Hold on, sir." Frelaine tapped on the door while the clerk looked up the information. "Yes, sir. We have her personal confirmation. Is there anything wrong, sir?"

"No," Frelaine said. "Just wanted to check."

After all, it was no one's business if the girl didn't want to defend herself.

He was still 'entitled to kill her.'

It was his turn.

He postponed it for that day, however, and went to a movie. After dinner, he returned to his room and read the ECB pamphlet. Then he lay on his bed and glared at the ceiling.

All he had to do was pump a bullet into her. Just ride by in a cab and kill her.

She was being a very bad sport about it, he decided resentfully, and went to sleep.

THE next afternoon, Frelaine walked by the cafe again. The girl was back, sitting at the same table. Frelaine caught a cab.

"Drive around the block very slowly," he told the driver.

"Sure," the driver said, grinning with sardonic wisdom.

From the cab, Frelaine watched for spotters. As far as he could tell, the girl had none. Both her hands were in sight upon the table.

An easy, stationary target.

Frelaine touched the button of his double-breasted jacket. A fold flew open and the gun was in his hand. He broke it open and checked the cartridges, then closed it with a snap.

"Slowly, now," he told the driver.

The taxi crawled by the cafe. Frelaine took careful aim, centering the girl in his sights. His finger tightened on the trigger.

"Damn it!" he said.

A waiter had passed by the girl. He didn't want to chance winging someone else.

"Around the block again," he told the driver.

The man gave him another grin and hunched down in his seat. Frelaine wondered if the driver would feel so happy if he knew that Frelaine was gunning for a woman.

This time there was no waiter around. The girl was lighting a cigarette, her mournful face intent on her lighter. Frelaine centered her in his sights, squarely above the eyes, and held his breath.

Then he shook his head and put the gun back in his pocket. The idiotic girl was robbing him of the full benefit of his catharsis.

He paid the driver and started to walk.

It's too easy, he told himself. He was used to a real chase. Most of the other six kills had been quite difficult. The Victims had tried every dodge. One had hired at least a dozen spotters. But Frelaine had gotten to them all by altering his tactics to meet the situation.

Once he had dressed as a milkman, another time as a

bill collector. The sixth Victim he had had to chase through the Sierra Nevadas. The man had clipped him, too. But Frelaine had done better than that.

How could he be proud of this one? What would the Tens Club say?

That brought Frelaine up with a start. He wanted to get into the club. Even if he passed up this girl, he would have to defend himself against a Hunter. Surviving that, he would still be four hunts away from membership. At that rate, he might never get in.

HE began to pass the cafe again, then, on impulse, stopped abruptly.

"Hello," he said.

Janet Patzig looked at him out of sad blue eyes, but said nothing.

"Say, look," he said, sitting down. "If I'm being fresh, just tell me and I'll go. I'm an out-of-towner. Here on a convention. And I'd just like someone feminine to talk to. If you'd rather I didn't—"

"I don't care," Janet Patzig said tonelessly.

"A brandy," Frelaine told the waiter. Janet Patzig's glass was still half full.

Frelaine looked at the girl and he could feel his heart throbbing against his ribs. This was more like it—having a drink with your Victim!

"My name's Stanton Frelaine," he said, knowing it didn't matter.

"Janet."

"Janet what?"

"Janet Patzig."

"Nice to know you," Frelaine said, in a perfectly

natural voice. "Are you doing anything tonight, Janet?"

"I'm probably being killed tonight," she said quietly.

Frelaine looked at her carefully. Did she realize who he was? For all he knew, she had a gun leveled at him under the table.

He kept his hand close to the fling-out button.

"Are you a Victim?" he asked.

"You guessed it," she said sardonically. "If I were you, I'd stay out of the way. No sense getting hit by mistake."

Frelaine couldn't understand the girl's calm. Was she a suicide? Perhaps she just didn't care. Perhaps she wanted to die.

"Haven't you got any spotters?" he asked, with the right expression of amazement.

"No." She looked at him, full in the face, and Frelaine saw something he hadn't noticed before.

She was very lovely.

"I am a bad, bad girl," she said lightly. "I got the idea I'd like to commit a murder, so I signed for ECB. Then—I couldn't do it."

FRELAINE shook his head, sympathizing with her.

"But I'm still in, of course. Even if I didn't shoot, I still have to be a Victim."

"But why don't you hire some spotters?" he asked.

"I couldn't kill anyone," she said. "I just couldn't. I don't even have a gun."

"You've got a lot of courage," Frelaine said, "coming out in the open this way." Secretly, he was amazed at her stupidity.

"What can I do?" she asked listlessly. "You can't hide

from a Hunter. Not a real one. And I don't have enough money to make a real disappearance."

"Since it's in your own defense, I should think—" Frelaine began, but she interrupted.

"No. I've made up my mind on that. This whole thing is wrong, the whole system. When I had my Victim in the sights—when I saw how easily I could—I could—"

She pulled herself together quickly.

"Oh, let's forget it," she said, and smiled.

Frelaine found her smile dazzling.

After that, they talked of other things. Frelaine told her of his business, and she told him about New York. She was twenty-two, an unsuccessful actress.

They had supper together. When she accepted Frelaine's invitation to go to the Gladiatorials, he felt absurdly elated.

He called a cab—he seemed to be spending his entire time in New York in cabs—and opened the door for her. She started in. Frelaine hesitated. He could have pumped a shot into her at that moment. It would have been very easy.

But he held his hand. Just for the moment, he told himself.

THE Gladiatorials were about the same as those held anywhere else, except that the talent was a little better. There were the usual historical events, swordsmen and netmen, duels with saber and foil. Most of these, naturally, were fought to the death.

Then bull fighting, lion fighting and rhino fighting, followed by the more modern events. Fights from behind barricades with bow and arrow. Dueling on a high wire.

The evening passed pleasantly.

Frelaine escorted the girl home, the palms of his hands sticky with sweat. He had never found a woman he liked better. And yet she was his legitimate kill.

He didn't know what he was going to do.

She invited him in and they sat together on the couch. The girl lighted a cigarette for herself with a large lighter, then settled back.

"Are you leaving soon?" she asked him.

"I suppose so," Frelaine said. "The convention is only lasting another day."

She was silent for a moment. "I'll be sorry to see you go. Send roses to my funeral."

They were quiet for a while. Then Janet went to fix him a drink. Frelaine eyed her retreating back. Now was the time. He placed his hand near the button.

But the moment had passed for him, irrevocably. He wasn't going to kill her. You don't kill the girl you love.

The realization that he loved her was shocking. He'd come to kill, not to find a wife.

She came back with the drink and sat down opposite him, staring at emptiness.

"Janet," he said. "I love you."

She sat, just looking at him. There were tears in her eyes.

"You can't," she protested. "I'm a Victim. I won't live long enough to—"

"You won't be killed. I'm your Hunter."

She stared at him a moment, then laughed uncertainly.

"Are you going to kill me?" she asked.

"Don't be ridiculous," he said. "I'm going to marry you."

Suddenly she was in his arms.

"Oh, Lord!" she gasped. "The waiting—I've been so frightened—"

"It's all over," he told her. "Think what a story it'll make for our kids. How I came to murder you and left marrying you."

She kissed him, then sat back and lighted another cigarette.

"Let's start packing," Frelaine said. "I want—"

"Wait," Janet interrupted. "You haven't asked if I love you."

"What?"

She was still smiling, and the cigarette lighter was pointed at him. In the bottom of it was a black hole. A hole just large enough for a .38 caliber bullet.

"Don't kid around," he objected, getting to his feet.

"I'm not being funny, darling," she said.

IN a fraction of a second, Frelaine had time to wonder how he could ever have thought she was not much over twenty. Looking at her now—*really* looking at her—he knew she couldn't be much less than thirty. Every minute of her strained, tense existence showed on her face.

"I don't love you, Stanton," she said very softly, the cigarette lighter poised.

Frelaine struggled for breath. One part of him was able to realize detachedly what a marvelous actress she really was. She must have known all along.

Frelaine pushed the button, and the gun was in his

hand, cocked and ready.

The blow that struck him in the chest knocked him over a coffee table. The gun fell out of his hand. Gasping, half-conscious, he watched her take careful aim for the *coup de grace.*

"Now I can join the Tens," he heard her say elatedly as she squeezed the trigger.

Diplomatic Immunity

He said he wasn't immortal—but nothing could kill him.
Still, if the Earth was to live as free world, he had to die.

"COME right in, gentlemen," the Ambassador waved them into the very special suite the State Department had given him. "Please be seated."

Colonel Cercy accepted a chair, trying to size up the individual who had all Washington chewing its fingernails. The Ambassador hardly looked like a menace. He was of medium height and slight build, dressed in a conservative brown tweed suit that the State Department had given him. His face was intelligent, finely molded and aloof.

As human as a human, Cercy thought, studying the alien with bleak, impersonal eyes.

"How may I serve you?" the Ambassador asked, smiling.

"The President has put me in charge of your case," Cercy said. "I've studied Professor Darrig's reports—" he nodded at the scientist beside him— "but I'd like to hear the whole thing for myself."

"Of course," the alien said, lighting a cigarette. He seemed genuinely pleased to be asked; which was interesting, Cercy thought. In the week since he had landed, every important scientist in the country had been at him.

But in a pinch they call the Army, Cercy reminded himself. He settled back in his chair, both hands jammed carelessly in his pockets. His right hand was resting on the butt of a .45, the safety off.

"I HAVE come," the alien said, "as an ambassador-at-large, representing an empire that stretches halfway across the Galaxy. I wish to extend the welcome of my people and to invite you to join our organization."

"I see," Cercy replied. "Some of the scientists got the impression that participation was compulsory."

"You will join," the Ambassador said, blowing smoke through his nostrils.

Cercy could see Darrig stiffen in his chair and bite his lip. Cercy moved the automatic to a position where he could draw it easily. "How did you find us?" he asked.

"We ambassadors-at-large are each assigned an unexplored section of space," the alien said. "We examine each star-system in that region for planets, and each planet for intelligent life. Intelligent life is rare in the Galaxy, you know."

Cercy nodded, although he hadn't been aware of the fact.

"When we find such a planet, we land, as I did, and prepare the inhabitants for their part in our organization."

"How will your people know that you have found intelligent life?" Cercy asked.

"There is a sending mechanism that is part of our

structure," the Ambassador answered. "It is triggered when we reach an inhabited planet. This signal is beamed continually into space, to an effective range of several thousand light-years. Follow-up crews are continually sweeping through the limits of the reception area of each Ambassador, listening for such messages. Detecting one, a colonizing team follows it to the planet."

He tapped his cigarette delicately on the edge of an ashtray. "This method has definite advantages over sending combined colonization and exploration teams obviously. It avoids the necessity of equipping large forces for what may be decades of searching."

"Sure." Cercy's face was expressionless. "Would you tell me more about this message?"

"There isn't much more you need know. The beam is not detectable by your methods and, therefore, cannot be jammed. The message continues as long as I am alive."

DARRIG drew in his breath sharply, glancing at Cercy.

"If you stopped broadcasting," Cercy said casually, "our planet would never be found."

"Not until this section of space was resurveyed," the diplomat agreed.

"Very well. As a duly appointed representative of the President of the United States, I ask you to stop transmitting. We don't choose to become part of your empire."

"I'm sorry," the Ambassador said. He shrugged his shoulders easily. Cercy wondered how many times he had played this scene on how many other planets.

"There's really nothing I can do." He stood up.

"Then you won't stop?"

"I can't. I have no control over the sending, once it's activated." The diplomat turned and walked to the window. "However, I have prepared a philosophy for you. It is my duty, as your Ambassador, to ease the shock of transition as much as possible. This philosophy will make it instantly apparent that—"

As the Ambassador reached the window, Cercy's gun was out of his pocket and roaring. He squeezed six rounds in almost a single explosion, aiming at the Ambassador's head and back. Then an uncontrollable shudder ran through him.

The Ambassador was no longer there!

CERCY and Darrig stared at each other. Darrig muttered something about ghosts. Then, just as suddenly, the Ambassador was back.

"You didn't think," he said, "that it would be as easy as all that, did you? We Ambassadors have, necessarily, a certain diplomatic immunity." He fingered one of the bullet holes in the wall. "In case you don't understand, let me put it this way. It is not in your power to kill me. You couldn't even understand the nature of my defense."

He looked at them, and in that moment Cercy felt the Ambassador's complete alienness.

"Good day, gentlemen," he said.

Darrig and Cercy walked silently back to the control room. Neither had really expected that the Ambassador would be killed so easily, but it had still been a shock when the slugs had failed.

"I suppose you saw it all, Malley?" Cercy asked, when he reached the control room.

The thin, balding psychiatrist nodded sadly. "Got it on film, too."

"I wonder what his philosophy is," Darrig mused, half to himself.

"It was illogical to expect it would work. No race would send an ambassador with a message like that and expect him to live through it. Unless—"

"Unless what?"

"Unless he had a pretty effective defense," the psychiatrist finished unhappily.

Cercy walked across the room and looked at the video panel. The Ambassador's suite was very special. It had been hurriedly constructed two days after he had landed and delivered his message. The suite was steel and lead lined, filled with video and movie cameras, recorders, and a variety of other things.

It was the last word in elaborate death cells.

In the screen, Cercy could see the Ambassador sitting at a table. He was typing on a little portable the Government had given him.

"Hey, Harrison!" Cercy called.

"Might as well go ahead with Plan Two."

Harrison came out of a side room where he had been examining the circuits leading to the Ambassador's suite. Methodically he checked his pressure gauges, set the controls and looked at Cercy. "Now?" he asked.

"Now." Cercy watched the screen. The Ambassador was still typing.

Suddenly, as Harrison sent home the switch, the room

was engulfed in flames. Fire blasted out of concealed holes in the walls, poured from the ceiling and floor.

In a moment, the room was like the inside of a blast furnace.

Cercy let it burn for two minutes, then motioned Harrison to cut the switch. They stared at the roasted room.

They were looking, hopefully, for a charred corpse.

But the Ambassador reappeared beside his desk, looking ruefully at the charred typewriter. He was completely unsinged.

"Could you get me another typewriter?" he asked, looking directly at one of the hidden projectors. "I'm setting down a philosophy for you ungrateful wretches."

He seated himself in the wreckage of an armchair. In a moment, he was apparently asleep.

"ALL right, everyone grab a seat," Cercy said. "Time for a council of war."

Malley straddled a chair backward. Harrison lighted a pipe as he sat down, slowly puffing it into life.

"Now, then," Cercy said. "The Government has dropped this squarely in our laps. We have to kill the Ambassador—obviously. I've been put in charge." Cercy grinned with regret. "Probably because no one higher up wants the responsibility of failure. And I've selected you three as my staff. We can have anything we want, any assistance or advice we need. All right. Any ideas?"

"How about Plan Three?" Harrison asked.

"We'll get to that," Cercy said. "But I don't believe it's going to work."

"I don't either," Darrig agreed. "We don't even know the nature of his defense."

"That's the first order of business, Malley, take all our data so far, and get someone to feed it into the Derichman Analyzer. You know the stuff we want. What properties has X, if X can do thus and thus?"

"Right," Malley said. He left, muttering something about the ascendancy of the physical sciences.

"Harrison," Cercy asked, "is Plan Three set up?"

"Sure."

"Give it a try:"

While Harrison was making his last adjustments, Cercy watched Darrig. The plump little physicist was staring thoughtfully into space, muttering to himself. Cercy hoped he would come up with something. He was expecting great things of Darrig.

Knowing the impossibility of working with great numbers of people, Cercy had picked his staff with care. Quality was what he wanted.

With that in mind, he had chosen Harrison first. The stocky, sour-faced engineer had a reputation for being able to build anything, given half an idea of how it worked.

Cercy had selected Malley, the psychiatrist, because he wasn't sure that killing the Ambassador was going to be a purely physical problem.

Darrig was a mathematical physicist, but his restless, curious mind had come up with some interesting theories in other fields. He was the only one of the four who was really interested in the Ambassador as an intellectual problem.

"He's like Metal Old Man," Darrig said finally.

"What's that?"

"Haven't you ever heard the story of Metal Old Man? Well, he was a monster covered with black metal armor. He was met by Monster-Slayer, an Apache culture hero. Monster-Slayer, after many attempts, finally killed Metal Old Man."

"How did he do it?"

"Shot him in the armpit. He didn't have any armor there."

"Fine," Cercy grinned. "Ask our Ambassador to raise his arm."

"All set!" Harrison called.

"Fine. Go."

In the Ambassador's room, an invisible spray of gamma rays silently began to flood the room with deadly radiation.

But there was no Ambassador to receive them.

"That's enough," Cercy said, after a while. "That would kill a herd of elephants."

But the Ambassador stayed invisible for five hours, until some of the radioactivity had abated. Then he appeared again.

"I'm still waiting for that typewriter," he said.

"HERE'S the Analyzer's report." Malley handed Cercy a sheaf of papers. "This is the final formulation, boiled down."

Cercy read it aloud: "The simplest defense against any and all weapons, is to *become* each particular weapon."

"Great," Harrison said. "What does it mean?"

"It means," Darrig explained, "that when we attack

the Ambassador with fire, he turns into fire. Shoot at him, and he turns into a bullet—until the menace is gone, and then he changes back again," he took the papers out of Cercy's hand and riffled through them.

"Hmm. Wonder if there's any historical parallel? Don't suppose so." He raised his head. "Although this isn't conclusive, it seems logical enough. Any other defense would involve recognition of the weapon first, then an appraisal, then a countermove predicated on the potentialities of the weapon. The Ambassador's defense would be a lot faster and safer. He wouldn't have to recognize the weapon. I suppose his body simply *identifies*, in some way, with the menace at hand."

"Did the Analyzer say there was any way of breaking this defense?" Cercy asked.

"The Analyzer stated definitely that there was no way, if the premise were true," Malley answered gloomily.

"We can discard that judgment," Darrig said. "The machine is limited."

"But we still haven't got any way of stopping him," Malley pointed out. "And he's still broadcasting that beam."

Cercy thought for a moment.

"Call in every expert you can find. We're going to throw the book at the Ambassador. I know," he said, looking at Darrig's dubious expression, "but we have to try."

DURING the next few days, every combination and permutation of death was thrown at the Ambassador. He was showered with weapons, ranging from Stone-Age axes to modern high-powered rifles, peppered with hand grenades, drowned in acid, suffocated in poison gas.

He kept shrugging his shoulders philosophically, and continued to work on the new typewriter they had given him.

Bacteria was piped in, first the known germ diseases, then mutated species.

The diplomat didn't even sneeze.

He was showered with electricity, radiation, wooden weapons, iron weapons, copper weapons, brass weapons, uranium weapons—anything and everything, just to cover all possibilities.

He didn't suffer a scratch, but his room looked as though a barroom brawl had been going on in it continually for fifty years.

Malley was working on an idea of his own, as was Darrig. The physicist interrupted himself long enough to remind Cercy of the Baldur myth. Baldur had been showered with every kind of weapon and remained unscathed, because everything on Earth had promised to love him. Everything, except the mistletoe. When a little twig of it was shot at him, he died.

Cercy turned away impatiently, but had an order of mistletoe sent up, just in case.

It was, at least, no less effective than the explosive shells or the bow and arrow. It did nothing except lend an oddly festive air to the battered room.

After a week of this, they moved the unprotesting Ambassador into a newer, bigger, stronger death cell. They were unable to venture into his old one because of the radioactivity and micro-organisms.

The Ambassador went back to work at his typewriter.

All his previous attempts had been burned, torn or eaten away.

"Let's go talk to him," Darrig suggested, after another day had passed. Cercy agreed. For the moment, they were out of ideas...

"COME, right in, gentlemen," the Ambassador said, so cheerfully that Cercy felt sick. "I'm sorry I can't offer you anything. Through an oversight, I haven't been given any food or water for about ten days. Not that it matters, of course."

"Glad to hear it," Cercy said.

The Ambassador hardly looked as if he had been facing all the violence Earth had to offer. On the contrary, Cercy and his men looked as though they had been under bombardment.

"You've got quite a defense there," Malley said conversationally.

"Glad you like it."

"Would you mind telling us how it works?" Darrig asked innocently.

"Don't you know?"

"We think so. You become what is attacking you. Is that right?"

"Certainly," the Ambassador said. "You see, I have no secrets from you."

"Is there anything we can give you," Cercy asked, "to get you to turn off that signal?"

"A bribe?"

"Sure," Cercy said. "Anything you—?"

"Nothing," the Ambassador replied.

"Look, be reasonable," Harrison said. "You don't

want to cause a war, do you? Earth is united now. We're arming—"

"With what?"

"Atom bombs," Malley answered him. "Hydrogen bombs. We're—"

"Drop one on me," the Ambassador said. "It wouldn't kill me. What makes you think it will have any effect on my people?"

The four men were silent. Somehow, they hadn't thought of that.

"A people's ability to make war," the Ambassador stated, "is a measure of the status of their civilization. Stage one is the use of simple physical extensions. Stage two is control at the molecular level. You are on the threshold of stage three, although still far from mastery of atomic and subatomic forces," he smiled ingratiatingly. "My people are reaching the limits of stage five."

"What would that be?" Darrig asked.

"You'll find out," the Ambassador said. "But perhaps you've wondered if my powers are typical? I don't mind telling you that they're not. In order for me to do my job and nothing more, I have certain built-in restrictions, making me capable only of passive action."

"Why?" Darrig asked.

"For obvious reasons. If I were to take positive action in a moment of anger, I might destroy your entire planet."

"Do you expect us to believe that?" Cercy asked.

"Why not? Is it so hard to understand? Can't you believe that there are forces you know nothing about?

And there is another reason for my passiveness. Certainly by this time you've deduced it?"

"To break our spirit, I suppose," Cercy said.

"Exactly. My telling you won't make any difference, either. The pattern is always the same. An Ambassador lands and delivers his message to a high-spirited, wild young race like yours. There is frenzied resistance against him, spasmodic attempts to kill him. After all these fail, the people are usually quite crestfallen. When the colonization team arrives, their indoctrination goes along just that much faster." He paused, then said, "Most planets are more interested in the philosophy I have to offer. I assure you, it will make the transition far easier."

He held out a sheaf of typewritten pages. "Won't you at least look through it?"

Darrig accepted the papers and put them in his pocket. "When I get time."

"I suggest you give it a try," the Ambassador said. "You must be near the crisis point now. Why not give it up?"

"Not yet," Cercy replied tonelessly.

"Don't forget to read the philosophy," the Ambassador urged them.

The men hurried from the room.

"NOW look," Malley said, once they were back in the control room, "there are a few things we haven't tried. How about utilizing psychology?"

"Anything you like," Cercy agreed, "including black magic. What did you have in mind?"

"The way I see it," Malley answered, "the

Ambassador is geared to respond, instantaneously, to any threat. He must have an all-or-nothing defensive reflex. I suggest first that we try something that won't trigger that reflex."

"Like what?" Cercy asked.

"Hypnotism. Perhaps we can find out something."

"Sure," Cercy said. "Try it. Try anything."

Cercy, Malley and Darrig gathered around the video screen as an infinitesimal amount of a light hypnotic gas was admitted into the Ambassador's room. At the same time, a bolt of electricity lashed into the chair where the Ambassador was sitting.

"That was to distract him," Malley explained. The Ambassador vanished before the electricity struck him, and then appeared again, curled up in his armchair.

"That's enough," Malley whispered, and shut the valve. They watched. After a while, the Ambassador put down his book and stared into the distance.

"How strange," he said. "Alfern dead. Good friend… just a freak accident. He ran into it, out there… Didn't have a chance. But it doesn't happen often."

"He's thinking out loud," Malley whispered, although there was no possibility of the Ambassador's hearing them. "Vocalizing his thoughts. His friend must have been on his mind for some time."

"Of course," the Ambassador went on, "Alfern had to die sometime. No immortality—yet. But that way—no defense. Out there in space they just pop up. Always there, underneath, just waiting for a chance to boil out."

"His body isn't reacting to the hypnotic as a menace yet," Cercy whispered.

"Well," the Ambassador told himself, "the regularizing principle has been doing pretty well, keeping it all down, smoothing out the inconsistencies—"

Suddenly he leaped to his feet, his face pale for a moment, as he obviously tried to remember what he had said. Then he laughed.

"Clever. That's the first time that particular trick has been played on me, and the last time. But, gentlemen, it didn't do you any good. I don't know, myself, how to go about killing me." He laughed at the blank walls.

"Besides," he continued, "the colonizing team must have the direction now. They'll find you with or without me."

He sat down again, smiling.

"THAT does it!" Darrig cried. "He's not invulnerable. Something killed his friend Alfern."

"Something out in space," Cercy reminded him. "I wonder what it was."

"Let me see," Darrig reflected aloud. "The regularizing principle. That must be a natural law we knew nothing about. And underneath—what would be underneath?"

"He said the colonization team would find us anyhow," Malley reminded them.

"First things first," Cercy said. "He might have been bluffing us…no, I don't suppose so. We still have to get the Ambassador out of the way."

"I think I know what is underneath!" Darrig exclaimed. "This is wonderful. A new cosmology, perhaps."

"What is it?" Cercy asked. "Anything we can use?"

"I think so. But let me work it out. I think I'll go back to my hotel. I have some books there I want to check, and I don't want to be disturbed for a few hours."

"All right," Cercy agreed. "But what—?"

"No, no, I could be wrong," Darrig said. "Let me work it out," he hurried from the room.

"What do you think he's driving at?" Malley asked.

"Beats me," Cercy shrugged. "Come on, let's try some more of that psychological stuff."

First they filled the Ambassador's room with several feet of water. Not enough to drown him, just enough to make him good and uncomfortable.

To this, they added the lights. For eight hours, lights flashed in the Ambassador's room. Bright lights to pry under his eyelids; dull, clashing ones to disturb him.

Sound came next—screeches and screams and shrill, grating noises. The sound of a man's fingernails being dragged across slate, amplified a thousand times, and strange, sucking noises, and shouts and whispers.

Then, the smells. Then, everything else they could think of that could drive a man insane.

The Ambassador slept peacefully through it all.

"Now look," Cercy said, the following day, "let's start using our damned heads." His voice was hoarse and rough. Although the psychological torture hadn't bothered the Ambassador, it seemed to have backfired on Cercy and his men.

"Where in hell is Darrig?"

"Still working on that idea of his," Malley said, rubbing his stubbled chin. "Says he's just about got it."

"We'll work on the assumption that he can't

produce," Cercy said. "Start thinking. For example, if the Ambassador can turn into anything, what is there he can't turn into?"

"Good question," Harrison grunted.

"It's the payoff question," Cercy said. "No use throwing a spear at a man who can turn into one."

"How about this?" Malley asked. "Taking it for granted he can turn into anything, how about putting him in a situation where he'll be attacked even *after* he alters?"

"I'm listening," Cercy said.

"Say he's in danger. He turns into the thing threatening him. What if *that thing* were itself being threatened? And, in turn, was in the act of threatening something else? What would he do then?"

"How are you going to put that into action?" Cercy asked.

"Like this." Malley picked up the telephone. "Hello? Give me the Washington Zoo. This is urgent."

The Ambassador turned as the door opened. An unwilling, angry, hungry tiger was propelled in. The door slammed shut.

The tiger looked at the Ambassador. The Ambassador looked at the tiger.

"Most ingenious," the Ambassador said.

At the sound of his voice, the tiger came unglued. He sprang like a steel spring uncoiling, landing on the floor where the Ambassador had been.

The door opened again. Another tiger was pushed in. He snarled angrily and leaped at the first. They smashed together in midair.

The Ambassador appeared a few feet off, watching.

He moved back when a lion entered the door, head up and alert. The lion sprang at him, almost going over on his head when he struck nothing. Not finding any human, the lion leaped on one of the tigers.

The Ambassador reappeared in his chair, where he sat smoking and watching the beasts kill each other.

In ten minutes the room looked like an abattoir.

But by then the Ambassador had tired of the spectacle, and was reclining on his bed, reading.

"I GIVE up," Malley said. "That was my last bright idea."

Cercy stared at the floor, not answering. Harrison was seated in the corner, getting quietly drunk.

The telephone rang.

"Yeah?" Cercy said.

"I've got it!" Darrig's voice shouted over the line. "I really think this is it. Look, I'm taking a cab right down. Tell Harrison to find some helpers."

"What is it?" Cercy asked.

"The chaos underneath!" Darrig replied, and hung up.

They paced the floor, waiting for him to show up. Half an hour passed, then an hour. Finally, three hours after he had called, Darrig strolled in.

"Hello," he said casually.

"Hello, hell!" Cercy growled. "What kept you?"

"On the way over," Darrig said, "I read the Ambassador's philosophy. It's quite a work."

"Is that what took you so long?"

"Yes. I had the driver take me around the park a few times, while I was reading it."

"Skip it. How about—"

"I can't skip it," Darrig said, in a strange, tight voice. "I'm afraid we were wrong. About the aliens, I mean. It's perfectly right and proper that they should rule us. As a matter of fact, I wish they'd hurry up and get here."

But Darrig didn't look certain. His voice shook and perspiration poured from his face. He twisted his hands together, as though in agony.

"It's hard to explain," he said. "Everything became clear as soon as I started reading it: I saw how stupid we were, trying to be independent in this interdependent Universe. I saw—oh, look, Cercy. Let's stop all this foolishness and accept the Ambassador as our friend."

"Calm down!" Cercy shouted at the perfectly calm physicist. "You don't know what you're saying."

"It's strange," Darrig said. "I know how I felt—I just don't feel that way any more. I think. Anyhow, I know *your* trouble. You haven't read the philosophy. You'll see what I mean, once you've read it." He handed Cercy the pile of papers. Cercy promptly ignited them with his cigarette lighter…

"It doesn't matter," Darrig said. "I've got it memorized. Just listen. Axiom one. All peoples—"

Cercy hit him, a short, clean blow, and Darrig slumped to the floor.

"Those words must be semantically keyed," Malley said. "They're designed to set off certain reactions in us, I suppose. All the Ambassador does is alter the philosophy to suit the peoples he's dealing with."

"Look, Malley," Cercy said. "This is your job now. Darrig knows, or thought he knew, the answer. You have to get that out of him."

"That won't be easy," Malley said. "He'd feel that he

was betraying everything he believes in if he were to tell us."

"I don't care how you get it," Cercy said. "Just get it."

"Even if it kills him?" Malley asked.

"Even if it kills you."

"Help me get him to my lab," Malley said.

THAT night Cercy and Harrison kept watch on the Ambassador from the control room. Cercy found his thoughts were racing in circles.

What had killed Alfern in space? Could it be duplicated on Earth? What was the regularizing principle? What was the chaos underneath?

What in hell am I doing here? he asked himself. But he couldn't start that sort of thing.

"What do you figure the Ambassador is?" he asked Harrison. "Is he a man?"

"Looks like one," Harrison said drowsily.

"But he doesn't act like one. I wonder if this is his true shape?"

Harrison shook his head, and lighted his pipe.

"What is there of him?" Cercy asked. "He looks like a man, but he can change into anything else. You can't attack him; he adapts. He's like water, taking the shape of any vessel he's poured into."

"You can boil water," Harrison yawned.

"Sure. Water hasn't any shape, has it? Or has it? What's basic?"

With an effort, Harrison tried to focus on Cercy's words. "Molecular pattern? The matrix?"

"Matrix," Cercy repeated, yawning himself. "Pattern.

Must be something like that. A pattern is abstract, isn't it?"

"Sure. A pattern can be impressed on anything. What did I say?"

"Let's see," Cercy said. "Pattern. Matrix. Everything about the Ambassador is capable of change. There must be some unifying force that retains his personality. Something that doesn't change, no matter what contortions he goes through."

"Like a piece of string," Harrison murmured with his eyes closed.

"Sure. Tie it in knots, weave a rope out of it, wind it around your finger; it's still string."

"Yeah."

"But how do you attack a pattern?" Cercy asked. And why couldn't he get some sleep? To hell with the Ambassador and his hordes of colonists, he was going to close his eyes for a moment…

"WAKE up, Colonel!"

Cercy pried his eyes open and looked up at Malley. Besides him, Harrison was snoring deeply. "Did you get anything?"

"Not a thing," Malley confessed. "The philosophy must've had quite an effect on him. But it didn't work all the way. Darrig knew that he *had wanted* to kill the Ambassador, and for good and sufficient reasons. Although he felt differently now, he still had the feeling that he was betraying us. On the one hand, he couldn't hurt the Ambassador; on the other, he wouldn't hurt us."

"Won't he tell anything?"

"I'm afraid it's not that simple," Malley said. "You know, if you have an insurmountable obstacle that *must* be surmounted... and also, I think the philosophy had an injurious effect on his mind."

"What are you trying to say?" Cercy got to his feet.

"I'm sorry," Malley apologized, "there wasn't a damned thing I could do. Darrig fought the whole thing out in his mind, and when he couldn't fight any longer, he—retreated. I'm afraid he's hopelessly insane."

"Let's see him."

They walked down the corridor to Malley's laboratory. Darrig was relaxed on a couch, his eyes glazed and staring.

"Is there any way of curing him?" Cercy asked.

"Shock therapy, maybe." Malley was dubious. "It'll take a long time. And he'll probably block out everything that had to do with producing this."

Cercy turned away, feeling sick. Even if Darrig could be cured, it would be too late. The aliens must have picked up the Ambassador's message by now and were undoubtedly heading for Earth.

"What's this?" Cercy asked, picking up a piece of paper that lay by Darrig's hand.

"Oh, he was doodling," Malley said. "Is there anything written on it?"

Cercy read aloud: "Upon further consideration I can see that Chaos and the Gorgon Medusa are closely related."

"What does that mean?" Malley asked.

"I don't know," Cercy puzzled. "He was always interested in folklore."

"Sounds schizophrenic," the psychiatrist said.

Cercy read it again. "Upon further consideration, I can see that Chaos and the Gorgon Medusa are closely related." He stared at it. "Isn't it possible," he asked Malley, "that he was trying to give us a clue? Trying to trick himself into giving and not giving at the same time?"

"It's possible," Malley agreed. "An unsuccessful compromise— But what could it mean?"

"Chaos." Cercy remembered Darrig's mentioning that word in his telephone call. "That was the original state of the Universe in Greek myth, wasn't it? The formlessness out of which everything came?"

"Something like that," Malley said. "And Medusa was one of those three sisters with the horrible faces."

Cercy stood for a moment, staring at the paper. Chaos… Medusa… and the organizing principle! Of course!

"I think—" He turned and ran from the room. Malley looked at him; then loaded a hypodermic and followed.

IN the control room, Cercy shouted Harrison into consciousness.

"Listen," he said, "I want you to build something, quick. Do you hear me?"

"Sure." Harrison blinked and sat up. "What's the rush?"

"I know what Darrig wanted to tell us," Cercy said. "Come on, I'll tell you what I want. And Malley, put down that hypodermic. I haven't cracked. I want you to get me a book on Greek mythology. And hurry it up."

Finding a Greek mythology isn't an easy task at two

o'clock in the morning. With the aid of FBI men, Malley routed a book dealer out of bed. He got his book and hurried back.

Cercy was red-eyed and excited, and Harrison and his helpers were working away at three crazy looking rigs. Cercy snatched the book from Malley, looked up one item, and put it down.

"Great work," he said. "We're all set now. Finished, Harrison?"

"Just about." Harrison and ten helpers were screwing in the last parts. "Will you tell me what this is?"

"Me too," Malley put in.

"I don't mean to be secretive," Cercy said. "I'm just in a hurry. I'll explain as we go along." He stood up. "Okay, let's wake up the Ambassador."

THEY watched the screen as a bolt of electricity leaped from the ceiling to the Ambassador's bed. Immediately, the Ambassador vanished.

"Now he's a part of that stream of electrons, right?" Cercy asked.

"That's what he told us," Malley said.

"But still keeping his pattern, within the stream," Cercy continued. "He has to, in order to get back into his own shape. Now we start the first disrupter."

Harrison hooked the machine into circuit, and sent his helpers away.

"Here's a running graph of the electron stream," Cercy said. "See the difference?" On the graph there was an irregular series of peaks and valleys, constantly shifting and leveling. "Do you remember when you hypnotized the Ambassador? He talked about his friend who'd been killed in space."

"That's right," Malley nodded. "His friend had been killed by something that had just popped up."

"He said something else," Cercy went on. "He told us that the basic organizing force of the Universe usually stopped things like that. What does that mean to you?"

"The organizing force," Malley repeated slowly. "Didn't Darrig say that that was a new natural law?"

"He did. But think of the implications, as Darrig did. If an organizing principle is engaged in some work, there must be something that opposes it. That which opposes organization is—"

"Chaos!"

"That's what Darrig thought, and what we should have seen. The chaos is underlying, and out of it there arose an organizing principle. This principle, if I've got it right, sought to suppress the fundamental chaos, to make all things regular.

"But the chaos still boils out in spots, as Alfern found out. Perhaps the organizational pattern is weaker in space. Anyhow, those spots are dangerous, until the organizing principle gets to work on them."

HE turned to the panel. "Okay, Harrison. Throw in the second disrupter." The peaks and valleys altered on the graph. They started to mount in crazy, meaningless configurations.

"Take Darrig's message in the light of that. Chaos, we know, is underlying. Everything was formed out of it. The Gorgon Medusa was something that *couldn't be looked upon.* She turned men into stone, you recall, destroyed them. So, Darrig found a relationship between chaos and that which can't be looked upon. All with regard to the Ambassador, of course."

"The Ambassador can't look upon chaos!" Malley cried.

"That's it. The Ambassador is capable of an infinite number of alterations and permutations. But *something*—the matrix—can't change, because then there would be nothing left. To destroy something as abstract as a pattern, we need a state in which no pattern is possible. A state of chaos."

The third disrupter was thrown into circuit. The graph looked as if a drunken caterpillar had been sketching on it.

"Those disrupters are Harrison's idea," Cercy said. "I told him I wanted an electrical current with absolutely no coherent pattern. The disrupters are an extension of radio jamming. The first alters the electrical pattern. That's its purpose: to produce a state of patternlessness. The second tries to destroy the pattern left by the first; the third tries to destroy the pattern made by the first two. They're fed back then, and any remaining pattern is systematically destroyed in circuit… I hope."

"This is supposed to produce a state of chaos?" Malley asked, looking into the screen.

For a while there was only the whining of the machines and the crazy doodling of the graph. Then, in the middle of the Ambassador's room, a spot appeared. It wavered, shrunk, expanded—

What happened was indescribable. All they knew was that everything within the spot had disappeared.

"Switch it off!" Cercy shouted. Harrison cut the switch.

The spot continued to grow.

"How is it we're able to look at it?" Malley asked, staring at the screen.

"The shield of Perseus, remember?" Cercy said. "Using it as a mirror, he could look at Medusa."

"It's still growing!" Malley shouted.

"There was a calculated risk in all this," Cercy said. "There's always the possibility that the chaos may go on, unchecked. If that happens, it won't matter much what—"

The spot stopped growing. Its edges wavered and rippled; and then it started to shrink.

"The organizing principle," Cercy said, and collapsed into a chair.

"Any sign of the Ambassador?" he asked, in a few minutes.

The spot was still wavering. Then it was gone. Instantly there was an explosion. The steel walls buckled inward, but held. The screen went dead.

"The spot removed all the air from the room," Cercy explained, "as well as the furniture and the Ambassador."

"He couldn't take it," Malley said. "No pattern can cohere, in a state of patternlessness. He's gone to join Alfern."

Malley started to giggle. Cercy felt like joining him, but pulled himself together.

"Take it easy," he said. "We're not through yet."

"Sure we are! The Ambassador—"

"Is out of the way. But there's still an alien fleet homing in on this region of space. A fleet so strong we couldn't scratch it with an H-bomb. They'll be looking for us."

He stood up.

"Go home and get some sleep. Something tells me that tomorrow we're going to have to start figuring out some way of camouflaging a planet."

One Man's Poison

They could eat a horse, only luckily there was none...it might have eaten them first!

HELLMAN plucked the last radish out of the can with a pair of dividers. He held it up for Casker to admire, then laid it carefully on the workbench beside the razor.

"Hell of a meal for two grown men," Casker said, flopping down in one of the ship's padded crash chairs.

"If you'd like to give up your share—" Hellman started to suggest.

Casker shook his head quickly. Hellman smiled, picked up the razor and examined its edge critically.

"Don't make a production out of it," Casker said, glancing at the ship's instruments. They were approaching a red dwarf, the only planet-bearing sun in the vicinity. "We want to be through with supper before we get much closer."

Hellman made a practice incision in the radish, squinting along the top of the razor. Casker bent closer, his mouth open.

Hellman poised the razor delicately and cut the radish cleanly in half.

"Will you say grace?" Hellman asked.

Casker growled something and popped a half in his mouth. Hellman chewed more slowly. The sharp taste seemed to explode along his disused taste buds.

"Not much bulk value," Hellman said.

Casker didn't answer. He was busily studying the red dwarf.

AS he swallowed the last of his radish, Hellman stifled a sigh. Their last meal had been three days ago… if two biscuits and a cup of water could be called a meal. This radish, now resting in the vast emptiness of their stomachs, was the last gram of food on board ship.

"Two planets," Casker said. "One's burned to a crisp."

"Then we'll land on the other."

Casker nodded and punched a deceleration spiral into the ship's tape.

Hellman found himself wondering for the hundredth time where the fault had been. Could he have made out the food requisitions wrong, when they took on supplies at Calao station? After all, he had been devoting most of his attention to the mining equipment. Or had the ground crew just forgotten to load those last precious cases?

He drew his belt in to the fourth new notch he had punched.

Speculation was useless. Whatever the reason, they were in a jam. Ironically enough, they had more than enough fuel to take them back to Calao. But they would be a pair of singularly emaciated corpses by the time the ship reached there.

"We're coming in now," Casker said.

And to make matters worse, this unexplored region of space had few suns and fewer planets. Perhaps there was a slight possibility of replenishing their water supply, but the odds were enormous against finding anything they could eat.

"Look at that place," Casker growled.

Hellman shook himself out of his reverie.

The planet was like a round gray-brown porcupine. The spines of a million needle-sharp mountains glittered in the red dwarf's feeble light. And as they spiraled lower, circling the planet, the pointed mountains seemed to stretch out to meet them.

"It can't be *all* mountains," Hellman said.

"It's not."

Sure enough, there were oceans and lakes, out of which thrust jagged island-mountains. But no sign of level land, no hint of civilization; or even animal life.

"At least it's got an oxygen atmosphere," Casker said.

Their deceleration spiral swept them around the planet, cutting lower into the atmosphere, braking against it. And still there was nothing but mountains and lakes and oceans and more mountains.

On the eighth run, Hellman caught sight of a solitary building on a mountaintop. Casker braked recklessly, and the hull glowed red hot. On the eleventh run, they made a landing approach.

"Stupid place to build," Casker muttered.

The building was doughnut-shaped, and fitted nicely over the top of the mountain. There was a wide, level lip around it, which Casker scorched as he landed the ship.

FROM the air, the building had merely seemed big.

On the ground, it was enormous. Hellman and Casker walked up to it slowly. Hellman had his burner ready, but there was no sign of life.

"This planet must be abandoned," Hellman said almost in a whisper.

"Anyone in his right mind would abandon this place," Casker said. "There're enough good planets around, without anyone trying to live on a needle point."

They reached the door. Hellman tried to open it and found it locked. He looked back at the spectacular display of mountains.

"You know," he said, "when this planet was still in a molten state, it must have been affected by several gigantic moons that are now broken up. The strains, external and internal, wrenched it into its present spined appearance and—"

"Come off it," Casker said ungraciously. "You were a librarian before you decided to get rich on uranium."

Hellman shrugged his shoulders and burned a hole in the doorlock. They waited.

The only sound on the mountain top was the growling of their stomachs.

They entered.

The tremendous wedge-shaped room was evidently a warehouse of sorts. Goods were piled to the ceiling, scattered over the floor, stacked haphazardly against the walls. There were boxes and containers of all sizes and shapes, some big enough to hold an elephant, others the size of thimbles.

Near the door was a dusty pile of books. Immediately, Hellman bent down to examine them.

"Must be food somewhere in here," Casker said, his

face lighting up for the first time in a week. He started to open the nearest box.

"This is interesting," Hellman said, discarding all the books except one.

"Let's eat first," Casker said, ripping the top off the box. Inside was a brownish dust. Casker looked at it, sniffed, and made a face.

"Very interesting indeed," Hellman said, leafing through the book.

Casker opened a small can, which contained a glittering green slime. He closed it and opened another. It contained a dull orange slime.

"Hmm," Hellman said, still reading.

"Hellman! Will you kindly drop that book and help me find some food?"

"Food?" Hellman repeated, looking up. "What makes you think there's anything to eat here? For all you know, this could be a paint factory."

"It's a warehouse!" Casker shouted.

He opened a kidney-shaped can and lifted out a soft purple stick. It hardened quickly and crumpled to dust as he tried to smell it. He scooped up a handful of the dust and brought it to his mouth.

"That might be extract of strychnine," Hellman said casually.

CASKER abruptly dropped the dust and wiped his hands.

"After all," Hellman pointed out, "granted that this is a warehouse—a cache, if you wish—we don't know what the late inhabitants considered good fare. Paris green salad, perhaps, with sulphuric acid as dressing."

"All right," Casker said, "but we gotta eat. What're you going to do about all this?" He gestured at the hundreds of boxes, cans and bottles.

"The thing to do," Hellman said briskly, "is to make a qualitative analysis on four or five samples. We could start out with a simple titration, sublimate the chief ingredient, see if it forms a precipitate, work out its molecular makeup from—"

"Hellman, you don't know what you're talking about. You're a librarian, remember? And I'm a correspondence school pilot. We don't know anything about titrations and sublimations."

"I know," Hellman said, "but we should. It's the right way to go about it."

"Sure. In the meantime, though, just until a chemist drops in, what'll we do?"

"This might help us," Hellman said, holding up the book. "Do you know what it is?"

"No," Casker said, keeping a tight grip on his patience.

"It's a pocket dictionary and guide to the Helg language."

"Helg?"

"The planet we're on. The symbols match up with those on the boxes."

Casker raised an eyebrow. "Never heard of Helg."

"I don't believe the planet has ever had any contact with Earth," Hellman said. "This dictionary isn't Helg-English. It's Helg-Aloombrigian."

Casker remembered that Aloombrigian was the home planet of a small, adventurous reptilian race, out near the center of the Galaxy.

"How come you can read Aloombrigian?" Casker asked.

"Oh, being a librarian isn't a completely useless profession," Hellman said modestly. "In my spare time—"

"Yeah. Now how about—"

"Do you know," Hellman said, "the Aloombrigians probably helped the Helgans leave their planet and find another. They sell services like that. In which case, this building very likely is a food cache!"

"Suppose you start translating," Casker suggested wearily, "and maybe find us something to eat."

They opened boxes until they found a likely looking substance. Laboriously, Hellman translated the symbols on it.

"Got it," he said. "It reads: — 'USE SNIFFNERS — THE BETTER ABRASIVE'".

"Doesn't sound edible," Casker said.

"I'm afraid not."

They found another, which read: VIGROOM! FILL ALL YOUR STOMACHS, AND FILL THEM RIGHT!

"What kind of animals do you suppose these Helgans were?" Casker asked.

Hellman shrugged his shoulders.

The next label took almost fifteen minutes to translate. It read: ARGOSEL MAKES YOUR THUDRA ALL TIZZY. CONTAINS THIRTY ARPS OF RAMSTAT PULZ, FOR SHELL LUBRICATION.

"There must be *something* here we can eat," Casker said with a note of desperation.

"I hope so," Hellman replied.

AT the end of two hours, they were no closer. They had translated dozens of titles and sniffed so many substances that their olfactory senses had given up in disgust.

"Let's talk this over," Hellman said, sitting on a box marked: VORMITISH—GOOD AS IT SOUNDS!

"Sure," Casker said, sprawling out on the floor. "Talk."

"If we could deduce what kind of creatures inhabited this planet, we'd know what kind of food they ate, and whether it's likely to be edible for us."

"All we do know is that they wrote a lot of lousy advertising copy."

Hellman ignored that. "What kind of intelligent beings would evolve on a planet that is all mountains?"

"Stupid ones!" Casker said.

That was no help. But Hellman found that he couldn't draw any inferences from the mountains. It didn't tell him if the late Helgans ate silicates or proteins or iodine-base foods or anything.

"Now look," Hellman said, "we'll have to work this out by pure logic—Are you listening to me?"

"Sure," Casker said.

"Okay. There's an old proverb that covers our situation perfectly: 'One man's meat is another man's poison.'"

"Yeah," Casker said. He was positive his stomach had shrunk to approximately the size of a marble.

"We can assume, first, that their meat is our meat."

Casket wrenched himself away from a vision of five juicy roast beefs dancing tantalizingly before him. "What if their meat is our *poison*? What then?"

"Then," Hellman said, "we will assume that their poison is our meat."

"And what happens if their meat *and* their poison are our poison?"

"We starve."

"All right," Casker said, standing up. "Which assumption do we start with?"

"Well, there's no sense in asking for trouble. This *is* an oxygen planet, if that means anything. Let's assume that we can eat some basic food of theirs. If we can't we'll start on their poisons."

"If we live that long," Casker said.

Hellman began to translate labels. They discarded such brands as ANDROGYNITES DELIGHT and VERBELL – FOR LONGER, CURLIER, MORE SENSITIVE ANTENNAE, until they found a small gray box, about six inches by three by three. It was called VALKORIN'S UNIVERSAL TASTE TREAT, FOR ALL DIGESTIVE CAPACITIES.

"This looks as good as any," Hellman said. He opened the box.

Casker leaned over and sniffed. "No odor."

WITHIN the box they found a rectangular, rubbery red block. It quivered slightly, like jelly.

"Bite into it," Casker said.

"Me?" Hellman asked. "Why not you?"

"You picked it."

"I prefer just looking at it," Hellman said with dignity. "I'm not too hungry."

"I'm not either," Casker said.

They sat on the floor and stared at the jellylike block.

After ten minutes, Hellman yawned, leaned back and closed his eyes.

"All right, coward," Casker said bitterly. "I'll try it. Just remember, though, if I'm poisoned, you'll never get off this planet. You don't know how to pilot."

"Just take a little bite, then," Hellman advised.

Casker leaned over and stared at the block. Then he prodded it with his thumb.

The rubbery red block giggled.

"Did you hear that?" Casker yelped, leaping back.

"I didn't hear anything," Hellman said, his hands shaking. "Go ahead."

Casker prodded the block again. It giggled louder, this time with a disgusting little simper.

"Okay," Casker said, "what do we try next?"

"Next? What's this?"

"I don't eat anything that giggles," Casker stated firmly.

"Now listen to me," Hellman said. "The creatures who manufactured this might have been trying to create an esthetic sound as well as a pleasant shape and color. That giggle is probably only for the amusement of the eater."

"Then bite into it yourself," Casker offered.

Hellman glared at him, but made no move toward the rubbery block. Finally he said, "Let's move it out of the way."

They pushed the block over to a corner. It lay there giggling softly to itself.

"Now what?" Casker said.

Hellman looked around at the jumbled stacks of incomprehensible alien goods. He noticed a door on either side of the room.

"Let's have a look in the other sections," he suggested.

Casker shrugged his shoulders apathetically.

Slowly they trudged to the door in the left wall. It was locked and Hellman burned it open with the ship's burner.

It was a wedge-shaped room, piled with incomprehensible alien goods.

The hike back across the room seemed like miles, but they made it only slightly out of wind. Hellman blew out the lock and they looked in.

It was a wedge-shaped room, piled with incomprehensible alien goods.

"All the same," Casker said sadly, and closed the door.

"Evidently there's a series of these rooms going completely around the building," Hellman said. "I wonder if we should explore them."

Casker calculated the distance around the building, compared it with his remaining strength, and sat down heavily on a long gray object.

"Why bother?" he asked.

HELLMAN tried to collect his thoughts. Certainly he should be able to find a key of some sort, a clue that would tell him what they could eat. But where was it?

He examined the object Casker was sitting on. It was about the size and shape of a large coffin, with a shallow depression on top. It was made of a hard, corrugated substance.

"What do you suppose this is?" Hellman asked.

"Does it matter?"

Hellman glanced at the symbols painted on the side of the object, then looked them up in his dictionary.

"Fascinating," he murmured, after a while.

"Is it something to eat?" Casker asked, with a faint glimmering of hope.

"No. You are sitting on something called THE MOROG CUSTOM SUPER TRANSPORT FOR THE DISCRIMINATING HELGAN WHO DESIRES THE BEST IN VERTICAL TRANSPORTATION. It's a vehicle!"

"Oh," Casker said dully.

"This is important! Look at it! How does it work?"

Casker wearily climbed off the Morog Custom Super Transport and looked it over carefully. He traced four almost invisible separations on its four corners. "Retractable wheels, probably, but I don't see—"

Hellman read on. "It says to give it three amphus of high-gain Integor fuel, then a van of Tonder lubrication, and not to run it over three thousand Ruls for the first fifty mungus."

"Let's find something to eat," Casker said.

"Don't you see how important this is?" Hellman asked. "This could solve our problem. If we could deduce the alien logic inherent in constructing this vehicle, we might know the Helgan thought pattern. This, in turn, would give us an insight into their nervous systems, which would imply their biochemical makeup."

Casker stood still, trying to decide whether he had enough strength left to strangle Hellman.

"For example," Hellman said, "what kind of vehicle would be used in a place like this? Not one with wheels, since everything is up and down. Anti-gravity? Perhaps, but what *kind* of anti-gravity? And why did the inhabitants devise a boxlike form instead—"

Casker decided sadly that he didn't have enough strength to strangle Hellman, no matter how pleasant it might be. Very quietly, he said, "Kindly stop making like a scientist. Let's see if there isn't *something* we can gulp down."

"All right," Hellman said sulkily.

CASKER watched his partner wander off among the cans, bottles and cases. He wondered vaguely where Hellman got the energy, and decided that he was just too cerebral to know when he was starving.

"Here's something," Hellman called out, standing in front of a large yellow vat.

"What does it say?" Casker asked.

"Little bit hard to translate. But rendered freely, it reads: MORISHILLE'S VOOZY, WITH LACTO-ECTO ADDED FOR A NEW TASTE SENSATION. EVERYONE DRINKS VOOZY. GOOD BEFORE AND AFTER MEALS, NO UNPLEASANT AFTER-EFFECTS. GOOD FOR CHILDREN! THE DRINK OF THE UNIVERSE!"

"That sounds good," Casker admitted, thinking that Hellman might not be so stupid after all.

"This should tell us once and for all if their meat *is* our meat," Hellman said. "This Voozy seems to be the closest thing to a universal drink I've found yet."

"Maybe," Casker said hopefully, "maybe it's just plain water!"

"We'll see." Hellman pried open the lid with the edge

of the burner.

Within the vat was a crystal-clear liquid.

"No odor," Casker said, bending over the vat.

The crystal liquid lifted to meet him.

Casker retreated so rapidly that he fell over a box. Hellman helped him to his feet, and they approached the vat again. As they came near, the liquid lifted itself three feet into the air and moved toward them.

"What've you done now?" Casker asked, moving back carefully. The liquid flowed slowly over the side of the vat. It began to flow toward him.

"Hellman!" Casker shrieked.

Hellman was standing to one side, perspiration pouring down his face, reading his dictionary with a preoccupied frown.

"Guess I bumbled the translation," he said.

"Do something!" Casker shouted. The liquid was trying to back him into a corner.

"Nothing I can do," Hellman said, reading on. "Ah, here's the error. It doesn't say 'Everyone drinks Voozy.' Wrong subject. 'Voozy drinks *everyone*.' That tells us something! The Helgans must have soaked liquid in through their pores. Naturally, they would prefer to be drunk, instead of to drink."

Casker tried to dodge around the liquid, but it cut him off with a merry gurgle. Desperately he picked up a small bale and threw it at the Voozy. The Voozy caught the bale and drank it. Then it discarded that and turned back to Casker.

Hellman tossed another box. The Voozy drank this one and a third and fourth that Casker threw in. Then, apparently exhausted, it flowed back into its vat.

Casker clapped down the lid and sat on it, trembling violently.

"Not so good," Hellman said. "We've been taking it for granted that the Helgans had eating habits like us. But, of course, it doesn't necessarily—"

"No, it doesn't. No, sir, it certainly doesn't. I guess we can see that it doesn't. Anyone can see that it doesn't—"

"Stop that," Hellman ordered sternly. "We've no time for hysteria."

"Sorry." Casker slowly moved away from the Voozy vat.

"I guess we'll have to assume that their meat is our poison," Hellman said thoughtfully. "So now we'll see if their poison is our meat."

Casker didn't say anything. He was wondering what would have happened if the Voozy had drunk him.

In the corner, the rubbery block was still giggling to itself.

"NOW here's a likely-looking poison," Hellman said, half an hour later.

Casker had recovered completely, except for an occasional twitch of the lips.

"What does it say?" he asked.

Hellman rolled a tiny tube in the palm of his hand. "It's called Pvastkin's Plugger. The label reads: WARNING! WARNING! HIGHLY DANGEROUS! PVASTKIN'S PLUGGER IS DESIGNED TO FILL HOLES OR CRACKS OF NOT MORE THAN TWO CUBIC VIMS. HOWEVER—THE PLUGGER IS NOT TO BE EATEN UNDER ANY KIND OF

CIRCUMSTANCES. THE ACTIVE INGREDIENT, RAMOTOL, WHICH MAKES PVASTKIN'S SO EXCELLENT A PLUGGER, WILL RENDER IT EXTREMELY DANGEROUS SHOULD IT BE TAKEN INTERNALLY."

"Sounds great," Casker said. "It'll probably blow us sky-high."

"Do you have any other suggestions?" Hellman asked.

Casker thought for a moment. The food of Helg was obviously unpalatable for humans. So perhaps was their poison… but wasn't starvation better than this sort of thing?

After a moment's communion with his stomach, he decided that starvation was not better.

"Go ahead," he said.

Hellman slipped the burner under his arm and unscrewed the top of the little bottle. He shook it.

Nothing happened.

"It's got a seal," Casker pointed out.

Hellman punctured the seal with his fingernail and set the bottle on the floor. An evil-smelling green froth began to bubble out.

Hellman looked dubiously at the froth. It was congealing into a glob and spreading over the floor.

"Yeast, perhaps," he said, gripping the burner tightly.

"Come, come. Faint heart never filled an empty stomach."

"I'm not holding *you* back," Hellman said.

The glob swelled to the size of a man's head.

"How long is that supposed to go on?" Casker asked.

"Well," Hellman said, "it's advertised as a Plugger. I suppose that's what it does—expands to plug up holes."

"Sure. But how *much*?"

"Unfortunately, I don't know how much two cubic vims are. But it can't go on much—"

Belatedly, they noticed that the Plugger had filled almost a quarter of the room and was showing no signs of stopping.

"We should have believed the label!" Casker yelled to him, across the spreading glob. "It *is* dangerous!"

As the Plugger produced more surface, it began to accelerate in its growth. A sticky edge touched Hellman, and he jumped back.

"Watch out!"

He couldn't reach Casker, on the other side of the gigantic sphere of blob. Hellman tried to run around, but the Plugger had spread, cutting the room in half. It began to swell toward the walls.

"Run for it!" Hellman yelled, and rushed to the door behind him.

HE flung it open just as the expanding glob reached him. On the other side of the room, he heard a door slam shut. Hellman didn't wait any longer. He sprinted through and slammed the door behind him.

He stood for a moment, panting, the burner in his hand. He hadn't realized how weak he was. That sprint had cut his reserves of energy dangerously close to the collapsing point. At least Casker had made it, too, though.

But he was still in trouble.

The Plugger poured merrily through the blasted lock, into the room. Hellman tried a practice shot on it, but the Plugger was evidently impervious… as, he realized, a good plugger should be.

It was showing no signs of fatigue.

Hellman hurried to the far wall. The door was locked, as the others had been, so he burned out the lock and went through.

How far could the glob expand? How much was two cubic vims? Two cubic miles, perhaps? For all he knew, the Plugger was used to repair faults in the crusts of planets.

In the next room, Hellman stopped to catch his breath. He remembered that the building was circular. He would burn his way through the remaining doors and join Casker. They would burn their way outside and…

Casker didn't have a burner!

Hellman turned white with shock. Casker had made it into the room on the right, because they had burned it open earlier. The Plugger was undoubtedly oozing into that room, through the shattered lock… and Casker couldn't get out! The Plugger was on his left, a locked door on his right!

Rallying his remaining strength, Hellman began to run. Boxes seemed to get in his way purposefully, tripping him, slowing him down. He blasted the next door and hurried on to the next. And the next. And the next.

The Plugger couldn't expand *completely* into Casker's room!

Or could it?

The wedge-shaped rooms, each a segment of a circle, seemed to stretch before him forever, a jumbled montage of locked doors, alien goods, more doors, more goods. Hellman fell over a crate, got to his feet and fell again. He had reached the limit of his strength, and passed it. But Casker was his friend.

Besides, without a pilot, he'd never get off the place.

Hellman struggled through two more rooms on trembling legs and then collapsed in front of a third.

"Is that you, Hellman?" he heard Casker ask, from the other side of the door.

"You all right?" Hellman managed to gasp.

"Haven't much room in here," Casker said, "but the Plugger's stopped growing. Hellman, get me out of here!"

HELLMAN lay on the floor panting. "Moment," he said.

"Moment, hell!" Casker shouted. "Get, me out, I've found water!"

"What? How?"

"Get me out of here!"

Hellman tried to stand up, but his legs weren't cooperating. "What happened?" he asked.

"When I saw that glob filling the room, I figured I'd try to start up the Super Custom Transport. Thought maybe it could knock down the door and get me out. So I pumped it full of high-gain Integor fuel."

"Yes?" Hellman said, still trying to get his legs under control.

"That Super Custom Transport is an animal, Hellman! And the Integer fuel is water! Now get me out!"

Hellman lay back with a contented sigh. If he had had a little more time, he would have worked out the whole thing himself, by pure logic. But it was all very apparent now. The most efficient machine to go over those vertical, razor-sharp mountains would be an animal, probably with retractable suckers. It was kept in hibernation between trips; and if it drank water, the other products designed for it would be palatable, too. Of course they still didn't know much about the late inhabitants, but undoubtedly…

"Burn down that door!" Casker shrieked, his voice breaking.

Hellman was pondering the irony of it all. If one man's meat—*and* his poison—are your poison, then try eating something else. So simple, really.

But there was one thing that still bothered him.

"How did you know it was an Earth-type animal?" he asked.

"Its breath, stupid! It inhales and exhales and smells as if it's eaten onions!" There was a sound of cans falling and bottles shattering. "Now hurry!"

"What's wrong?" Hellman asked, finally getting to his feet and poising the burner.

"The Custom Super Transport. It's got me cornered behind a pile of cases. Hellman, it seems to think that I'm *its* meat!"

Broiled with the burner—well done for Hellman, medium rare for Casker—it was their meat, with enough left over for the trip back to Calao.

The Perfect Woman

Somebody once came up with a song title we have never forgotten: "For every man there is woman, so why did I get stuck with you?"

Not that Mr. Morcheck felt that way about Myra. He not only believed she was absolutely perfect; you could get a punch in the nose for doubting it!

And he was so *right—for a while!*

MR. MORCHECK awoke with a sour taste in his mouth and a laugh ringing in his ears. It was George Owen-Clark's laugh, the last thing he remembered from the Triad-Morgan party. And what a party it had been! All Earth had been celebrating the turn of the century. The year Three Thousand! Peace and prosperity to all, and happy life…

"How happy is your life?" Owen-Clark had asked, grinning slyly, more than a little drunk. "I mean, how is life with your sweet wife?"

That had been unpleasant. Everyone knew that Owen-Clark was a Primitivist, but what right had he to rub people's noses in it? Just because he had married a Primitive Woman…

"I love my wife," Morcheck had said stoutly. "And she's a hell of a lot nicer and more responsive than that bundle of neuroses you call *your* wife."

But of course, you can't get under the thick hide of a Primitivist. Primitivists love the faults in their women as much as their virtues—more, perhaps. Owen-Clark had grinned ever more slyly, and said, "You know, Morcheck old man, I think your wife needs a checkup. Have you noticed her reflexes lately?"

Insufferable idiot! Mr. Morcheck eased himself out of bed, blinking at the bright morning sun that hid behind his curtains. Myra's reflexes—the hell of it was, there was a germ of truth in what Owen-Clark had said. Of late, Myra had seemed rather—out of sorts.

"Myra!" Morcheck called. "Is my coffee ready?" There was a pause. Then her voice floated brightly upstairs. "In a minute!"

Morcheck slid into a pair of slacks, still blinking sleepily. Thank Stat the next three days were celebration-points. He'd need all of them just to get over last night's party.

Downstairs, Myra was bustling around, pouring coffee, folding napkins, pulling out his chair for him. He sat down, and she kissed him on his bald spot. He liked being kissed on his bald spot.

"How's my little wife this morning?" he asked.

"Wonderful, darling," she said after a little pause. "I made Seffiners for you this morning. You like Seffiners."

Morcheck bit into one, done to a turn, and sipped his coffee.

"How do you feel this morning?" he asked her.

Myra buttered a piece of toast for him, then said, "Wonderful darling. You know, it was a perfectly wonderful party last night. I loved every moment of it."

"I got a little bit veery," Morcheck said with a wry grin.

"I love you when you're veery," Myra said. "You talk like an angel like a very clever angel, I mean. I could listen to you forever," she buttered another piece of toast for him.

Mr. Morcheck beamed on her like a benignant sun, then frowned. He put down his Seffiner and scratched his cheek. "You know," he said, "I had a little ruck-in with Owen-Clark. He was talking about Primitive Women."

Myra buttered a fifth piece of toast for him without answering, adding it to the growing pile. She started to reach for a sixth, but he touched her hand lightly. She bent forward and kissed him on the nose.

"Primitive Women!" she scoffed. "Those neurotic creatures! Aren't you happier with me, dear? I may be Modern—but no Primitive Woman could love you the way I do—and I adore you!"

What she said was true. Man had never, in all recorded history, been able to live happily with unreconstructed Primitive Woman. The egoistic, spoiled creatures demanded a lifetime of care and attention. It was notorious that Owen-Clark's wife made him dry the dishes. And the fool put up with it! Primitive Women were forever asking for money with which to buy clothes and trinkets, demanding breakfast in bed, dashing off to bridge games, talking for hours on the telephone, and Stat knows what else. They tried to take over men's jobs. Ultimately, they proved their equality.

Some idiots like Owen-Clark insisted on their excellence.

Under his wife's enveloping love, Mr. Morcheck felt his hangover seep slowly away. Myra wasn't eating. He knew that she had eaten earlier, so that she could give her full attention to feeding him. It was little things like that that made all the difference.

"He said your reaction time had slowed down."

"He did?" Myra asked, after a pause. "Those Primitives think they know everything."

It was the right answer, but it had taken too long. Mr. Morcheck asked his wife a few more questions, observing her reaction time by the second hand on the kitchen clock. She *was* slowing up!

"Did the mail come?" he asked her quickly. "Did anyone call? Will I be late for work?"

After three seconds she opened her mouth, then closed it again.

Something was terribly wrong.

"I love you," she said simply.

Mr. Morcheck felt his heart pound against his ribs. He loved her! Madly, passionately! But that disgusting Owen-Clark had been right. She needed a checkup. Myra seemed to sense his thought. She rallied perceptibly, and said, "All I want is your happiness, dear. I think I'm sick… Will you have me cured? Will you take me back after I'm cured—and not let them change me—I wouldn't want to be changed!" Her bright head sank on her arms. She cried—noiselessly, so as not to disturb him.

"It'll just be a checkup, darling," Morcheck said, trying to hold back his own tears. But he knew—as well as she knew—that she was really sick.

It was so unfair, he thought. Primitive Woman, with her coarse mental fibre, was almost immune to such ailments. But delicate Modern Woman, with her finely balanced sensibilities, was all too prone. So monstrously unfair! Because Modern Woman contained all the finest, dearest qualities of femininity.

Except stamina.

Myra rallied again. She raised herself to her feet with an effort. She was very beautiful. Her sickness had put a high color in her cheeks, and the morning sun highlighted her hair.

"My darling," she said. "Won't you let me stay a little longer? I may recover by myself." But her eyes were fast becoming unfocused.

"Darling..." She caught herself quickly, holding on to an edge of the table. "When you have a new wife—try to remember how much I loved you," she sat down, her face blank.

"I'll get the car," Morcheck murmured, and hurried away. Any longer and he would have broken down himself.

Walking to the garage he felt numb, tired, broken. Myra—gone! And modern science, for all its great achievements, unable to help.

He reached the garage and said, "All right, back out." Smoothly his car backed out and stopped beside him.

"Anything wrong, boss?" his car asked. "You look worried. Still got a hangover?"

"No—it's Myra. She's sick."

The car was silent for a moment. Then it said softly,

"I'm very sorry, Mr. Morcheck. I wish there were something I could do."

"Thank you," Morcheck said, glad to have a friend at this hour. "I'm afraid there's nothing anyone can do."

The car backed to the door and Morcheck helped Myra inside. Gently the car started.

It maintained a delicate silence on the way back to the factory.

Cost of Living

If easy payment plans were to be really efficient, patrons' lifetimes had to be extended!

CARRIN decided that he could trace his present mood to Miller's suicide last week. But the knowledge didn't help him get rid of the vague, formless fear in the back of his mind. It was foolish. Miller's suicide didn't concern him.

But why had that fat, jovial man killed himself? Miller had had everything to live for—wife, kids, good job, and all the marvelous luxuries of the age. Why had he done it?

"Good morning, dear," Carrin's wife said as he sat down at the breakfast table.

"Morning, honey. Morning, Billy."

His son grunted something.

You just couldn't tell about people, Carrin decided, and dialed his breakfast. The meal was gracefully prepared and served by the new Avignon Electric Autocook.

His mood persisted, annoyingly enough since Carrin wanted to be in top form this morning. It was his day off, and the Avignon Electric finance man was coming. This was an important day.

He walked to the door with his son.

"Have a good day, Billy."

His son nodded, shifted his books and started to school without answering. Carrin wondered if something was bothering him, too. He hoped not. One worrier in the family was plenty.

"See you later, honey." He kissed his wife as she left to go shopping.

At any rate, he thought, watching her go down the walk, at least she's happy. He wondered how much she'd spend at the A. E. store.

Checking his watch, he found that he had half an hour before the A. E. finance man was due. The best way to get rid of a bad mood was to drown it, he told himself, and headed for the shower.

THE shower room was a glittering plastic wonder, and the sheer luxury of it eased Carrin's mind. He threw his clothes into the A. E. automatic Kleen-presser, and adjusted the shower spray to a notch above "brisk." The five-degrees-above-skin-temperature water beat against his thin white body. Delightful! And then a relaxing rub-dry in the A. E. Auto-towel.

Wonderful, he thought, as the towel stretched and kneaded his stringy muscles. And it should be wonderful, he reminded himself. The A. E. Auto-towel with shaving attachments had cost three hundred and thirteen dollars, plus tax.

But worth every penny of it, he decided, as the A. E. shaver came out of a corner and whisked off his rudimentary stubble. After all, what good was life if you couldn't enjoy the luxuries?

His skin tingled when he switched off the auto-towel. He should have been feeling wonderful, but he wasn't, Miller's suicide kept nagging at his mind, destroying the peace of his day off.

Was there anything else bothering him? Certainly there was nothing wrong with the house. His papers were in order for the finance man.

"Have I forgotten something?" he asked out loud.

"The Avignon Electric finance man will be here in fifteen minutes," his A. E. bathroom Wall-reminder whispered.

"I know that. Is there anything else?"

The Wall-reminder reeled off its memorized data—a vast amount of minutiae about watering the lawn, having the Jet-lash checked, buying lamb chops for Monday, and the like. Things he still hadn't found time for.

"All right, that's enough." He allowed the A. E. Auto-dresser to dress him, skillfully draping a new selection of fabrics over his bony frame. A whiff of fashionable masculine perfume finished him and he went into the living room, threading his way between the appliances that lined the walls.

A quick inspection of the dials on the wall assured him that the house was in order. The breakfast dishes had been sanitized and stacked, the house had been cleaned, dusted, polished, his wife's garments had been hung up, his son's model rocket ships had been put back in the closet.

Stop worrying, you hypochondriac, he told himself angrily.

The door announced, "Mr. Pathis from Avignon Finance is here."

Carrin started to tell the door to open when he noticed the Automatic Bartender.

Good God, why hadn't he thought of it!

The Automatic Bartender was manufactured by Castile Motors. He had bought it in a weak moment. A.E. wouldn't think very highly of that, since they sold their own brand.

HE wheeled the bartender into the kitchen, and told the door to open.

"A very good day to you, sir," Mr. Pathis said.

Pathis was a tall, imposing man, dressed in a conservative tweed drape. His eyes had the crinkled corners of a man who laughs frequently. He beamed broadly and shook Carrin's hand, looking around the crowded living room.

"A beautiful place you have here, sir. Beautiful! As a matter of fact, I don't think I'll be overstepping the company's code to inform you that yours is the nicest interior in this section."

Carrin felt a sudden glow of pride at that, thinking of throws of identical houses, on this block and the next, and the one after that.

"Now, then, is everything functioning properly?" Mr. Pathis asked, setting his briefcase on a chair. "Everything in order?"

"Oh, yes," Carrin said enthusiastically. "Avignon Electric never goes out of whack."

"The phone all right? Changes records for the full seventeen hours?"

"It certainly does," Carrin said. He hadn't had a chance to tryout the phone, but it was a beautiful piece of furniture.

"The Solido-projector all right? Enjoying the programs?"

"Absolutely perfect reception." He had watched a program just last month, and it had been startlingly lifelike.

"How about the kitchen? Auto-cook in order? Recipe-master still knocking 'em out?"

"Marvelous stuff. Simply marvelous."

Mr. Pathis went on to inquire about his refrigerator, his vacuum cleaner, his car, his helicopter, his subterranean swimming pool, and the hundreds of other items Carrin had bought from Avignon Electric.

"Everything is swell," Carrin said, a trifle untruthfully since he hadn't unpacked every item yet. "Just wonderful."

"I'm so glad," Mr. Pathis said, leaning back with a sigh of relief. "You have no idea how hard we try to satisfy our customers. If a product isn't right, back it comes, no questions asked. We believe in pleasing our customers."

"I certainly appreciate it, Mr. Pathis."

CARRIN hoped the A. E. man wouldn't ask to see the kitchen. He visualized the Castile Motors Bartender in there, like a porcupine in a dog show.

"I'm proud to say that most of the people in this neighborhood buy from us," Mr. Pathis was saying. "We're a solid firm."

"Was Mr. Miller a customer of yours?" Carrin asked.

"That fellow who killed himself?" Pathis frowned briefly. "He was, as a matter of fact. That amazed me, sir, absolutely amazed me. Why, just last month the fellow bought a brand-new Jet-lash from me, capable of doing three hundred and fifty miles an hour on a straightaway. He was as happy as a kid over it, and then to go and do a thing like that! Of course, the Jet-lash brought up his debt a little."

"Of course."

"But what did that matter? He had every luxury in the world. And then he went and hung himself."

"Hung himself?"

"Yes," Pathis said, the frown coming back. "Every modern convenience in his house, and he hung himself with a piece of rope. Probably unbalanced for a long time."

The frown slid off his face, and the customary smile replaced it. "But enough of that! Let's talk about you."

The smile widened as Pathis opened his briefcase. "Now, then, your account. You owe us two hundred and three thousand dollars and twenty-nine cents, Mr. Carrin, as of your last purchase. Right?"

"Right," Carrin said, remembering the amount from his own papers. "Here's my installment."

He handed Pathis an envelope, which the man checked and put in his pocket.

"Fine. Now you know, Mr. Carrin, that you won't live long enough to pay us the full two hundred thousand, don't you?"

"No, I don't suppose I will," Carrin said soberly.

He was only thirty-nine, with a full hundred years of life before him, thanks to the marvels of medical science. But at a salary of three thousand a year, he still couldn't pay it all off and have enough to support a family on at the same time.

"Of course, we would not want to deprive you of necessities, which in any case is fully protected by the laws we helped formulate and pass. To say nothing of the terrific items that are coming out next year. Things you wouldn't want to miss, sir!"

Mr. Carrin nodded. Certainly he wanted new items.

"Well, suppose we make the customary arrangement. If you will just sign over your son's earnings for the first thirty years of his adult life, we can easily arrange credit for you."

MR. Pathis whipped the papers out of his briefcase and spread them in front of Carrin.

"If you'll just sign here, sir."

"Well," Carrin said, "I'm not sure. I'd like to give the boy a start in life, not saddle him with—"

"But my dear sir," Pathis interposed, "this is for your son as well. He lives here, doesn't he? He has a right to enjoy the luxuries, the marvels of science."

"Sure," Carrin said. "Only—"

"Why, sir, today the average man is living like a king. A hundred years ago the richest man in the world couldn't buy what any ordinary citizen possesses at present. You mustn't look upon it as a debt. It's an investment."

"That's true," Carrin said dubiously.

He thought about his son and his rocket ship models, his star charts, his maps. Would it be right he asked himself?

"What's wrong?" Pathis asked cheerfully.

"Well, I was just wondering," Carrin said. "Signing

over my son's earnings—you don't think I'm getting in a little too deep, do you?"

"Too deep? My dear sir!" Pathis exploded into laughter. "Do you know Mellon down the block? Well, don't say I said it, but he's already mortgaged his grandchildren's salary for their full life expectancy! And he doesn't have half the goods he's made up his mind to own! We'll work out something for him. Service to the customer is our job and we know it well."

Carrin wavered visibly.

"And after you're gone, sir, they'll all belong to your son."

That was true, Carrin thought. His son would have all the marvelous things that filled the house. And after all, it was only thirty years out of a life expectancy of a hundred and fifty.

He signed with a flourish.

"Excellent!" Pathis said. "And by the way, has your home got an A. E. Master-operator?"

It hadn't. Pathis explained that a Master-operator was new this year, a stupendous advance in scientific engineering. It was designed to take over all the functions of housecleaning and cooking, without its owner having to lift a finger.

"Instead of running around all day, pushing half a dozen different buttons, with the Master-operator all you have to do is push *one*! A remarkable achievement!"

Since it was only five hundred and thirty-five dollars, Carrin signed for one, having it added to his son's debt.

Right's right, he thought, walking Pathis to the door. This house will be Billy's some day. His and his wife's. They certainly will want everything up-to-date.

Just one button, he thought. That *would* be a time-saver!

AFTER Pathis left, Carrin sat back in an adjustable chair and turned on the solido. After twisting the Ezi-dial, he discovered that there was nothing he wanted to see. He tilted back the chair and took a nap.

The something on his mind was still bothering him.

"Hello, darling!" He awoke to find his wife was home. She kissed him on the ear. "Look."

She had bought an A. E. Sexitizer-negligee. He was pleasantly surprised that that was all she had bought. Usually, Leela returned from shopping laden down.

"It's lovely," he said.

She bent over for a kiss, then giggled—a habit he knew she had picked up from the latest popular solido star. He wished she hadn't.

"Going to dial supper," she said, and went to the kitchen. Carrin smiled, thinking that soon she would be able to dial the meals without moving out of the living room. He settled back in his chair, and his son walked in.

"How's it going, Son?" he asked heartily.

"All right," Billy answered listlessly.

"What'sa matter, Son?" The boy stared at his feet, not answering. "Come on, tell Dad what's the trouble."

Billy sat down on a packing case and put his chin in his hands. He looked thoughtfully at his father.

"Dad, could I be a Master Repairman if I wanted to be?"

Mr. Carrin smiled at the question. Billy alternated between wanting to be a Master Repairman and a rocket pilot. The repairmen were the elite. It was their job to fix the automatic repair machines. The repair machines could fix just about anything, but you couldn't have a machine fix the machine that fixed the machine. That was where the Master Repairmen came in.

But it was a highly competitive field and only a very few of the best brains were able to get their degrees. And, although the boy was bright, he didn't seem to have an engineering bent.

"It's possible, Son. Anything is possible."

"But is it possible for me?"

"I don't know," Carrin answered, as honestly as he could.

"Well, I don't want to be a Master Repairman anyway," the boy said, seeing that the answer was no. "I want to be a space pilot."

"A space pilot, Billy?" Leela asked, coming in to the room. "But there aren't any."

"Yes, there are," Billy argued. "We were told in school that the government is going to send some men to Mars."

"They've been saying that for a hundred years," Carrin said, "and they still haven't gotten around to doing it."

"They will this time."

"Why would you want to go to Mars?" Leela asked, winking at Carrin. "There are no pretty girls on Mars."

"I'm not interested in girls. I just want to go to Mars."

"You wouldn't like it, honey." Leela said. "It's a nasty old place with no air."

"It's got some air. I'd like to go there," the boy

insisted sullenly. "I don't like it here."

"What's that?" Carrin asked, sitting up straight. "Is there anything you haven't got? Anything you want?"

"No, sir. I've got everything I want." Whenever his son called him sir, Carrin knew that something was wrong.

"Look, Son, when I was your age I wanted to go to Mars, too. I wanted to do romantic things. I even wanted to be a Master Repairman."

"Then why didn't you?"

"Well, I grew up. I realized that there were more important things. First I had to payoff the debt my father had left me, and then I met your mother—"

Leela giggled.

"—and I wanted a home of my own. It'll be the same with you. You'll payoff your debt and get married, the same as the rest of us."

BILLY was silent for a while. Then he brushed his dark hair—straight, like his father's—back from his forehead and wet his lips.

"How come I have debts, sir?"

Carrin explained carefully. About the things a family needed for civilized living, and the cost of those items. How they had to be paid. How it was customary for a son to take on apart of his parent's debt, when he came of age.

Billy's silence annoyed him. It was almost as if the boy were reproaching him. After he had slaved for years to give the ungrateful whelp every luxury!

"Son," he said harshly, "have you studied history in school? Good. Then you know how it was in the past.

Wars. How would you like to get blown up in a war?"

The boy didn't answer.

"Or how would you like to break your back for eight hours a day, doing work a machine should handle? Or be hungry all the time? Or cold, with the rain beating down on you, and no place to sleep?"

He paused for a response, got none and went on. "You live in the most fortunate age mankind has ever known. You are surrounded by every wonder of art and science. The finest music, the greatest books and art, all at your fingertips. All you have to do is push a button." He shifted to a kindlier tone. "Well, what are you thinking?"

"I was just wondering how I could go to Mars," the boy said. "With the debt, I mean. I don't suppose I could get away from that."

"Of course not."

"Unless I stowed away on a rocket."

"But you wouldn't do that."

"No, of course not," the boy said, but his tone lacked conviction.

"You'll stay here and marry a very nice girl," Leela told him.

"Sure I will," Billy said. "Sure." He grinned suddenly. "I didn't mean any of that stuff about going to Mars. I really didn't."

"I'm glad of that," Leela answered.

"Just forget I mentioned it," Billy said, smiling stiffly. He stood up and raced upstairs.

"Probably gone to play with his rockets," Leela said. "He's such a little devil."

THE Carrins ate a quiet supper, and then it was time for Mr. Carrin to go to work. He was on night shift this month. He kissed his wife good-by, climbed into his Jet-lash and roared to the factory. The automatic gates recognized him and opened. He parked and walked in.

Automatic lathes, automatic presses—everything was automatic. The factory was huge and bright, and the machines hummed softly to themselves, doing their job and doing it well.

Carrin walked to the end of the automatic washing machine assembly line, to relieve the man there.

"Everything all right?" he asked.

"Sure," the man said. "Haven't had a bad one all year. These new models here have built-in voices. They don't light up like the old ones."

Carrin sat down where the man had sat and waited for the first washing machine to come through. His job was the soul of simplicity. He just sat there and the machines went by him. He pressed a button on them and found out if they were all right. They always were. After passing him, the washing machines went to the packaging section.

The first one slid by on the long slide of rollers. He pressed the starting button on the side.

"Ready for the wash," the washing machine said.

Carrin pressed the release and let it go by.

That boy of his, Carrin thought. Would he grow up and face his responsibilities? Would he mature and take his place in society? Carrin doubted it. The boy was a born rebel. If anyone got to Mars, it would be his kid.

But the thought didn't especially disturb him.

"Ready for the wash." Another machine went by.

Carrin remembered something about Miller. The jovial man had always been talking about the planets, always kidding about going off somewhere and roughing it. He hadn't, though. He'd committed suicide.

"Ready for the wash."

Carrin had eight hours in front of him, and he loosened his belt to prepare for it. Eight hours of pushing buttons and listening to a machine announce its readiness.

"Ready for the wash."

He pressed the release.

"Ready for the wash."

Carrin's mind strayed from the job, which didn't need much attention in any case. He wished he had done what he had longed to do as a youngster.

It would have been great to be a rocket pilot, to push a button and go to Mars.

What a Man Believes

Man is endowed with free will: but after death—the reckoning. What will it be? Man has forever pondered the price of a sin and the value of a good deed in the final auditing beyond the grave. We hope the good in us will weigh heavily, but we fear that our sinfulness will bear down. Hope—our greatest comfort. And now Robert Sheckley tell us it can be our ultimate punishment.

YOU must forgive me," Mr. Archer said, his lips peeled back in a grin. "I shouldn't be smiling—smirking." He laughed out loud, high-pitched. "But it'll take a moment. I just hadn't expected—even on my deathbed—"

"Of course," the man behind the desk said. He smiled encouragingly. In the tremendous room there was only Mr. Archer, the desk he stood before, and the man who sat behind it. The ceiling of the room was a soaring, limitless arch, as far above Archer's head as the blue sky had seemed when he was alive. The walls were misty, far-away things. And in the center of it all, there he was —Edward Moran Archer.

"A very usual reaction, I assure you," the man behind the desk said, looking down at the lapels of his suit to give Archer time to straighten his face.

"We make allowances for it. Your present age of

sophistication is wary of anthropomorphisms, such as this. People are no longer raised in the belief of a heaven and a hell; they view such things as convenient fictions for the preachers and writers. Naturally, when they die and find themselves catapulted into the one or the other, the reaction is hysteria. Some cry. Others laugh."

"I see," Mr. Archer said. He had himself under control now, but a grin was still tugging at the corners of his broad mouth. "Well, I haven't been a particularly good chap. Broke a number of the Ten Commandments, including the more serious ones. Where's your fire and brimstone?" He pursed his lips, because the grin was threatening to crack any moment. Imagine! After all, he was going to be burned in a good old-fashioned hell of the sort his grandfather had described in such loving detail. But he still couldn't take it seriously. The situation was so bizarre, so basically humorous.

"Do you *want* fire and brimstone?" the man behind the desk asked.

"Not particularly," Mr. Archer said. "Is there any choice?"

"Of course!" the man told him, looking very undiabolical in his neat gray business suit, with his smoothly combed hair. "Free will is manifest in the universe—even here. You have many alternatives to choose among."

"Different punishments?" Archer asked. "A choice of the thumbscrews or the iron maiden? The rack or the hot irons?"

"All those come under a single category," the man

behind the desk said. "Allow me to show you."

Instantly, Archer discovered himself to be a disembodied intellect. He was in a small, low-ceilinged room. The only light was provided by smoking torches, which threw jagged streaks of red and yellow across the stone walls.

Poesque, Archer thought, and complimented himself on his coolness.

In the center of the room was a tableau. A man, a single rag wrapped around his loins, was stretched across a great wheel, his body drawn tight as a taut bowstring. His tormenters, motionless, were on either side of him. One held a hot iron, a bare fraction of an inch from the flesh. Another was tightening an iron boot to his foot while still another had his hand on the lever that moved the wheel; and all were frozen in mid-action.

The faces of the tormenters were hooded and dark; the man's agonized face was turned to the ceiling, and all Archer could see was the white line of his jaw and corded neck. He strained his eyes to catch a movement, but for long seconds could make out none. Then he noticed that, imperceptibly, the rack was being drawn tighter; the boot was being screwed on the foot, the steaming iron coming closer, searing the flesh by degrees so gradual as to be imperceptible.

The scene vanished.

"Not laughing now?" the man behind the desk asked in a friendly tone.

Archer shook his head.

"We show that scene first. There's nothing like a little good old-fashioned torture to sober a man up. Of course, they say that no physical torment can compare to the psychological, and I believe it is true. Still, for those who can't stand the others, *we do* have the torture chambers."

"You said there were other choices?" Archer asked. He caught himself shuddering. Physical torture—it had always terrified him. Ever since he had been a little boy. Even the thought of being hurt—a splintered arm, a blasted leg…

"Of course there are others," the man said. "And you may choose anyone of them. Allow me to present the selection."

Archer's mind was immediately in space, moving in on the side of a mountain. He came in closer, and saw a dot on the white stone face. The dot resolved itself into a man.

Standing beside him in spirit, Archer watched him climb. He moved slowly, carefully, up the sheer face of the cliff. There was barely a handhold on the smooth rock, hardly a single roughness to give purchase. Like a giant ant, the man struggled on.

Looking up, Archer could see that the top of the mountain was wreathed in mist. There was mist below, covering the bottom. Between the two mists was sheer, bare rock, and the climbing man.

The man moved upward, and Archer saw that he *must* move up, or slip down. And once started, there would be nothing to break the descent.

Would he fall, Archer wondered, watching him cling to the rock, scrambling for a grip. Or would he win through to the top? Archer watched, and felt a surge of sympathy grow within him. "Beat them!" he shouted through silent lips. "Get there!"

And the scene vanished.

"A variation," the man behind the desk said, "On the theme of Sisyphus. But instead of a stone, the man pulls himself."

"What happens when he reaches the top?" Archer asked, feeling better already. The mountain was a far better alternative to the torture, he thought, leaning against the desk.

"To tell you the truth," the man said, "It has never been definitely established that the mountain *has* a top. Although I suppose it has."

"No top?" Archer breathed.

He stood erect, suddenly. "You mean that the man will just climb and climb—for all eternity?"

"I never said it had no top. I just mentioned that it has never been definitely established. As for climbing and climbing, he will climb, yes. Unless he wishes to let go, in which case he will fall. And eternity is one of your sophistications, which I, personally, have no belief in. There is no proof of it."

The next scene was a boat on an ocean. The water was gray, and the waves were gray, with no whitecaps. In front of the little boat was a wall of gray mist; behind it and on all sides was gray water, stretching as far as the eye could see.

There was a man in the mastless little boat, sitting at the helm, staring into the mist. The boat moved gently, over the gray waves, into the mist, which retreated in front of it.

"Pleasant, eh?" the man behind the desk asked, when

the scene disappeared. "Romantic, isn't it? A ship at sea, the mysterious water."

"I suppose the ocean has no end?" Archer said wryly, feeling he had caught on to the place.

"I really don't know," the man said. "The ocean undoubtedly has an end somewhere. But it is entirely possible that the boat is moving in gigantic circles."

"And he'll never find out," Archer said.

"He expects to," the man told him. "If he has faith, he thinks that just beyond the wall of mist may be the shore. A mile, a dozen miles, a hundred miles. Or only a few yards."

"Show me more," Archer said. "I'm catching on."

There was a small, well-lighted room with a closed door in one wall. A conveyor belt ran through an opening, across the room, and out another opening. A man stood in front of the belt, putting bolts in the mechanisms that rode past. His work wasn't difficult; every second a part would come by, he would slip a bolt into it, and wait for the next.

"The influence of the machine age," the man said. "It suits some."

"When the last bolt is in, he's finished?"

"Right."

"But," Archer said, "The conveyor belt is endless. And someone—some other victim, perhaps, has the job of taking out the bolts; at a different part of the belt." Archer permitted himself a sour smile. He had the place figured out, exactly as he had figured out every place he had ever been in his life; every place except the hospital, that is, where no amount of money would give him a new heart.

"Why doesn't he go through that door?" Archer asked. "Is it locked?"

"No, there are no locked doors here. But he must not leave his work. The door is there when he is finished."

"The old anticipation game," Archer said. "Keep them hoping, keep them thinking it's going to be all right in the end. Clever devils!"

"It may well be," the man behind the desk said. He looked at the lapels of his suit until Archer had stopped smiling. "But I, personally, don't know."

There were other things; ingenious things, amazing things, even terrifying things. Archer saw the choice of the ancients; a clearing in a forest where a man could stand, sword in hand. Then, through the trees, a gigantic wolf would bound forth. With one sweep—evidently he was in practice—the man would cut down the wolf. Mortally wounded, the animal would drag itself away.

The man would stand, sword poised, listening. Some barely perceptible sound—the rustle of a twig, the pounding of a heart—would give the warning, and he would turn at the instant another wolf leaped through the trees from a different point. And cut him down, and wait for another.

"It would be amusing," Archer said, "If it were the same wolf, over and over again."

"But it may not be," the man reminded him. "There may well be a number of foes to kill—a hundred, a thousand, a million. He may someday reach the end of them, and be able to continue through the forest to his destiny."

"Or he may not," Archer said sardonically. "Especially if it is the same wolf. As you and I know."

The man shrugged his shoulders. "That is not my concern. Faith, or the lack of it, is not for me. You have seen—choose!"

Psychological torture, Archer mused. Wasn't it always that way? Wasn't hell just another way of keeping the other fellow anticipating, hoping, waiting? So that was how it was. Well then.

But what idiot, he wondered, would choose the torture chamber? A masochist, perhaps? A man like himself, who saw through the eternity of anticipation? Oh, no!

The mountain? Strenuous, to say the least. And so stupid, as was the conveyor belt. The swordsman's lot was a little better, but who wanted to spend eternity stabbing wolves? With the possibility that one might be a trifle careless, and get bitten in the process.

The others were no better.

"I believe the boat is the best thing," Archer said. "So if you haven't any—"

Instantly he was in a small boat, sailing over a gray sea, into a mist.

Damn! There were some more questions he wanted to ask. Well, no matter; he might as well settle down to spend eternity comfortably.

After a while he looked over the boat. There was nothing to see. No ropes, no rudder, no provisions. Just a wooden hull and himself. There was enough room to lie down, though, and he did so. Perhaps he could sleep.

With a gray, expressionless sky over him, the gray sea under him, and the gray boat on all sides, Archer slept.

He awoke, to find the same sea and sky, the same boat and mist.

He wasn't hungry or thirsty.

Reaching down with his hand, he felt the water. It was real water. He tasted it. Salt. An ocean of tears? He settled down to wait.

Time passed, and he reviewed his situation. Anticipation was the key to the torture, he was sure. For all eternity he was supposed to peer into the mist, waiting, expecting the shore to come any minute, dark against the gray water. But he resolved not to think of it. It was absurd to hold hopes in this place.

Perhaps he should have chosen something else, he thought, after a time. There was no denying that the boat ride was monotonous. At least, lopping off heads or putting in bolts he would have something to do.

Archer reviewed his life. He went over it in minute detail, reliving every moment, stretching it out. Grimly he reviewed the steps that had brought him here, the many crossroads in his life. He thought about everything, the good, the bad and the indifferent.

In a way, he was glad that many decisions had brought him to this place. It gave him much to think about.

Time passed, unnoticed on the sea, the advancing boat, the retreating mist.

Thought ran on.

Time passed, and Archer lay or sat or stood in the boat, feeling as human as ever, except that he was never hungry or thirsty. But bored!

So much time passed that it seemed as though eternity must be starting over again. Archer had exhausted every thought, every combination and permutation of thought that he was capable of. And nothing changed in the gray boat, or on the gray sea, or in the gray mist.

Time passed.

Slowly…

TIME PASSED!

"This is too much," Archer said out loud again. He had been talking aloud for some time.

"I can't stand this," he repeated. For the ten millionth time he speculated on what was in the water. What dangers? What horrors?

Time passed.

"But I think I can go overboard." After thinking about it for the billionth time, Archer lowered himself over the side of the boat into the gray sea. He had long considered how it would feel, the water lapping around him, the thoughts it would bring, and the thoughts *they* would bring.

For a moment it was wonderful.

He paddled, keeping himself up in the water, watching the boat continue without him. Then something happened.

Ahead, the mists parted. The boat cleaved through them, and there was the shore, long and dark on the horizon. Archer could make out trees, a beach. The boat sped on, and grounded itself. Archer saw the shapes of other boats, and thought he glimpsed people.

"There was an end!" he gasped. "The boat wasn't going in circles!"

And the climber—Archer knew that he had reached the top of his mountain, if he had the courage to go on long enough. And the worker had placed his last bolt, and the swordsman killed his last wolf.

All, a test of faith! Faith, in hell!

He struck out for the shore, but the water was like thick jelly, weighing down his arms and legs, keeping his head below the surface. He took one last, despairing look at the shore, and began to sink.

Of course he couldn't drown. Not once dead. All he could do was sink, and sink, and sink. To where? To the bottom.

And what would be waiting for him on the bottom? Why, for those without faith or hope—

The torture chamber, of course.

What Goes Up

What goes up must come down, as they say about even the stock market. It was true enough, until Edgarson found a world where the law of averages was repealed. They ran strictly to flat top square waves: very square.

"All right, space rat, out you go," the junior officer said with a wide, boyish grin.

"Couldn't we talk this over?" Edgarson asked, edging down the gangplank with a certain dignity. "I mean, to leave me in this backwoods—" He gestured at the dusty, deserted landing field, the raw brick buildings, the tar road; all the signs of a low-order atomic civilization.

"I assure you," Edgarson went on, "I would be glad to work my passage if you'd just take me to some civilized—"

The port closed with a clang. Edgarson sighed and walked away from the ship. My God, he thought. I don't even know the name of the planet where they've gone and dumped me!

He pushed back his shoulders as he reached the tar road. Behind him the ship lifted, silently and efficiently, and was gone. Once the ship was out of sight, Edgarson allowed his back to slump.

Those damned starships…

But he couldn't blame them. A stowaway has no rights. He had known that. But what else could he have done?

After his businesses had gone bankrupt on Moira II, Edgarson had to get out, but fast. The fastest way without capital was to hide aboard a long-haul transport.

The ship had taken off just in time. The authorities of the Belt Stars, of which Moira II was the proudest jewel, were quite strict with what they termed 'irresponsible' bankruptcies.

Unfortunately, the ship's captain was equally strict with unpaid-for weight. They had dropped Edgarson's scrawny 132 pounds on the first oxygen planet on their course.

What was he going to do now?

Edgarson glanced back at the signs in front of the little spaceport. Luckily they were in Fammish, one of the great interstellar tongues. The planet was called Porif. He had never heard of it.

One of the signs pointed to the city of Mif. Edgarson followed it, hands in his pockets, scuffing his feet along the rough tar.

This, he told himself was the end. The absolute end. He'd never get off this place. Four times he had made fortunes, and four times lost them in the maddening uncertainties of Beltstar finances.

I'm through, he thought. Might as well hang myself.

A passing vehicle almost made hanging unnecessary. An antique gas job, it was rolling along at a good seventy miles an hour. Edgarson heard it, turned, and there it was, swaying over the entire road. His eyes bulged. It was coming straight for him.

At the last moment he unparalyzed his muscles enough to leap into the ditch beside him.

The car ground to a halt a hundred feet up the road.

"You maniac!" Edgarson screamed in passable Fammish. Suicide was all very well. But when one is almost killed—

"What are you doing now?" he shouted at the man, who was backing his car. "Coming back for another try?"

"Terribly sorry," the man said, smiling pleasantly. He was large, red-faced and redheaded. "Did not mean to frighten you."

"Frighten me!" Edgarson said. "The hell with that. You almost killed me."

"Oh, no," the man said, eyeing him closely. "You're not old enough."

"Sure I'm old enough," Edgarson said. "Anyone is old enough to die."

"You must be an outworlder," the redheaded man said. "I should have noticed your accent. Well, friend, you can't die here. Not yet."

"I can die any place or time I want," Edgarson said, feeling silly.

The redheaded man thought that over for a moment, rubbing the side of his nose with a freckled forefinger. "How old are you?" he asked.

"Thirty-six."

"I thought you were about my age. Here on Porif you can't die before you're fifty-four. At least, not during this cycle."

Edgarson didn't have any immediate answer for that. He just gaped.

"My name's Fals," the man told him. "Could I offer you a ride into town?" Edgarson climbed into the car. In a few moments Fals had it careening crazily over the road.

"You'll kill us both," Edgarson gasped as the landscape whizzed by.

"Well, I *am* a touch euphoric," Fals said. "But the statistics are against it. I won't kill either of us. And the car's insured."

Edgarson rode the rest of the way in stoical silence. He didn't know what sort of place Porif was, and until he found out, he determined to keep quiet. He didn't want to break any taboos. He knew that in the bewildering array of planets in the civilized galaxy, there were some pretty odd spots. Places where reason and common sense went to hell on a trolley. Places where the law of gravity was repealed for six months out of the year, and the verities of Earth science were looked upon as polite fiction.

Natural law, as defined by Earth and Belt scientists, didn't mean much to old mother nature. Perhaps she just hadn't wanted to construct a logical, consistent type of universe.

Edgarson was prepared to accept, tentatively, that he couldn't die before the age of fifty-four. On Porif.

"Here we are," Fals said cheerfully, pulling up in front of a small brick house in what must have been a suburb of the city. "Is there anything I can do for you? Any favor, anything?"

He *must* be euphoric, Edgarson thought. But he wasn't going to let the opportunity slip past him.

"I'm temporarily embarrassed for funds," he began smoothly. "If you could—"

"Say no more," Fals said. "Be my guest. Stay at my house. I couldn't refuse you anything, right now."

"You couldn't?" Edgarson asked, his eyes narrowing.

"Practically nothing. I'm at the extreme peak of an altruist upswing. One of my personality characteristics. It'll pass in a day or two, of course. I'll probably regret all this exceedingly. But come in."

Just outside the doorway he stopped. "Don't mind my sister," he said in a confiding whisper. "Hetta's not feeling so good. You know how ectomorphs can be? Well, she's just coming out of the bottom of a depressive trough. Be nice to her." He laughed uproariously and kicked open the door.

Inside, it was what he had expected of a lower atomic age dwelling. Lumpy couches, blobby pictures on the wall, ridiculous curtains and overstuffed chairs.

Edgarson looked around warily, trying to figure out his next move. Either his patron was slightly off his track, or there was something unique about this planet. *Depressive trough.* Even citizens of the more sophisticated regions didn't have that sort of knowledge at their fingertips.

"Are you a psychologist?" he asked Fals, sitting down on a chair.

"No," Fals said. "I'm a fireman, usually."

"Usually?"

"Yes. I'm on a vacation now. All of us are."

"Then who fights the fires?"

"What fires?" Fals asked, surprised.

Edgarson was about to start over when the depressive sister came in.

"Oh, I'm tired," she said, ignoring Edgarson and collapsing on the couch. "Tired and unhappy."

Edgarson stared at her for a moment, before remembering his manners and standing up. The girl was as redheaded as her brother, but slim where he was corpulent. Ectomorph, had he said? Well, Hetta was slender, but she was also filled where a female ectomorph should be filled.

Edgarson felt his spirits brighten. Suicide could wait. This might prove interesting. There might even be some exploitable commercial angle.

For a while conversation was desultory. Fals turned on a little screen, which seemed to be a primitive brother of solidovision. He was soon engrossed in what purported to be a comedy program.

The redheaded girl, Hetta, didn't stir. Once she murmured something about the cruelty of the world, but it was too vague for Edgarson to answer.

Finally, she lifted herself off the couch and essayed a tentative smile.

"You see?" Fals whispered. "She's out of the trough."

Edgarson shook his head. A fireman who didn't fight fires, but who had a pretty accurate psychological knowledge. Well, he'd have to find out.

"I think I'll make supper," Hetta said, and jumped off the couch.

The meal was very pleasant. Hetta was fascinated by the great outside world she had never seen. She listened breathlessly to Edgarson's tales of interstellar commerce, and of the ridiculous drop in the stock market on Moira II that had wrecked him.

She put the soup on the table and asked, "How could that happen?" Edgarson smiled at her charming naivete. "Weren't you in a cycle?" she wanted to know. "Didn't you *know* the market was going to drop?"

Edgarson did his best to explain how business worked. How you could occasionally detect trends, calculate rises, prepare for drops. But not always. And that, even at best, market calculation was guesswork.

"But that's ridiculous," Hetta said, frowning prettily. "How can you live in such an uncertain world? I'm glad it's not that way here."

"You must excuse my sister," Fals said, smiling. "She doesn't know anything of the outside world—"

Edgarson ignored him. "How does it work here?" he asked the girl.

"Why, it's down in the books," she said, as one would instruct a child. "The statistics books. If a business is going to be good, the statistics books tell you."

"Aren't the books ever wrong?" Edgarson asked, gently.

She shook her head. "Not during the cycle."

Just then a bell clamored. Fals got up and answered the telephone.

"Yes. yes, yes. Hm. All right, I'll check it." He put down the receiver. "Fire in the 31st Warehouse district." He thought for a moment. "I don't believe it's going to spread."

"You might as well be sure," Hetta said. "I'll bring in the book."

"Hang on," Fals said into the telephone. Hetta struggled back with a fat volume. Edgarson walked over and watched.

The book was entitled *Fire Statistics, City of Mif, Cycle B.*

"Here it is," Fals said, turning a page. "Margat Building, 31st Warehouse district. Just as I thought."

Looking over his shoulder, Edgarson read: "Margat Building, probability 78.4% against a major fire before 18 Arget."

"Hello," Fals said into the telephone. "You're not due for a fire before 18 Arget, and here it isn't even Hovl yet. Don't worry about it. It will burn itself out pretty soon."

The man on the other end seemed to be giving him an argument. Fals said into the phone, sharply, "Don't tell *me*, pal. I'm a fireman. It's in the book. Probability 78.4 against. Call me if it spreads." He hung up.

"That's how it goes," he said to Edgarson. "These warehouse owners would root a man out of bed for every little flash fire. I don't know why they don't read the statistics on their own buildings."

"I don't get it," Edgarson said. "Was there a fire in that warehouse?"

"That's what *he* said," Fals said, finishing his soup. Hetta cleared the plates and brought in the meat course. "Probably a wastebasket or something. They always look bigger than they are."

"But if he reported a fire—" Edgarson began.

"It can't be a big fire," Hetta told him. "Otherwise it

would be down in the statistics."

"Statistics can be wrong," Edgarson said, remembering several beatings he had taken on sure things.

"Not these," Fals said...

The telephone rang again. "Hello?" Fals said. "I thought so. Of course it burned itself out. No, you didn't disturb me. Don't worry about it. But please, buy a fire statistics book. That way, you won't have to be calling the fire station all the time. I assure you, when a real fire is due, we'll be on the spot—*before* it happens. Good night."

"Could I see this fire book?" Edgarson asked. Fals handed him the big volume, and Edgarson leafed through it, reading entries at random.

"Joenson farm," one entry read. "Probability 56% no major fire before 7 Hovl."

"Mif State Park," read another. "Prob. 64% no major fire before 1 Egl. Prob. 89% fire by 19 Egl, destroying fifty-four acres NE corner."

The rest of the entries followed the same pattern.

"I don't understand this," Edgarson said, closing the book. "I know you can determine a probability, even about fires. That's how insurance works. But how can you know there won't be a fire before the date the book gives? I mean, even if the probability is seventy percent—and I don't see how that's arrived at—there's still a thirty percent chance that there'll be a fire sooner."

"Not here," Fals said, with a touch of local pride. "Not on Porif. Any probability of fifty-one percent or better is as good as one hundred percent during the cycle. We don't believe in exceptions here. What's probable is certain."

"Does that work with everything?" Edgarson asked.

"Of course," Fals told him. "That's why I knew I wouldn't kill you with the car. The statistics for this cycle show that no one under fifty-four is going to be killed, except under certain specified circumstances which you didn't come under."

"How long is the cycle?" Edgarson asked.

"Ten years. Then a new one starts. Come in the library. I'll show you some of the other books."

Lining one whole wall was a set of books called *Business Statistics, Cycle B.* Leafing through them, Edgarson found that they contained predictions for every business on the planet through the present cycle. They showed the probable profit and loss figures weekly. The businesses that would bankrupt were down, as well as the ones that would boom.

Skimming, Edgarson read: "Jeenings Carbon, common stock. Selling, 145, 1 Marstt. In two weeks, prob. 56% to 189. Constant to Egl, 89% prob., then rise to 720. A period of leveling at 700, then a short steep incline to 842—" That was a summary, of course. A week by week breakdown followed.

"Is this true?" Edgarson asked.

Hetta glanced over his shoulder. "Oh, of course. The stock is at 189 right now. And the rest will follow."

"My Lord," Edgarson said, and closed the book. If the entry were true, a man could make a fortune by investing now. Invest and sell when it reached 842. Make a profit of—

"Wait a minute," he said. "This can't be true. Everyone on the planet would buy this stuff. That would change the prediction."

"No," Fals said, grinning. "The probable purchases of stocks are estimated pretty closely. No one's going to overload on one stock. We scatter our money around, buy good and bad. We Porifans don't care so much for quick profits."

Edgarson thought it over. He'd have to find out if this prediction business worked every time. If it did, he had stumbled on a gold mine.

A *predictable* stock market, he told himself. Predictable businesses, fire losses. They probably predicted earthquakes and floods, too. A smart man could make a fortune in a year. Or less.

Of course, he'd need some capital to invest at the start. He'd have to find some way of getting that.

Edgarson discovered, suddenly that Hetta was glancing at him. That was significant. But she was also pretending that she wasn't looking at him. That was even more significant.

Edgarson decided that it might not be too difficult to raise the initial capital.

The next morning, Edgarson went to Fals' library. The Porifan didn't own all the statistics books, but he did have everything that pertained to the city of Mif, and its immediate area.

Ignoring breakfast, Edgarson began to read, skipping back and forth between the 190 volumes *of Business Statistics, Cycle B.* It was quite a book.

It told the future history of every business on the planet, and Edgarson was unable to doubt its validity. The conservative, quiet air of the books was almost proof in itself.

"Jacnx Mauf. Co. Common 23. 13 Luggat, rise to 26, prob. 76% 19 Luggat, rise to 28, prob. 93% 1 Mener, drop to 18, prob. 98%."

How could he doubt it?

Edgarson made the attempt, in the spirit of caution. He ate breakfast at lunchtime and went to the Mif central library. According to the evidence in old newspapers and outdated statistics books, all previous predictions had been one hundred percent correct. One hundred percent!

Edgarson checked further. He found that a cycle lasted for ten revolutions of the planet around its primary—ten years. That there was a gap between cycles, evidently for the purpose of collecting and publishing the statistics for the next cycle. The cycles were always labeled A and B, one following another.

Checking one cycle against another, Edgarson found that there wasn't much difference. Some new businesses, the closing of some old ones; a few points change in probability-ratings. But no real turnover.

Edgarson wasn't interested in theories; he wanted profits. Still, he felt obliged to find out some of the reasons why. Accordingly, he dug into a stack of reference book.

Late that night, he walked back to Fals' house. He had skimmed the history and psychology of Porif, and he was able to extrapolate a few answers from it.

According to their own psychology books, the people of Porif were simpler, less unpredictable than the complex peoples of Earth and the Belt Stars. It was possible to get a coherent, predictable picture of a

Porifan's personality; a feat impossible with an Earthman.

The hard thing, Edgarson knew, was individual psychology. Once you have that mastered, the psychology of aggregates is far simpler.

Edgarson found that the Porifans were conformists. Consciously and unconsciously they believed their own statistics, and wanted to preserve them. Individuals went out of their way to fit into their predicted niche. On perverse Moira II that would never work.

The favorite hobby of most planets is war. A very few are more interested in art, or religion. On Porif the passion was, and had always been, statistics and probabilities.

And nature seemed to help them. The perverse old lady had repealed the usual law of averages on Porif. Instead of a constant leveling process, high predictions stayed constant. So, if a fire started ahead of time, there was never a draft to fan it into conflagration. If a man was in an auto accident before his predicted moment, he somehow was thrown clear.

Nature conspired to make Porif an understandable, predictable place to live.

A perfect place for an Earthman to make a quick fortune.

Edgarson slept on it. The next morning he walked down to Fals' library to consider his problem again. Seating himself in Fals' overstuffed chair, he popped a native variety of plum in his mouth and thought.

The first step in making a fortune was to raise capital, and the first step in raising capital was to marry Hetta.

Securing some of her funds through marriage, he could speculate—if a sure thing can be called speculation. He had about six months until the end of cycle B. He could be rich by that time.

And marrying Hetta wouldn't be too unpleasant a task, either. Edgarson liked ectomorphic redheads, properly filled.

No time like the present, he told himself. Hetta had gone to town, shopping, and Fals was off waiting for a fire to start on an outlying farm.

Edgarson pulled down the index to the *Human Statistics* book, Cycle B. (170 volumes, cross indexed). Hetta, he found, was on page 1189 of volume 23. Her classification was *unstable ectomorph, female, auburn, 32-saa3b.*

According to the book, a person of Hetta's makeup had a primary five-day elation-depression cycle; normal for auburn ectomorphs. The trough usually occurred at sunset of the third day. During that time, auburn ectomorphs desired comfort, poetry and understanding, soft music and beautiful sunsets.

Edgarson grinned, jotted the information on a pad and read on.

The elation-high occurred on the fifth day, and lasted for most of two hours. There was a strong tendency toward amorousness at such times (89% probability), and a desire for adventure, mystery, the unknown.

Edgarson grinned even wider, and read on.

Superimposed on all this was a longer, gentler cycle, characterized as a secondary tenderness swing, over a period of thirty-five days.

And a great deal more pertinent data.

Edgarson drew up a graph of Hetta's cycles for the next month, with appropriate comments and advice to himself, and read the last paragraph.

Hetta's instability was one common to ectomorphic redheads. A pathological tendency, very repressed, probability 7%.

Which, he knew, was Porif double-talk for never.

Armed with this data, Edgarson began his wooing.

"Let me tell you about the great planets," he said to her at the height of her elation period. "Let me tell you about space."

"Oh, please do," Hetta said. "I so wish I could travel!"

"And why not?" Edgarson said, sliding his arm gently across the top of the couch. "Why not speed between the stars in a two-bunk scouter? Know the adventure of strange ports! The thrill of distant places!"

"How wonderful," Hetta said, and didn't flinch when the arm gently touched her shoulder.

When he wasn't wooing Hetta, Edgarson was busy with Business Statistics. He made up a list of ten businesses that were going to boom, figured out how long he would hold stock, what he would invest the profits in, how much he could buy on margin.

His profits at the end of a month, he estimated, would be in the hundred thousands.

"You are so delicate," he said to her, at the extreme tip of her tenderness swing. "So fair, so gentle."

"Am I?" Hetta asked.

"Yes," Edgarson said, with a sigh. "I wish—"

"What?"

"Oh, nothing." He sighed again, and proceeded to give her a fictitious account of his childhood. It served its purpose. All Hetta's latent tenderness came to the fore.

"You poor boy," she said.

The omnipresent arm was around her.

"I care for you, you know," Edgarson said huskily, feeling ridiculous. He was used to the breezy give-and-take approach of Earth and Moira II. On civilized planets a definite understanding was reached within five minutes or so. But that wouldn't work on Porif, or on a girl with Hetta's character coefficients.

Edgarson proceeded as a tenderhearted lover, wondering when Porif would emerge from its purple period.

While he wooed her, Edgarson extrapolated an easy ten billion-dollar profit from the *Business Statistics.* He had it all figured out now; how he would make his initial profits, how much he would plough back, how much he would extend himself on margin, how much he'd save.

And the other things. Land he was going to buy, farms and waterways. Insurance companies, banks, federal investments. The ten-year cycle had only a few months to go. He wanted a measure of security during the gap between cycle.

The climax of his lovemaking came at the trough of Hetta's depression. He bought her candy; he showered her with tenderness, love and understanding. A phonograph was playing Hetta's favorite song at the moment Edgarson proposed. And to top it all, before their eyes was a magnificent, multicolored sunset; a sunset lovers dream of.

It wasn't chance, of course. Edgarson had planned it carefully. The sunset had been listed in *Weather Statistics, Cycle B, combined with Holinim's Greater Book of Sunsets.*

The proposal was a predictable success, odds 89.7% for. They were married three days later.

Armed with more of his wife's money than even he had expected, Edgarson started to invest. He had five months to go, and he was going to make the most of it.

The statistics books were one hundred percent accurate. Edgarson's profits came through exactly as he had planned. Down to the last decimal point, the books were right.

He tried to put his brother-in-law on to a few good things, but Fals was in a sullen period. He held on to a small block of mediocre stocks, resolutely, and refused to speculate.

"What's the matter with you?" Edgarson asked him, one day when his profit had hit eight hundred thousand. "Don't you believe in your own statistics?"

"Of course I do," Fals said, glowering at him. "But this isn't the way we do business here."

Edgarson stared at him, baffled. He was unable to understand a man who didn't take money when it was practically handed to him. It was the Porifans most inhuman characteristic.

"Aren't you going to invest in anything?" Edgarson asked.

"Of course I am," Fals said. "I'm buying a block of Heemstl limited."

Edgarson went over to *Business Statistics*—now his bible—and looked up the concern. The book gave it a

75 percent probability of a sizeable loss during the cycle.

"What the hell are you buying *that* for?" Edgarson asked.

"Well," Fals said, "They need some more operating capital. Young concern, you know. I figure—"

"Please stop, you weary me," Edgarson said. Fals looked even more sullen and left.

What could you do, Edgarson asked himself. Of course you had to have people investing in poor stocks. Not *everyone* can get rich. And it was very noble of the Porifans, to support their failing businesses. But what could you do with people like that?

Take their money, he told himself.

The next months were feverish ones for Edgarson. It was necessary to buy at exactly the right time, sell at the right time. The Porifan stock market was like an orchestra. Delicacy in timing had to be observed, to get everything possible out of it.

Edgarson's businesses spread.

He didn't have much time for Hetta during these months. Building a great fortune was absorbing, night-and-day work. But he figured he would make it all up to her later.

Besides, she thought he was wonderful.

With the cycle nearing its end, Edgarson planned out his procedure for the hiatus. During the year gap, new predictions would be assembled and published. But Edgarson wasn't going to be caught napping.

Most of his businesses he felt, were bound to bridge the gap between cycle B and A. They were sound concerns with high probability ratings. But he wanted to be sure, so he sold his fluctuating wildcat stocks and put money in farms, city real estate, hotels, parks, government bonds, anything that looked sound.

He put excess profits in the banks. It was possible, he supposed, for a ninety-five-percent-good bank to go busted. But not five of them! Not ten of them!

"I've got a good tip for you," his brother-in-law said, two days before the end of the cycle. "Buy some Verstt. Buy it big."

Upon looking it up, Edgarson discovered that Verstt was on the verge of receivership. He looked at Fals coldly. The Porifan probably resented his presence here. Didn't approve of the way he was cleaning up the cash, and wanted to slow him down.

"I'll think it over," Edgarson said, ushering Fals to the door.

How could you argue with an idiot?

The day came, ending Cycle B. Edgarson spent the morning at his telephones, waiting for news.

The phone rang.

"Yes?" Edgarson asked.

"Sir, Markinson company stock dropping."

Edgarson smiled, and put down the telephone. Markinson had been a good investment. He'd ride any loss down. After he got through this depression—if that was what it was—he'd have ten more years to recoup in. And then he'd get out!

Take a lot, leave a little, that was his motto.

The telephones started ringing constantly. More of his businesses were failing, dropping, going bankrupt. The bottom had dropped out of manufacturing. Iron ore was slag on the market. Mines were worthless.

Still, Edgarson wasn't alarmed. There was still real estate, farms, insurance, waterways, federal projects—

A telephone call informed him that his largest farm had burned to the ground, crops and all.

"Good," Edgarson said. "Collect the insurance."

Another call informed him that his chief insurance company had gone bankrupt, as had its underwriters.

Edgarson started to sweat. He was having a few bad breaks, but—

It did go on. Telephones rang night and day. The banks started to fail! One after another, Edgarson's gilt-edged concerns dwindled and dropped. And the damndest things happened to Edgarson's other concerns.

Farms were burnt to the ground, roads were flooded, canals were exploded. People were hurt on his line, and sued. Tornadoes hit, earthquakes followed. Dams built to last a century burst. Buildings collapsed.

Coincidence, Edgarson told him, holding on to his morale with a death-like grip.

Then the federal government announced that it would go into temporary receivership, if anyone would take it.

That killed a few more of Edgarson's billions.

It made depressions in the belt group seem like mild prosperity.

It took just under a month to strip Edgarson of most of his holdings. Too numb to think, he stumbled into Fals' library. His wife was there, curled up in a corner. Evidently she was depressive again. Fals was standing, arms folded across his chest, staring at him self-righteously.

"What happened?" Edgarson croaked.

"During the hiatus," Fals told him, "All odds are reversed."

"Huh?"

"Didn't you know that?" Fals said. "I thought you were a big finance man."

"Give," Edgarson said.

"How do you think the statisticians get their figures?" Fals told him. "If the major predictions came true all the time, they'd be one hundred percent. During the gap, every thing that was below fifty percent probability—and therefore never came about—obtains."

"Gah," said Edgarson.

"Look, suppose you wanted certain odds to average out, as they must. Something is ninety percent certain. It works out one hundred percent of the time for ten years. In order for the prediction of ninety percent to be right, it would have to be ten percent wrong for ten years, or 100 percent wrong for one year.

"Understand? If a business is ninety percent sure of success for the ten-year cycle, it has to be 100 percent sure of failure for that year. It *must* fail."

"Say it again," Edgarson mumbled.

"I think you understand it now," Fals said. "That's why all of us buy low-probability stocks during the cycle. They work out fine during the gap."

"Oh, Lord," Edgarson said, and sat down.

"You didn't think your stocks would go up forever, did you?" Fals asked.

Edgarson had thought just that. Or rather, he had

taken it for granted. Logically, he knew Fals was right. On other planets, odds are constantly averaging. Not on Porif. Here, everything went one way or the other. Ten years, during which time all the highs obtained. Then a year, during which the former lows obtained.

Of course, it averaged quite nicely. But what a way to do it!

He was dimly aware that Fals had left the room.

Somewhere a telephone was ringing.

"Yeh?" Edgarson said, taking it on the library extension. He listened for a while, then, hung up.

He had just been informed that he was several billion dollars in debt, largely due to marginal buying. On Porif they had prisons for irresponsible bankruptcies.

"Well," Edgarson said, "I guess I'll just have to—"

"Stand still, damn you," Hetta said, getting to her feet. She was holding a pistol in both hands. It was an old, chemically operated revolver, of a sort that civilized nations hadn't used in centuries. But it was as capable of killing as a more modern arm.

"Oh, how I hate you," Hetta said, in her flamboyant style. "I hate everyone, but you the worst. Stand still!"

Edgarson was calculating the odds against his jumping out the library window safely. Unfortunately he didn't have a book handy to give him the figures.

"I'm going to shoot you in the stomach," Hetta said, with a smile that made his flesh crawl. "I want to see you die slowly."

That did it. Hetta's seven percent instability was coming out, exactly as the minor odds against tornadoes, floods and earthquakes had come out. She was a murderess!

No wonder, Edgarson thought, she had been so easy to marry.

"Stop swaying," Hetta said, taking careful aim.

Edgarson crashed through the window, the explosion of the gun deafening him. He didn't stop to see whether he was dead or not, but ran full tilt for the spaceport.

He hoped the odds were in his favor.

"OK, space rat," the grinning young officer said. "Out you go." He pushed Edgarson down the gangplank.

"Where am I?" Edgarson asked. He had climbed aboard the ship before an irate mob seized him. The captain had taken him one stop, but no further.

"What's it matter?" the officer asked, prodding him.

"If you'd consider taking me to a civilized port—" Edgarson began.

The port slammed behind him.

Well, this is the end, he told himself. This was the end of the road, the absolute blank wall. Here he was, on another backwoods planet. He'd never get off this one. Might as well commit suicide.

"Hello," someone said. Edgarson looked up. In front of him was a green skinned native. On each of his three arms the native wore a bracelet of what looked like platinum. In each bracelet was what looked like a gigantic diamond.

The native was wheeling a wheelbarrow filled with dirt. The wheelbarrow seemed to be made of solid gold.

"How do you do, friend?" Edgarson said, walking up to the native and smiling.

Warrior Race

Destroying the spirit of the enemy is the goal of war and the aliens had the best way!

THEY never did discover whose fault it was. Fannia pointed out that if Donnaught had had the brains of an ox, as well as the build, he would have remembered to check the tanks. Donnaught, although twice as big as him, wasn't quite as fast with an insult. He intimated, after a little thought, that Fannia's nose might have obstructed his reading of the fuel gauge.

This still left them twenty light-years from Thetis, with a cupful of transformer fuel in the emergency tank.

"All right," Fannia said presently. "What's done is done. We can squeeze about three light-years out of the fuel before we're back on atomics. Hand me *The Galactic Pilot*—unless you forgot that, too."

Donnaught dragged the bulky microfilm volume out of its locker, and they explored its pages.

The Galactic Pilot told them they were in a sparse, seldom-visited section of space, which they already knew. The nearest planetary system was Hatterfield; no intelligent life there. Sersus had a native population, but no refueling facilities. The same with Illed, Hung and Porderai.

"Ah-ha!" Fannia said. "Read that, Donnaught. If you can read, that is."

"Cascella," Donnaught read, slowly and clearly, following the line with a thick forefinger. "Type M sun. Three planets, intelligent (AA3C) human-type life on second. Oxygen-breathers. Non-mechanical. Religious. Friendly. Unique social structure, described in Galactic Survey Report 33877242. Population estimate: stable at three billion. Basic Cascellan vocabulary taped under Cas33b2. Scheduled for resurvey 2375A.D. Cache of transformer fuel left, beam coordinate 8741 kgl. Physical descript: Unocc. flatland."

"Transformer fuel, boy!" Fannia said gleefully. "I believe we will get to Thetis, after all," he punched the new direction on the ship's tape. "If that fuel's still there."

"Should we read up on the unique social structure?" Donnaught asked, still poring over *The Galactic Pilot.*

"Certainly," Fannia said. "Just step over to the main galactic base on Earth and buy me a copy."

"I forgot," Donnaught admitted slowly.

"Let me see," Fannia said, dragging out the ship's language library. "Cascellan, Cascellan… Here it is. Be good while I learn the language," he set the tape in the hypnophone and switched it on. "Another useless tongue in my overstuffed head," he murmured, and then the hypnophone took over.

COMING out of transformer drive with at least a drop of fuel left, they switched to atomics. Fannia rode the beam right across the planet, locating the slender metal spire of the Galactic Survey cache. The plain was no longer unoccupied, however. The Cascellans had built a city around the cache, and the spire dominated the crude wood-and-mud buildings.

"Hang on," Fannia said, and brought the ship down on, the outskirts of the city, in a field of stubble.

"Now look," Fannia said, unfastening his safety belt. "We're just here for fuel. No souvenirs, no side-trips, no fraternizing."

Through the port, they could see a cloud of dust from the city. As it came closer, they made out figures running toward their ship.

"What do you think this unique social structure is?" Donnaught asked, pensively checking the charge in a needler gun.

"I know not and care less," Fannia said, struggling into space armor. "Get dressed."

"The air's breathable."

"Look, pachyderm, for all we know, these Cascellans think the proper way to greet visitors is to chop off their heads and stuff them with green apples. If Galactic says unique, it probably means unique."

"Galactic said they were friendly."

"That means they haven't got atomic bombs. Come on, get dressed." Donnaught put down the needler and struggled into an oversize suit of space armor. Both men strapped on needlers, paralyzers, and a few grenades.

"I don't think we have anything to worry about," Fannia said, tightening the last nut on his helmet. "Even if they get rough, they can't crack space armor. And if they're not rough, we won't have any trouble. Maybe these gewgaws will help," he picked up a box of trading articles —mirrors, toys and the like.

Helmeted and armored, Fannia slid out the port and raised one hand to the Cascellans. The language, hypnotically placed in his mind, leaped to his lips.

"We come as friends and brothers. Take us to the chief."

The natives clustered around, gaping at the ship and the space armor. Although they had the same number of eyes, ears and limbs as humans, they completely missed looking like them.

"If they're friendly," Donnaught asked, climbing out of the port, "why all the hardware?" The Cascellans were dressed predominantly in a collection of knives, swords and daggers. Each man had at least five, and some had eight or nine.

"Maybe Galactic got their signals crossed," Fannia said, as the natives spread out in an escort. "Or maybe the natives just use the knives for mumblypeg."

THE city was typical of a nonmechanical culture. Narrow, packed-dirt streets twisted between ramshackle huts. A few two-story buildings threatened to collapse at any minute. A stench filled the air, so strong that Fannia's filter couldn't quite eradicate it. The Cascellans bounded ahead of the heavily laden Earthmen, dashing around like a pack of playful puppies. Their knives glittered and clanked.

The chief's house was the only three-story building in the city. The tall spire of the cache was right behind it.

"If you come in peace," the chief said when they entered, "you are welcome," he was a middle-aged Cascellan with at least fifteen knives strapped to various parts of his person. He squatted cross-legged on a raised dais.

"We are privileged," Fannia said. He remembered from the hypnotic language lesson that "chief" on Cascella meant more than it usually did on Earth. The chief here was a combination of king, high priest, deity and bravest warrior.

"We have a few simple gifts here," Fannia added, placing the gewgaws at the king's feet. "Will his majesty accept?"

"No," the king said. "We accept no gifts." Was that the unique social structure? Fannia wondered. It certainly was not human. "We are a warrior race. What we want, we take."

Fannia sat cross-legged in front of the dais and exchanged conversation with the king while Donnaught played with the spurned toys. Trying to overcome the initial bad impression, Fannia told the chief about the stars and other worlds, since simple people usually liked fables. He spoke of the ship, not mentioning yet that it was out of fuel. He spoke of Cascella, telling the chief how its fame was known throughout the Galaxy.

"That is as it should be," the chief said proudly. "We are a race of warriors, the like of which has never been seen. Every man of us dies fighting."

"You must have fought some great wars," Fannia said politely, wondering what idiot had written up the galactic report.

"I have not fought a war for many years," the chief said. "We are united now, and all our enemies have joined us."

Bit by bit, Fannia led up to the matter of the fuel.

"What is this 'fuel?'" the chief asked, haltingly because there was no equivalent for it in the Cascellan language.

"It makes our ship go."

"And where is it?"

"In the metal spire," Fannia said. "If you would just allow us—"

"In the holy shrine?" the chief exclaimed, shocked. "The tall metal church which the gods left here long ago?"

"Yeah," Fannia said sadly, knowing what was coming. "I guess that's it."

"It is sacrilege for an outworlder to go near it," the chief said. "I forbid it."

"We need the fuel." Fannia was getting tired of sitting cross-legged. Space armor wasn't built for complicated postures. "The spire was put here for such emergencies."

"Strangers, know that I am god of my people, as well as their leader. If you dare approach the sacred temple, there will be war."

"I was afraid of that," Fannia said, getting to his feet.

"And since we are a race of warriors," the chief said, "at my command, every fighting man of the planet will move against you. More will come from the hills and from across the rivers."

Abruptly, the chief drew a knife. It must have been a signal, because every native in the room did the same.

FANNIA dragged Donnaught away from the toys. "Look, lummox. These friendly warriors can't do a damn thing to us. Those knives can't cut space armor, and I doubt if they have anything better. Don't let them pile up on you, though. Use the paralyzer first, the needler if they really get thick."

"Right." Donnaught whisked out and primed a paralyzer in a single coordinated movement. With weapons, Donnaught was fast and reliable, which was virtue enough for Fannia to keep him as a partner.

"We'll cut around this building and grab the fuel. Two cans ought to be enough. Then we'll beat it fast."

They walked out the building, followed by the Cascellans. Four carriers lifted the chief, who was barking orders. The narrow street outside was suddenly jammed with armed natives. No one tried to touch them yet, but at least a thousand knives were flashing in the sun.

In front of the cache was a solid phalanx of Cascellans. They stood behind a network of ropes that probably marked the boundary between sacred and profane ground.

"Get set for it," Fannia said, and stepped over the ropes.

Immediately the foremost temple guard raised his knife. Fannia brought up the paralyzer, not firing it yet, still moving forward.

The foremost native shouted something, and the knife swept across in a glittering arc. The Cascellan gurgled something else, staggered and fell. Bright blood oozed from his throat."

"I *told* you not to use the needler yet!" Fannia said.

"I didn't," Donnaught protested. Glancing back, Fannia saw that Donnaught's needler was still holstered.

"Then I don't get it," said Fannia bewilderedly.

Three more natives bounded forward, their knives

held high. They tumbled to the ground also. Fannia stopped and watched as a platoon of natives advanced on them.

Once they were within stabbing range of the Earthmen, the natives were slitting their own throats!

Fannia was frozen for a moment, unable to believe his eyes. Donnaught halted behind him.

Natives were rushing forward by the hundreds now, their knives poised, screaming at the Earthmen. As they came within range, each native stabbed himself, tumbling on a quickly growing pile of bodies. In minutes the Earthmen were surrounded by a heap of bleeding Cascellan flesh, which was steadily growing higher.

"All right!" Fannia shouted. "Stop it," he yanked Donnaught back with him, to profane ground. "Truce!" he yelled in Cascellan.

The crowd parted and the chief was carried through. With two knives clenched in his fists, he was panting from excitement.

"We have won the first battle!" he said proudly. "The might of our warriors frightens even such aliens as yourselves. You shall not profane our temple while a man is alive on Cascella!"

The natives shouted their approval and triumph.

The two aliens dazedly stumbled back to their ship.

"SO that's what Galactic meant by a unique social structure," Fannie said morosely. He stripped off his armor and lay down on his bunk. "Their way of making war is to suicide their enemies into capitulation."

"They must be nuts," Donnaught grumbled. "That's no way to fight."

"It works, doesn't it?" Fannia got up and stared out a porthole. The sun was setting, painting the city a charming red in its glow. The beams of light glistened off the spire of the Galactic cache. Through the open doorway they could hear the boom and rattle of drums. "Tribal call to arms," Fannia said.

"I still say it's crazy." Donnaught had some definite ideas on fighting. "It ain't human."

"I'll buy that. The idea seems to be that if enough people slaughter themselves, the enemy gives up out of sheer guilty conscience."

"What if the enemy doesn't give up?"

"Before these people united, they must have fought it out tribe to tribe, suiciding until someone gave up. The losers probably joined the victors; the tribe must have grown until it could take over the planet by sheer weight of numbers." Fannia looked carefully at Donnaught, trying to see if he understood. "It's anti-survival, of course; if someone didn't give up, the race would probably kill themselves," he shook his head. "But war of any kind is antisurvival. Perhaps they've got rules."

"Couldn't we just barge in and grab the fuel quick?" Donnaught asked. "And get out before they all killed themselves?"

"I don't think so," Fannia said. "They might go on committing suicide for the next ten years, figuring they were still fighting us," he looked thoughtfully at the city. "It's that chief of theirs… He's their god and he'd probably keep them suiciding until he was the only man left. Then he'd grin, say, 'We are great warriors,' and kill himself."

Donnaught shrugged his big shoulders in disgust.

"Why don't we knock him off?"

"They'd just elect another god." The sun was almost below the horizon now. "I've got an idea, though," Fannia said. He scratched his head. "It might work. All we can do is try."

AT midnight, the two men sneaked out of the ship, moving silently into the city. They were both dressed in space armor again. Donnaught carried two empty fuel cans. Fannia had his paralyzer out.

The streets were dark and silent as they slid along walls and around posts, keeping out of sight. A native turned a corner suddenly, but Fannia paralyzed him before he could make a sound.

They crouched in the darkness, in the mouth of an alley facing the cache.

"Have you got it straight?" Fannia asked. "I paralyze the guards. You bolt in and fill up those cans. We get the hell out of here, quick. When they check, they find the cans still there. Maybe they won't commit suicide then."

The men moved across the shadowy steps in front of the cache. There were three Cascellans guarding the entrance, their knives stuck in their loincloths. Fannia stunned them with a medium charge, and Donnaught broke into a run.

Torches instantly flared, natives boiled out of every alleyway, shouting, waving their knives.

"We've been ambushed!" Fannia shouted. "Get back here, Donnaught!"

Donnaught hurriedly retreated. The natives had been waiting for them. Screaming, yowling, they rushed at the

Earthmen, slitting their own throats at five-foot range. Bodies tumbled in front of Fannia, almost tripping him as he backed up. Donnaught caught him by an arm and yanked him straight. They ran out of the sacred area.

"Truce, damn it!" Fannia called out. "Let me speak to the chief. Stop it! Stop it! I want a truce!"

Reluctantly, the Cascellans stopped their slaughter.

"This is war," the chief said, striding forward. His almost human face was stern under the torchlight. "You have seen our warriors. You know now that you cannot stand against them. The word has spread to all our lands. My entire people are prepared to do battle."

He looked proudly at his fellow-Cascellans, then back to the Earthmen. "I myself will lead my people into battle now. There will be no stopping us. We will fight until you surrender yourselves completely, stripping off your armor."

"Wait, chief," Fannia panted, sick at the sight of so much blood. The clearing was a scene out of the Inferno. Hundreds of bodies were sprawled around. The streets were muddy with blood.

"Let me confer with my partner tonight. I will speak with you tomorrow."

"No." the chief said. "You started the battle. It must go to its conclusion. Brave men wish to die in battle. It is our fondest wish. You are the first enemy we have had in many years, since we subdued the mountain tribes."

"Sure," Fannia said. "But let's talk about it—"

"I myself will fight you," the chief said, holding up a dagger. "I will die for my people, as a warrior must!"

"Hold it!" Fannia shouted. "Grant us a truce. We are

allowed to fight only by sunlight. It is a tribal taboo."

The chief thought for a moment, then said, "Very well. Until tomorrow."

The beaten Earthmen walked slowly back to their ship amid the jeers of the victorious populace.

NEXT morning, Fannia still didn't have a plan. He knew that he had to have fuel; he wasn't planning on spending the rest of his life on Cascella, or waiting until the Galactic Survey sent another ship, in fifty years or so. On the other hand, he hesitated at the idea of being responsible for the death of anywhere up to three billion people. It wouldn't be a very good record to take to Thetis. The Galactic Survey might find out about it. Anyway, he just wouldn't do it.

He was stuck both ways.

Slowly, the two men walked out to meet the chief. Fannia was still searching wildly for an idea while listening to the drums booming.

"If there was only someone we could fight," Donnaught mourned, looking at his useless plasters.

"That's the deal," Fannia said. "Guilty conscience is making sinners of us all, or something like that. They expect us to give in before the carnage gets out of hand," he considered for a moment. "It's not so crazy, actually. On Earth, armies don't usually fight until every last man is slaughtered on one side. Someone surrenders when they've had enough."

"If they'd just fight *us*!"

"Yeah, if they only—" He stopped. "We'll fight each other!" he said. "These people look at suicide as war. Wouldn't they look upon war—real fighting—as suicide?"

"What good would that do us?" Donnaught asked.

They were coming into the city now and the streets were lined with armed natives. Around the city there were thousands more. Natives were filling the plain, as far as the eye could see. Evidently they had responded to the drums and were here to do battle with the aliens.

Which meant, of course, a wholesale suicide.

"Look at it this way," Fannia said. "If a guy plans on suiciding on Earth, what do we do?"

"Arrest him?" Donnaught asked.

"Not at first. We offer him anything he wants, if he just won't do it. People offer the guy money, a job, their daughters, anything, just so he won't do it. It's taboo on Earth."

"So?"

"So," Fannia went on, "maybe fighting is just as taboo here. Maybe they'll offer us fuel, if we'll just stop."

Donnaught looked dubious, but Fannia felt it was worth a try.

THEY pushed their way through the crowded city, to the entrance of the cache. The chief was waiting for them, beaming on his people like a jovial war god.

"Are you ready to do battle?" he asked. "Or to surrender?"

"Sure," Fannia said. "Now, Donnaught!"

He swung, and his mailed fist caught Donnaught in the ribs. Donnaught blinked.

"Come on, you idiot, hit me back."

Donnaught swung, and Fannia staggered from the force of the blow. In a second they were at it like a pair of blacksmiths, mailed blows ringing from their armored hides.

"A little lighter," Fannia gasped, picking himself up from the ground. "You're denting my ribs," he belted Donnaught viciously on the helmet.

"Stop it!" the chief cried. "This is disgusting!"

"It's working," Fannia panted. "Now let me strangle you. I think that might do it."

Donnaught obliged by falling to the ground. Fannia clamped both hands around Donnaught's armored neck, and squeezed.

"Make believe you're in agony, idiot," he said.

Donnaught groaned and moaned as convincingly as he could.

"You must stop!" the, chief screamed. "It is terrible to kill another!"

"Then let me get some fuel," Fannia said, tightening his grip on Donnaught's throat.

The chief thought it over for a little while. Then he shook his head.

"No."

"What?"

"You are aliens. If you want to do this disgraceful thing, do it. But you shall not profane our religious relics."

DONNAUGHT and Fannia staggered to their feet. Fannia was exhausted from fighting in the heavy space armor; he barely made it up.

"Now," the chief said, "surrender at once. Take off your armor or do battle with us."

The thousands of warriors—possibly millions,

because more were arriving every second—shouted their blood-wrath. The cry was taken up on the outskirts and echoed to the hills where more fighting men were pouring down into the crowded plain.

Fannia's face contorted. He couldn't give himself and Donnaught up to the Cascellans. They might be cooked at the next church supper. For a moment he considered going after the fuel and letting the damned fools suicide all they pleased.

His mind an angry blank, Fannia staggered forward and hit the chief in the face with a mailed glove.

The chief went down, and the natives backed away in horror. Quickly, the chief snapped out a knife and brought it up to his throat. Fannia's hands closed on the chief's wrists.

"Listen to me," Fannia croaked. "We're going to take that fuel. If any man makes a move—if anyone kills himself—I'll kill your chief."

The natives milled around uncertainly. The chief was struggling wildly in Fannia's hands, trying to get a knife to his throat, so he could die honorably.

"Get it," Fannia told Donnaught, "and hurry it up."

The natives were uncertain just what to do. They had their knives poised at their throats, ready to plunge if battle was joined.

"Don't do it," Fannia warned. "I'll kill the chief and then he'll never die a warrior's death."

The chief was still trying to kill himself. Desperately, Fannia held on, knowing he had to keep him from suicide in order to hold the threat of death over him.

"Listen, Chief," Fannia said, eyeing the uncertain crowd. "I must have your promise there'll be no more war between us. Either I get it or I kill you."

"Warriors!" the chief roared. "Choose a new ruler. Forget me and do battle!"

The Cascellans were still uncertain, but knives started to lift.

"If you do it," Fannia shouted in despair, "I'll kill your chief. *I'll kill all of you*!"

That stopped them.

"I have powerful magic in my ship. I can kill every last man, and then you won't be able to die a warrior's death. Or get to heaven!"

The chief tried to free himself with a mighty surge that almost tore one of his arms free, but Fannia held on, pinning both arms behind his back.

"Very well," the chief said, tears springing into his eyes. "A warrior must die by his own hand. You have won, alien."

The crowd shouted curses as the Earthmen carried the chief and the cans of fuel back to the ship. They waved their knives and danced up and down in a frenzy of hate.

"Let's make it fast," Fannia said, after Donnaught had fueled the ship.

He gave the chief a push and leaped in. In a second they were in the air, heading for Thetis and the nearest bar at top speed.

The natives were hot for blood —their own. Every man of them pledged his life to wiping out the insult to their leader and god, and to their shrine.

But the aliens were gone. There was nobody to fight.

Writing Class

"Never use cliches in describing alien life-forms," Professor Carner admonished his class. But Eddie persisted—with good reason!

EDDIE McDermott paused at the door, then caught his breath and tiptoed into the classroom and to his seat. Mort Eddison, his best friend, looked at him reprovingly; the class had been in session for almost fifteen minutes, and one just didn't come late to Professor Carner's lecture. Especially on the first day.

Eddie breathed easier as he saw that Professor Carner's back was to the class as he completed a diagram on the blackboard.

"Now then," Carner said. "Suppose you were writing about the—ah—the Venusian Threngener, which, as you know, has three legs. How would you describe it?"

One of the students raised his hand. "I'd call it a three-legged monstrosity, spawned in the deepest hells of—"

"No," Carner said quietly. "That kind of writing might have been all right in the earliest days of our subject. But remember: You are no longer dealing with a simple, credulous audience. To achieve the proper effects nowadays, you must *underplay*! Understand?

Underplay! Now, someone else?"

Mort raised his hand, threw a glance at Eddie, and said: "How about, 'this tri-pedal blob of orange protoplasm, octopus like in its gropings—'"

"That's better," Carner said. "Tripedal is very nice, very exact. But must you compare it to an octopus?"

"Why not?" Mort asked.

"An octopus," the professor said, "is a well-known form of Earth life. It inspires no terror, no wonder. You might better compare the Threngener to *another* strange monster; a Callistan Eddel-splayer, for example." He smiled winningly at the class.

Eddie frowned and scratched his blonde crewcut. He had liked it better the first way. But Carner should know, of course. He was one of the best-known writers in the entire field, and he had done the college a favor by agreeing to teach the course. Eddie remembered reading some of Carner's stuff. It had scared the living daylights out of him when he was younger. That description of Saturnian brains immobilizing Earth-confederation ships, for example. That had been a great yarn.

THE trouble is, Eddie thought, I'm just not interested. He had had serious doubts about this course. Actually, he had signed up only because Mort had insisted.

"Any questions at this point?" Carner asked. One of the students—a serious-looking fellow wearing black horn-rimmed glasses—raised his hand.

"Suppose," he asked, "suppose you were writing a story speculating on an interstellar combine formed with the purpose of taking over Earth? Would it be permissible, for greater contrast, to make Earth's enemies black-hearted villains?"

A political thinker, Eddie thought with a sneer. He glanced hopefully at the clock.

"It wouldn't be advisable." Carner sat casually on the corner of his desk. "Make them human also; show the reader that these aliens—whether they have one head or five—have emotions understandable to them. Let them feel joy and pain. Show them as being misguided. Pure evil in your characters has gone out of fashion."

"But could I make their leader pure evil?" the young man asked, busily jotting down everything Carner had said.

"I suppose so," Carner said thoughtfully. "But give him motivations also. By the way, in dealing with that sort of story—the panoramic kind—remember not to oversimplify the aliens' problems. If they amass an army of twenty million, all have to be fed. If the rulers of fifty scattered star systems meet in conclave, remember that different star systems have different languages, and different races have different nervous systems. Bear in mind also, that there would be little logical reason for attacking earth; the galaxy is filled with so many stars and planets, what is the necessity of fighting for one?"

The horn-rimmed fellow nodded dubiously, writing his notes with tremendous speed. Eddie stifled a yawn. He preferred to think of his villains as pure unadulterated evil; it made characterization so much easier. And he was getting tremendously bored.

Carner answered questions for the next half-hour. He told them not to describe Venus as a 'jungle-choked green hell,' never, never to calf the moon 'pock-marked,' 'small-pox pitted,' or 'scarred from centuries of meteoric bombardment.'

"All this has been said," he explained. "Millions of times. *Do not* use cliches."

He went on to explain that the red spot of Jupiter need not be called a malevolent red eye, that Saturn's rings don't necessarily resemble a halo, and that the inhabitants of Venus are not Venetians.

"All common errors," he said. "I want a thousand words from each of you next time. I suggest that you choose a planet and write a fresh study of it, avoiding with care all the cliches I mentioned. Class dismissed."

"Well, whadja think?" Mort asked Eddie in the hall. "Isn't he great? I mean, he really *knows!*"

"I'm dropping out of the class," Eddie said, making up his mind.

"What! Why?"

"Well," Eddie said, "There's no reason why I shouldn't call the red spot on Jupiter a malevolent red eye. I put that in a story last month, and it sounded good. And that Venetian Threngener—I think it's a *monstrosity*, and I'm going to write about it that way."

He paused, and his face hardened with conviction.

"But the real reason—well, I'm just not interested in journalism. I'm dropping Carner's course in fact feature-article writing, because I want to write fiction!"

Final Examination

If you saw the stars in the sky vanishing by the millions, and knew you had but five days to prepare for your judgment—what would you do?

I suppose it started some time back, even before the astronomers discovered it, and certainly long before I found out. How far back I have no idea; thousands of years, perhaps, or more. But the first I knew about it was one March evening when I opened the newspaper.

Jane was in the kitchen, cleaning up, and I was settled back in the easy chair, reading through the lead articles. I skimmed through all the war talk, price controls, suicides, murders, and then glanced through the rest of the paper. One small article in the back caught my eye.

ASTRONOMERS LOSING STARS, the caption read. It was a human-interest story I suppose, because it went on in that maddening coy style the newspapers use for that sort of stuff.

"DR. Wilhelm Mentzner, at the Mount St. James Observatory, says that he has been unable, in recent weeks, to find some of the Milky Way stars. It would seem, Dr. Mentzner tells us, that they have vanished. Repeated photographs of certain portions of space do not show the presence of these dim, faraway stars. They were in place and intact in photographs made as recently as April, 1942, and…"

The article gave the names of some of the stars—they didn't mean a thing to me—and chided the scientists on their absentmindedness. "Imagine," it went on, "losing something as big as a star. Although," the writer summed up, "it doesn't really matter. They have a few hundred billion left to play around with."

I thought it was sort of cute at the time, although in questionable taste. I don't know a thing about science—I'm in the dress line—but I've always looked upon it with the greatest respect. The way I see it, you start laughing at scientists and they come up with something like the atom bomb. Better to treat them with a little respect.

I can't remember if I showed the article to my wife. If I did, she didn't say anything in particular.

Life went along as usual. I went to work in Manhattan and came home to Queens. In a few days there was another article. This one was written by a Phd., and it had dropped the kidding style.

It said that stars appeared to be disappearing from our Milky Way galaxy at a tremendous rate. Observatories in both hemispheres had estimated that a few million of the farthest stars had vanished in the past five weeks.

I stepped out the backdoor to have a look. Everything seemed in order to me. The Milky Way was still up there, smeared across the sky as thick as ever. The Big Dipper was shining away, and the North Star was still pointing toward Westchester. No difference. The ground was frozen under my feet, but the air was almost warm. Spring would be coming along soon, and Spring fashions.

In the distance I could see the red glow of Manhattan, across the 59th Street Bridge. That seemed to settle it. The only problem I had was dresses, and I went back inside to worry about them.

In a few more days the star-story had reached the front page. STARS DISAPPEARING, the headlines read. WHAT NEXT?

It seemed that millions of stars were vanishing from the Milky Way every day and night. The other galaxies seemed to be unaffected, although it was hard to tell; but they were definitely dropping out of ours. Most of them were so far away they could only be caught with a high-powered telescope, or a camera; but hundreds could still be seen disappearing by anybody with a pair of eyes. Not blowing up or fading out; just click—and they were gone.

This article—written by an astronomer *and* a Phd.—reminded everybody that only the light was stopping. The stars themselves must have been snubbed out hundreds of millions of years ago, and that the light was finally stopping, after travelling all that distance across space. I think it was hundreds of millions, although it might have been thousands.

The article didn't even speculate on the cause of it all.

I went stargazing that night. Everyone else in the neighborhood was out in their backyards, too. And sure enough, in the gigantic spread of stars I could see little specks of light winking out. They were barely noticeable; if I hadn't been looking for them I would never have seen anything different.

"Hey Jane," I called in the back door. "Come on out and have a look."

My wife came out and stood hands on hips, looking at the sky. She was frowning, as though she resented the whole business.

"I don't see anything," she said.

"Look carefully," I said. "Watch one section at a time. There was one! Did you see it?"

"No."

"Watch for little winks," I said. But it wasn't until the Thomas kid came from next door and loaned her his telescope that she saw it.

"Here, Mrs. Ostersen, use this," the kid said. He had three or four telescopes in his hands, a pair of binoculars, and a handful of charts. Quite a kid.

"You too, Mr. Ostersen," he said.

Through the telescope I could really see it. One moment a pinpoint of light would be there, and then—bing! It was gone. It was down right weird. For the first time I started getting worried.

It didn't bother Jane, though. She went back into her kitchen.

OF course, even with the galaxy collapsing, the dress business had to go on, but I found myself buying a newspaper four or five times a day and keeping the radio on in the store to find out what was going on. Everybody else was doing the same. People were even arguing about it on street corners.

The newspapers had about a thousand different theories. There were scientific articles on the red shift, and intergalactic dust; there were articles on stellar evolution and visual hallucination; the psychologists were trying to prove that the stars hadn't been there in the first place, or something like that.

I didn't know what to believe. The only article that made any sense to me was one written by a social commentator, and he wasn't even a full-fledged scientist. He said it looked as if someone was doing a big job of housecleaning in our galaxy.

The Thomas kid had his own theories. He was sure it was the work of invaders from another dimension. He told me they were sucking our galaxy into theirs, which was in another dimension, like dust into a vacuum cleaner.

"It's perfectly clear, Mr. Ostersen," he told me one evening after work. "They've started sucking in the outside stars at the other side of the Milky Way, and they're working through the centre. They'll reach us last, because we're at the far end."

"Well..." I said.

"After all," he told me, "*Astonishing Yarns and Weird Science Stories* practically agree on it, and they're the leaders in the sci-fic field."

"But they're not scientists," I said.

"That doesn't matter," the kid told me. "They predicted the submarine before there was one. They predicted airplanes when scientists were saying the bumblebee couldn't fly. And rockets and radar and atom bombs. They've got the truth about this too."

He paused for breath. "Someone's gotta stop the invaders," he went on in a tone of utter conviction. He looked at me sharply. "You know, since they're dimension-changers, they can take the appearance of humans." Again he looked at me, suspiciously.

"Anyone might be one. *You* might be one."

I could see he was getting nervous, and maybe on the verge of handing me over to some committee or other, so I fed him milk and cake. That just made him more suspicious, but there wasn't anything I could do about it.

The newspapers took up the science-fiction theory just as the Thomas kid had told it to me, and added their own embellishments. Some guy said he knew how the invaders could be stopped. He had been approached by them, he said, and they'd offered him controllership of a small galaxy if he'd cooperate... Of course, he wouldn't.

It sounds foolish, but the sky was getting pretty bare. People in every country were saying foolish things and doing foolish things. We were starting to wonder how soon our own sun would go.

I watched every night, and the stars disappeared faster and faster. The thing seemed to increase at a geometric rate. Soon the sky was just filled with little lights going out, faster than you could count. Almost all of it could be seen with the naked eye now, because it was getting a lot closer to us.

In two weeks the only part of the Milky Way left were the Magallenic clouds, and the astronomers said that they weren't a part of our galaxy anyhow. Betelguese and Actares and Rigel winked out, and Sirius and Vega. Then Alpha Centauri disappeared, and that was our closest neighbor. Aside from the moon, the sky was pretty bare at night, just a few dots and patches here and there.

I don't know what would have happened if the voice hadn't been heard then. It would be anybody's guess.

But the voice came the day after Alpha Centauri vanished.

I first heard it on my way to the store. I was walking down Lexington Avenue from the 59th Street station, looking in the dress windows to see what my competitors had to offer. Just as I was passing *Mary-Belle's Frocks*, and wondering how soon they'd have their Summer line in, I heard it.

It was a pleasant voice, friendly. It seemed to come from just behind me, about three feet over my shoulder.

"*Judgment of the inhabitants of the planet Earth*," it said, "*will be held in five days. Please prepare yourselves for final examination and departure. This announcement will be repeated*."

I looked around at once to find out who was speaking. I half expected to find a tall, cadaverous fanatic at my shoulder, some fiery-eyed fellow with flowing hair and a beard. But there was no one at all. The nearest person was about fifteen feet from me. For a moment I thought I was having a hallucination, hearing voices, that sort of thing. Then I saw that everyone else must have heard it, too.

Lexington Avenue is a pretty busy place at nine o'clock in the morning. There are plenty of people hurrying back and forth, kids going to school, subways roaring beneath you, cars and buses honking. Not now. You couldn't hear a sound. Every car had stopped, right where it was. The people on the sidewalks seemed frozen practically in mid-stride.

The man nearest me walked up. He was well dressed, about my age in his early forties. He was eyeing me with suspicion, as though I might have been responsible for the whole thing. I suppose I was looking at him in the same way.

"Did you hear it?" he asked me.

"Yes," I said.

"Did you do it?"

"No. Did you?"

"Most certainly not," he said indignantly. We stood for a few seconds, just looking at each other. I think we—everybody—knew, right there and then, that it was no hoax. What with the stars disappearing, I mean.

A pretty girl in a fur coat walked up to me. She was young; she looked scared, and very defiant.

"Did you hear it?" she asked us.

"Yes," I said, and the man nodded.

"Is it possible that she was operating on a loudspeaker?" the girl asked.

She?" we both said.

"That woman's voice," the girl said, looking a little exasperated. "A young woman—she said, 'Judgment of the inhabitants—'"

"It was a man's voice," the man said. "Of that I'm certain." He looked at me, and I nodded.

"Oh no," the girl told us. "A girl—she even had a slight New England accent—it was unmistakable." She looked around for support.

The people on Lexington Avenue had gathered in small groups. There were knots of people up and down the sidewalks as far as I could see. The cars still weren't moving. Most of the drivers had gotten out to ask someone else about the voice.

"Say, pardon me," some man said to me. "Am I hearing things or did you hear—"

That's how it was for the next hour. Everyone, it seemed, had heard it. But every woman was sure it had been a woman's voice, and every man was sure it had been a man's. I left finally, and went to my store.

Minnie, the salesgirl, and Frank, my stock boy, were already there. They had the radio on, but they were talking over it.

"Say, Mr. Ostersen," Frank called as I walked in. "Did *you* hear it?"

I sat down and discussed it with them, but we couldn't tell each other much. Frank had been in the store when he heard it. Minnie had just been walking in, her hand on the doorknob. Minnie was sure it was a girl's voice, about her own age, with just the trace of a Bronx accent. Frank and I held out for a man's voice, but where I was sure the man was in his early forties or late thirties, Frank was positive it was a young man, about twenty or twenty-two.

We noticed the radio, finally. It had been broadcasting all that time, but we hadn't paid any attention.

"...voice was heard in all parts of the country, at nine-oh-three this morning, Eastern Standard Time. This voice, purporting to be that of—of the, ah, Deity, announcing the Judgment Day, was heard—ah, was heard in all parts of the country." The voice hesitated, then continued. "In place of our usual program, we now bring you the Reverend Joseph Morrison, who will speak on—" The voice stopped for a moment, then came back with renewed vigor. "The Reverend Joseph Morrison!"

We listened to the radio most of the morning. The

Reverend Joseph Morrison seemed as confused as the rest of us, but he was followed by news announcements. The voice had been heard, as far as they could make out, in every country on earth. It had spoken in every language, every dialect and sub-dialect.

Minnie looked dazed as the reports piled in, and Frank looked shocked. I suppose I looked as startled as my normal deadpan would show. At eleven-forty-five I decided to call my wife. No use. I couldn't even get the operator.

"...possibilities that this is a hoax," a voice was saying from the radio in an unconvincing tone. "Mass hallucinations are far from unknown, and the chance must be considered. In the Middle Ages..."

Cutting through our conversation, and through the blaring radio, smooth as a knife through butter, the voice came again.

"*Judgment of the inhabitants of the planet Earth will be held in five days. Please prepare yourselves for final examination and departure. This announcement will be repeated.*"

Departure! I thought. Where were we going?

"There!" Frank shouted. "You see—it *was* a young man!"

"You're crazy!" Minnie screamed at him. Her hair had fallen over her eyes; she looked like an impassioned cocker spaniel.

"*You're* crazy!" Frank shouted back. They stood glaring at each other. Minnie seemed about ready to throw the cash register at him.

"Easy now," I said. "It seems—it seems like the voice speaks in everybody's language, and sounds like the sort of voice everybody would know."

"But how's that possible?" Frank asked me.

"I don't know. But it's certainly logical. If the voice spoke just in Latin or Hebrew or English, none of the Arabs would understand. Or the Armenians. So, while it's speaking everybody's language, it might as well speak everybody's dialect at the same time."

"Should we call it *it*?" Frank asked in a whisper. He glanced over his shoulder, as though he expected to find an avenging angel there. "Shouldn't we refer to it as *Him*?"

"She, you mean," Minnie said. "The old masculine idea that God must be a man is just so much ego-wash. Why, the feminine principle is evident all through the universe. Why, why, you just can't say Him when—when—"

Minnie had never been too strong on ideas. She ran out of breath and stood, panting and pushing back her hair.

After a while we talked about it calmly, and listened to the radio. There were more speakers and another survey of the countries that had heard the second announcement. At two o'clock I told them to go home. It was no use trying to get any work done that day. Besides, there were no customers.

The subways were running again when I reached the BMT, and I rode to my home in Queens.

"Of course you heard it?" My wife asked me at the door.

"Of course," I said. "Was it spoken by a woman in her middle-thirties, with just the trace of a Queens accent?"

"Yes!" Jane said. "Thank God we can agree on

something!" But of course we couldn't.

We talked about it all through supper, and we talked about it after supper. At nine o'clock the announcement came again, from behind and above our shoulders.

"*Judgment of the inhabitants of the planet Earth will be held in five days. Please prepare yourselves for final examination and departure. That is all.*"

"Well," Jane said. "I guess She means it."

"I guess He does," I said. So we went to bed.

THE next day I went in to work, although I don't know why. I knew that this was It, and everyone else knew it too. But it seemed right to go back to work, end of the world or not. Most of my adult life had been bound up in that store, and I wanted a day more with it. I had some idea of getting my affairs in order, although I knew it couldn't matter.

The subway ride was murderous. New York is always a crowded city, but it seemed as though the whole United States had moved in. The subways were so tightly jammed the doors couldn't even close. When I finally got out, the streets were filled from one curb to the other. Traffic had given up, and people were piling out of cars and buses anywhere they were stopped, adding to the jam in the streets.

In the store, Frank and Minnie were already there. I guess they had the same idea—about gathering up loose ends.

"Gee, Mr. Ostersen," Frank said. "What do you think He'll do—about our sins, I mean?" Frank was twenty-one, and I couldn't see how he could have committed an unusual number of sins. But he was worried about them. The way he frowned and paced around, he might have been the devil himself.

Minnie didn't have any sins on her mind, as far as I could see. She was wearing what must have been her best dress—she hadn't bought it in my store—and her hair was a lighter brown than it had been yesterday. I suspected she wanted to look her best in front of the Almighty, be He man or woman.

We talked about sins most of the morning, and listened to the radio. The radio had a lot to say about sins, but no two speakers agreed.

Around lunchtime, Ollie Bernstein dropped in.

"Hiya, ex-competitor," he said, standing in the doorway. "How's business?"

"I sold five dozen halos," I told him. "How's with you?"

"What's it matter?" he asked, coming sideways through the doorway. "Four days before Judgment, who cares? Come have lunch with me, ex-competitor."

Ollie and I had never been on really friendly terms. We sold the same price line, and our stores were too close for mutual comfort. Also, he was fat and I've always been suspicious of fat men. But suddenly, I found myself liking him. It seemed a shame I hadn't recognized his solid qualities years ago.

We went to Lotto's, a classy place on East 73rd Street. We had hoped to avoid some of the crowd by going uptown, but there wasn't a chance of it. Lotto's was very packed, and we stood around three-quarters of an hour waiting for a table.

Seated, we ordered roast duck, but had to settle for hamburger steak. The waiter told us people had been walking in and ordering roast duck all morning.

Lotto's had a radio—probably for the first time in its existence—and a minister or rabbi was speaking. He was interrupted by a news announcement.

"The war in Indo-China is over," the announcer said. "Peace was declared at 7:30 this morning. Also, a general truce has been called in Mongolia, and in Tanganyika." There was a lot of that. In Indo-China, it seemed that the rebels had given up the country to the French, declaring that all men should live in peace. The French immediately announced they were withdrawing their forces as fast as they could get planes for them. Every Frenchman was going to spend the last three days before Judgment in Paris.

For a moment I wished I was in Paris.

The announcer also said, the Russian airforce had agreed to pilot the Frenchmen home.

It was the same everywhere. Every country was leaning over backward, giving up this and that, offering land to its neighbors, shipping food to less fortunate areas, and so forth.

We listened over a bottle of Moselle—all the champagne had been drunk that morning. I think I got a little high. Anyhow, I walked back with my arms around two total strangers. We were assuring each other that peace, it was wonderful.

And it was at that.

I went home early, to miss the evening rush. It was still rough going. I grinned at my wife as I reached the door, and she grinned back. Jane was a little high, also.

THE next day I brought my wife into the city. With

three days left to go, two really because you couldn't count the Day itself, we figured we'd move into a good hotel, buy an armload of classical records and have our own private, quiet celebration. I thought we deserved it; although I could have been wrong.

Frank was already at the store when we got there. He was all dressed up; and he had a suitcase with him.

"What's up, Frank?" I asked.

"Well, Mr. Ostersen," he said, "with only two days left, I'm going to go on my first airplane trip. I'm flying to Texas."

"Oh?" I asked.

"Yessir," Frank said. He shuffled his feet, as if he knew he was doing something foolish. But his face was set. He was waiting for me to tell him not to go.

"I'm going out where I can ride a horse. Mr. Ostersen, I've always dreamed of going to Texas and riding a horse. It isn't just the horses, I want the airplane ride too, and I want to see what all that land looks like. I was figuring on doing it this summer, on my vacation, but now—well, I'm going."

I walked to the back of the store and opened the safe. I had four thousand dollars there; the rest was in the bank. I came back and handed Frank two thousand.

"Here, kid," I said. "Buy a horse for me." He just stared at me for a second, then dashed out. There wasn't much to say. Besides, it was an easy gesture. The stuff was as good as worthless. Might as well see the other fellow have a good time.

For once my wife seemed to agree with me. She smiled.

Minnie came in almost as soon as Frank left. She was

all dressed up, too, in another dress she hadn't bought in my store. There was a young fellow with her. He wasn't good-looking or bad-looking; just the sort of fellow you'd see anywhere. But Minnie seemed to think he was something pretty special, to judge by the way she was clutching his arm.

"Are you going to Texas too?" I asked.

"Oh, no," she said. "I'm getting married."

"Oh?" Jane asked.

"Yes ma'am," Minnie said. "Herb and I were going to wait 'til he finished dental school, so he shouldn't be living off his parents. But now—" She looked very cute, I must say. Her hair was a light blonde. It looked fine on her.

"Here, Minnie," my wife said. She took the other two thousand out of my hand and gave it to her. "Have a good time these last days."

"Hey!" I said, when Minnie and her young man had gone. "How about us? We'll never be able to get in a bank. What'll we do?"

"Quit worrying," Jane told me. "Don't you believe in young love?" She found the one comfortable chair in the place—the one we reserve for customers—and sat down.

"I've been too careful," she said when she saw me looking at her.

"I see," I said.

"And as far as money goes," she continued. "Haven't you any faith? The Lord will provide."

"That's fine by me," I said, and sat down beside her. The door opened, and in walked a short man. He was oldish, and dressed like a banker, but I knew right away he was in the dress line. There's something about the dress line, you can always tell.

"Not much business?" he asked.

"Not much." There hadn't been a customer in all day—or all yesterday, now that I thought about it.

"That's understandable," he told me. "It's because everyone is storming the big stores, the expensive stores. Everyone wants to wear the best dresses on their last days."

"Sounds logical," I said.

"Logical, but not entirely right," he said, frowning seriously through little pince-nez. "Why should the big, expensive stores drive the middle-class retailer out of business? I am here as a representative of Bonzelli's—to reimburse you for your financial loss." With that he dropped a thick manilla envelope on the counter, smiled, and left.

"Bonzelli's," my wife commented coolly. "They're—expensive."

Inside the envelope there was eight thousand dollars.

THAT wasn't the end of it. Strangers dropped in every few minutes, leaving money. After a while, I started handing it back. I went down the block to Ollie Bernstein's store, with twenty thousand dollars in a paper bag. I met him on the way. He had a fistful of bills.

"I've got a little gift for you, ex-competitor," he said. It was about fifteen thousand dollars. Everyone with money was handing it over, and getting it back from someone else.

"I've got an idea," I said. "How about the

unfortunate?"

"You mean the Bronx dress shops?" he asked.

"No, I mean the derelicts, the bums. Why shouldn't they share?"

"Count me in for fifteen thousand," he said without hesitation. We talked it over. Plans for going down to the Bowery and handing it out didn't seem so good. The streets were still impossible, and I didn't want to leave Jane for long. We finally decided to give it to the nearest church. They'd see it got into the proper hands.

The church on 65th and Madison was closest, so we went right there and formed on the end of the line. It stretched halfway down the block, but it was moving fast.

"I had no idea it was like this," Ollie said. He shook his head. Perspiration was dripping from him. He was working harder handing out money than he had ever worked to make it in his life.

"What kind of church is this?" he asked me.

"I don't know." I tapped the man in front of me. "What kind of church is this, mac?"

The man turned around. He was almost as big as Ollie but older, tireder looking. "How should I know?" he said. "I'm from Brooklyn."

We reached the inside of the church and a man took our money. He didn't have time to thank us; there were too many behind, clamoring for their chance. The man just threw the bills on a table. Another man, a Reverend of some kind, was walking back and forth, picking up handfuls of it and carrying it off, then coming back for more. We followed him, just out of curiosity. I didn't have any doubt they'd dispose of it in the right way, but a fellow likes to know where his charity is going. Besides, Jane would probably ask me.

At the side entrance of the church there was a line of poorly clad, red-faced men. Their clothes were in tatters, but their faces were shining. The Reverend was handing each man a handful of bills, then rushing back for more.

"Be simpler if they formed the line inside," I said to Ollie as we headed back for our stores. "Just have the guys with money lined up in front of the guys without. Faster."

"Listen," Ollie said. "You always have a middle man. Can't avoid it." He coughed three or four times. I could see that the strain was getting him. A man Ollie's size shouldn't run around handing out money that way.

On my way back to the store someone handed me five thousand dollars. He just grinned, shoved it in my hands and hurried on. I did a double take. It was one of the bums who had just got it.

Back in the store there was more money piled up on the counter. My wife was still in the same chair, reading a magazine.

"It's been piling up since you left," she said.

I threw my five thousand on the pile.

"You should have heard the radio," she said. "Congress passed about two dozen laws in the last hour. They've given everybody every right you could think of, and a few I never dreamed existed."

"It's the age of the common man," I told her.

FOR an hour I stood at the door handing out money, but it was just plain foolishness. The streets were mobbed with people handing out the stuff. Everyone wanted to give it away. It was a game; the rich gave it to the poor, and the poor turned around and handed it back to the rich. By two o'clock it was impossible to tell who had been rich and who poor.

In the meantime, Jane kept me posted on what was going on over the radio. Every country on the face of the earth was passing emancipation acts as quick as they could get a quorum together. The age of the common man had really come in—two days before deadline.

Jane and I left for lunch at three o'clock. We both knew it would be the last time we'd see the store. As a final gesture, we piled fifty thousand dollars or so on the counter, and left the doors open. It seemed the only thing we could do.

We ate in an East Sixty-third street restaurant. The regular help had left, but people wandered in off the streets, cooked for a while, ate and left. Jane fixed a few dozen club sandwiches for our share, and then we ate. The next problem was where to sleep. I was sure all the hotels would be full, but we had to try. In an emergency we could sleep in the store.

We walked into the Stanton-Carler, one of the biggest hotels in New York. There was a young man behind the main desk, reading *The World as Will and Idea*, by Schopenhauer.

"Any chance of a room?" I asked him.

"Here's a pass key," he said. "Take any vacant room you can find."

"How much?" I asked, fanning a few thousand-dollar bills.

"Are you kidding?" he said, and returned to his book. He looked like a very serious young man.

We found a vacant room on the fifteenth floor, and sat down as soon as we were inside. Immediately, Jane jumped up again.

"Records," she said. "I want to spend the day before Judgment listening to good music."

I was dog-tired, but I wanted the same thing. Jane and I had never had enough time to listen to all the music we wanted to hear. Somehow, we had never gotten around to it.

Jane wanted to go with me, but I thought, what with the jam New York was in, it would be easier if I went alone.

"Lock the door until I get back," I told her. "It may be the day before Judgment, but not everyone's an angel yet." She winked at me. She hadn't winked in years.

I scrambled through the crowd to a music store. It was deserted. I picked up a long-playing recorder and all the records I could carry. Then I came back. I had to walk to the fifteenth floor, because some guy was zooming up and down in one elevator, and the rest were out of order.

"Put on the Debussey," I told Jane when I got back, throwing myself in an armchair. It was a joy and a pleasure to be off my feet.

That's how we spent the rest of the day, and the evening. We played records. I had gotten some Bach, Debussey, Mozart, Hayden, and a few others I never heard of. I listened to more music in that day than I'd heard in five years previously.

WE woke up late the next day, about one-thirty in the afternoon. I felt guilty. It didn't seem right to sleep away the day before Judgment.

"Seems as good as any other way," Jane said. Perhaps she was right. Anyhow, we were both ravenously hungry. Jane's feet were blistered, because she hadn't moved around so much since we were courting.

"Stay put," I said. "You're shining knight will bring you lunch. My last good deed."

"Your first," she told me, smiling.

"Lock that door," I said, and left. I just don't trust people very much. I don't know why. Even on the day before Judgment, I couldn't trust everyone.

The streets were empty when I finally got down. A few people were walking around, peering nervously over their shoulders. A few more had joyous smiles on their faces. But the streets were very bare. Cars, taxis and buses had been left haphazardly all over the street. The traffic lights were still clicking red and green, but there was no traffic to regulate.

I saw no sign of a policeman, and remembered that I hadn't seen any since shortly after the announcement. I didn't know if I liked that, but I supposed that cops are human too. They might like to spend their last days with their families, also. And who was going to steal anything?

It might be a good idea, I thought, to drop into a church and offer up a prayer. Not that it would make any difference, or even that I especially wanted to. But I thought Jane would like me to. I tried three churches, but they were all packed, with hundreds waiting outside. Now I knew where everybody was.

I think I might have waited too, but Jane was expecting her lunch. I went on to a restaurant.

On my way back with a bundle of food, five people stopped me and tried to give me money. They seemed desperate. They explained that they had to get rid of it—and they had no idea how to. After working for it all their lives, it didn't seem right just to throw it away. And no one would take it now. They were really perplexed.

One man in particular struck me.

"Please take it, old man," he said. "I've been unfortunate—I've accumulated so much of it, it's almost impossible to dispose of it all. And I don't want it on my—hands. I really don't. Won't you accept a portion of it?"

I recognized him. He was an actor, and a well-known one. I had always enjoyed watching him, so I took a pile of bills off his hands, leaving it on the desk of the hotel. The young man who had been reading Schopenhauer was no longer there.

Jane and I ate, and listened to some more music. We listened to it the rest of the day, and didn't talk much. Towards evening Jane's eyes were soft. I knew she was thinking back over our life. I thought back too. It didn't seem so bad. Not really. I had made a few mistakes, but still not so bad.

Night came, and we made supper out of leftovers. We didn't want to go out for anything, and we didn't want to go to sleep.

"It'll come just at dawn," Jane said. I tried to tell her you can't predict the ways of the Almighty, but she wasn't going to sell out her woman's intuition for anything. She was sure.

That was a long night, and not a very good one. I felt as though I were a prisoner at the bar. It wasn't a very good way to feel, but I was frightened. I suppose everybody was.

Standing at the window I saw the first light of the false dawn. It was going to be a beautiful day over New York. There were no visible stars, but every light in the city was on, making stars of its own. It was as though the city was burning candles to the unknown.

"Goodbye, Jane," I said. I knew she was right. The announcement would come just at dawn. I hoped Minnie was in her husband's arms; and Frank—I felt he was probably on a horse, standing up in the unfamiliar saddle and looking toward the East. I hoped he was.

"Goodbye, dear," Jane said, and kissed me. There was a cool breeze from the open window, and darkness in the sky. It was beautiful, at that moment. It should have ended just like that.

"*There will be a slight delay*," the voice said from behind my shoulder, as pleasant as ever, and as distant, "*in settling the affairs of the inhabitants of the planet Earth. The final examination and departure will be held ten years from this date.*"

I stood at the window, my arm around Jane. We couldn't say anything for perhaps ten minutes.

"Well," I said to her finally. "Well, well."

"Well," she said. We were silent for a few more minutes. Then she said, "Well," again.

There was nothing else to say.

I looked out the window. Below me the city was sparkling with lights; the sun was coming up, and everything was deadly quiet. The only sound I could hear was the buzzing of an electric sign. It sounded like a broken alarm clock, or like a time bomb, perhaps.

"You'll have to go back to work," Jane said. She started to cry. "Although I suppose ten years is only a second in eternity. Only a second to Her."

"Less," I said. "A fraction of a second. Less."

"But not to us," Jane said.

* * *

It certainly should have ended there. Judgment day should have come, bringing with it whatever it brought. We were ready. All the worldly goods were disposed of, in New York and I suppose, in the rest of the world. But ten years was too long, too much a strain on goodness.

We should have been able to carry on. There was no reason why not. We could have gone back to our jobs. The farmers were still on the farms, the grocers and clerks were still around.

We could have done such a bang-up job of it. We could have pointed to that ten years with pride, and said, "You see! Our recorded history of thousands of years of avarice, cruelty and hate isn't the whole story. For ten years were good and clean and noble. For ten years we were brothers!"

Unfortunately, it wasn't that way.

The farmers didn't want to go back to their farms, and the grocers didn't want to return to their groceries. Oh, some did. Many did, for a while. But not for long. Everyone talked about high ideals, but it was just talk, just like before.

For six months Jane and I struggled along, not getting

much to eat, frightened by the mobs that surged around New York. Finally, we decided to move out. We joined the exodus leaving New York, drifted through Pennsylvania, and headed North.

The country was disrupted, but it pulled itself together again, after a fashion. Thousands were starving, then millions. Some had food, but they weren't very willing to share it. They were figuring what they'd do for ten years, if they shared their food. Money they'd still hand out in basketfuls. It wasn't worth anything. In nine months a million dollars wouldn't buy a rotten turnip.

As time passed, fewer and fewer stayed on the job. The money they got wouldn't buy anything. Besides, why work when the end was so near? Why work for someone else?

In about a year there was the Bulgaria incident. An American in Sophia disappeared. He just vanished. The American Embassy complained. They were told to go home. The Bulgarians didn't want any interference for their last nine years of existence. Besides, they added that they didn't know where the man was. Maybe they were telling the truth. People vanish even here.

Anyhow, after our third ultimatum we bombed them. The attack coincided with a bombing launched on us by China, who decided we were interfering with her trade with Japan.

Great Britain was bombed, and bombed someone else. Everyone started bombing everyone else.

I took Jane out of the city where we were staying, and headed for the open country. We ran and stumbled over the fields, with the roar of the planes above us. We hid in ditches. Jane was cut down by machine gun bullets in one raid. Perhaps she was fortunate. She missed the atom bombs the next week, and she missed the hydrogen bombs a week later.

I wasn't around when they dropped the H-bomb. I was in central Canada, and heading for open country. But I heard the noise, I saw the smoke. They had bombed New York.

After that, everyone threw the biggest bombs they had, as fast as they could, at anything that might be called a target. Radioactive dust followed, and bacteria followed that. Gas was used, some stuff that hung close to the ground for days; only a good-sized storm or two would blow it away.

All this time I was heading North. Most of the traffic was South, because there was a famine in the North. But I figured I'd rather take my chances with starvation than with the bacteria and dust. As it was, the germs almost got me. I was sick for a day. I wanted to die. If I'd had a gun I would have shot myself. But I lived and the bacteria never touched me again.

I joined up with a few men below the Arctic Circle, but had to leave them. One of them fell sick a day after I joined, and another followed him. I figured I was a carrier, so I left in the night, still heading North.

They bombed the North, too, to make sure no one got the pitchblende. I ran through the woods; I hid in caves. At night I would look at the moon, and the little sprinkling of stars left across the sky.

After the fourth year I didn't see any more human beings. I didn't have time to look. All my day was spent filling my belly. It was a full-time job, just to gather grasses, and perhaps kill a rabbit with a stone. I became pretty handy with stones.

I didn't even know when the ten years were up.

To sum up, I don't suppose I'm the last man on earth. There must be others, hiding in caves in other parts of the world, waiting on islands, on mountaintops. You can check my story with them, if you can find them, but I think you'll find it pretty accurate.

Now as for me…

I suppose I've been as sinful as most, but that's for you to judge, Sir.

My name is Adam Ostersen. I was born in Pine Grove, Maine, in June of…

The Specialist

Recruiting all the parts of a ship works great...unless you suddenly run out of recruits!

THE photon storm struck without warning, pouncing upon the Ship from behind a bank of giant red stars. Eye barely had time to flash a last second warning through Talker before it was upon them.

It was Talker's third journey into deep space, and his first light-pressure storm. He felt a sudden pang of fear as the Ship yawed violently, caught the force of the wave-front and careened end for end. Then the fear was gone, replaced by a strong pulse of excitement.

Why should he be afraid, he asked himself—hadn't he been trained for just this sort of emergency?

He had been talking to Feeder when the storm hit, but he cut off the conversation abruptly. He hoped Feeder would be all right. It was the youngster's first deep space trip.

The wire-like filaments that made up most of Talker's body were extended throughout the Ship. Quickly he withdrew all except the ones linking him to Eye, Engine, and the Walls. This was strictly their job now. The rest of the Crew would have to shift for themselves until the storm was over.

Eye had flattened his disklike body against a Wall, and had one seeing organ extended outside the Ship. For greater concentration, the rest of his seeing organs were collapsed, clustered against his body.

Through Eye's seeing organ, Talker watched the storm. He translated Eye's purely visual image into a direction for Engine, who shoved the Ship around to meet the waves. At appreciably the same time, Talker translated direction into velocity for the Walls, who stiffened to meet the shocks.

The coordination was swift and sure—Eye measuring the waves, Talker relaying the messages to Engine and Walls, Engine driving the ship nose-first into the waves, and Walls bracing to meet the shock.

Talker forgot any fear he might have had in the swiftly functioning teamwork. He had no time to think. As the Ship's communication system, he had to translate and flash his messages at top speed, coordinating information and directing action.

In a matter of minutes, the storm was over.

"ALL right," Talker said. "Let's see if there was any damage." His filaments had become tangled during the storm, but he untwisted and extended them through the Ship, plugging everyone into circuit. "Engine?"

"I'm fine," Engine said. The tremendous old fellow had dampened his plates during the storm, easing down the atomic explosions in his stomach. No storm could catch an experienced spacer like Engine unaware.

"Walls?"

The Walls reported one by one, and this took a long time. There were almost a thousand of them, thin, rectangular fellows making up the entire skin of the Ship. Naturally, they had reinforced their edges during the storm, giving the whole Ship resiliency. But one or two were dented badly.

Doctor announced that he was all right. He removed Talker's filament from his head, taking himself out of circuit, and went to work on the dented Walls. Made mostly of hands, Doctor had clung to an Accumulator during the storm.

"Let's go a little faster now," Talker said, remembering that there still was the problem of determining where they were. He opened the circuit to the four Accumulators. "How are you?" he asked.

There was no answer. The Accumulators were asleep. They had had their receptors open during the storm and were bloated on energy. Talker twitched his filaments around them, but they didn't stir.

"Let me," Feeder said. Feeder had taken quite a beating before planting his suction cups to a Wall, but his cockiness was intact. He was the only member of the Crew who never needed Doctor's attention; his body was quite capable of repairing itself.

He scuttled across the floor on a dozen or so tentacles, and booted the nearest Accumulator. The big, conial storage unit opened one eye, then closed it again. Feeder kicked him again, getting no response. He reached for the Accumulator's safety valve and drained off some energy.

"Stop that," the Accumulator said.

"Then wake up and report," Talker told him.

The Accumulators said testily that they were all right, as any fool could see. They had been anchored to the floor during the storm.

THE rest of the inspection went quickly. Thinker was fine, and Eye was ecstatic over the beauty of the storm. There was only one casualty.

Pusher was dead. Bipedal, he didn't have the stability of the rest of the Crew. The storm had caught him in the middle of a floor, thrown him against a stiffened Wall, and broken several of his important bones. He was beyond Doctor's skill to repair.

They were silent for a while. It was always serious when a part of the Ship died. The Ship was a cooperative unit, composed entirely of the Crew. The loss of any member was a blow to all the rest.

It was especially serious now. They had just delivered a cargo to a port several thousand light-years from Galactic Center. There was no telling where they might be.

Eye crawled to a Wall and extended a seeing organ outside. The Walls let it through, then sealed around it. Eye's organ pushed out, far enough from the Ship so he could view the entire sphere of stars. The picture traveled through Talker, who gave it to Thinker.

Thinker lay in one corner of the room, a great shapeless blob of protoplasm. Within him were all the memories of his space-going ancestors. He considered the picture, compared it rapidly with others stored in his cells, and said, "No galactic planets within reach."

Talker automatically translated for everyone. It was what they had feared.

Eye, with Thinker's help, calculated that they were several hundred light-years off their course, on the galactic periphery.

Every Crew member knew what that meant. Without

a Pusher to boost the Ship to a multiple of the speed of light, they would never get home. The trip back, without a Pusher, would take longer than most of their lifetimes.

"What would you suggest?" Talker asked Thinker.

This was too vague a question for the literal-minded Thinker. He asked to have it rephrased. "What would be our best line of action," Talker asked, "to get back to a galactic planet?"

Thinker needed several minutes to go through all the possibilities stored in his cells. In the meantime, Doctor had patched the Walls and was asking to be given something to eat.

"In a little while we'll all eat," Talker said, twitching his tendrils nervously. Even though he was the second youngest Crew member—only Feeder was younger—the responsibility was largely on him. This was still an emergency; he had to coordinate information and direct action.

ONE of the Walls suggested that they get good and drunk. This unrealistic solution was vetoed at once. It was typical of the Walls' attitude, however. They were fine workers and good shipmates, but happy-go-lucky fellows at best. When they returned to their home planets, they would probably blow all their wages on a spree.

"Loss of Ship's Pusher cripples the Ship for sustained faster-than-light speeds," Thinker began without preamble. "The nearest galactic planet is four hundred and five light-years off."

Talker translated all this instantly along his wave-packet body.

"Two courses of action are open. First, the Ship can proceed to the nearest galactic planet under atomic power from Engine. This will take approximately two hundred years. Engine might still be alive at this time although no one else will.

"Second, locate a primitive planet in this region, upon which are latent Pushers. Find one and train him. Have him push the Ship back to galactic territory."

Thinker was silent, having given all the possibilities he could find in the memories of his ancestors.

They held a quick vote and decided upon Thinker's second alternative. There was no choice, really. It was the only one, which offered them any hope of getting back to their homes.

"All right," Talker said. "Let's eat. I think we all deserve it."

The body of the dead Pusher was shoved into the mouth of Engine, who consumed it at once, breaking down the atoms to energy. Engine was the only member of the Crew who lived on atomic energy.

For the rest, Feeder dashed up and loaded himself from the nearest Accumulator. Then he transformed the food within him into the substances each member ate. His body chemistry changed, altered, adapted, making the different foods for the Crew.

Eye lived entirely on a complex chlorophyl chain. Feeder reproduced this for him, then went over to give Talker his hydrocarbons, and the Walls their chlorine compound. For Doctor he made a facsimile of a silicate fruit that grew on Doctor's native planet.

FINALLY, feeding was over and the Ship back in

order. The Accumulators were stacked in a corner, blissfully sleeping again. Eye was extending his vision as far as he could, shaping his main seeing organ for high-powered telescopic reception. Even in this emergency, Eye couldn't resist making verses. He announced that he was at work on a new narrative poem, called *Peripheral Glow*. No one wanted to hear it, so Eye fed it to Thinker, who stored everything, good or bad, right or wrong.

Engine never slept. Filled to the brim on Pusher, he shoved the Ship along at several times the speed of light.

The Walls were arguing among themselves about who had been the drunkest during their last leave.

Talker decided to make himself comfortable. He released his hold on the Walls and swung in the air, his small round body suspended by his crisscrossed network of filaments.

He thought briefly about Pusher. It was strange. Pusher had been everyone's friend and now he was forgotten. That wasn't because of indifference; it was because the Ship was a unit. The loss of a member was regretted, but the important thing was for the unit to go on.

The Ship raced through the suns of the periphery.

Thinker laid out a search spiral, calculating their odds on finding a Pusher planet at roughly four to one. In a week they found a planet of primitive Walls. Dropping low, they could see the leathery, rectangular fellows basking in the sun, crawling over rocks, stretching themselves thin in order to float in the breeze.

All the Ship's Walls heaved a sigh of nostalgia. It was just like home.

These Walls on the planet hadn't been contacted by a

galactic team yet, and were still unaware of their great destiny—to join in the vast Cooperation of the Galaxy.

There were plenty of dead worlds in the spiral, and worlds too young to bear life. They found a planet of Talkers. The Talkers had extended their spidery communication lines across half a continent.

Talker looked at them eagerly, through Eye. A wave of self-pity washed over him. He remembered home, his family, his friends. He thought of the tree he was planning to buy when he got back.

For a moment, Talker wondered what he was doing here, part of a Ship in a far corner of the Galaxy.

He shrugged off the mood. They were bound to find a Pusher planet, if they looked long enough.

At least, he hoped so.

THERE was a long stretch of arid worlds as the Ship pushed through the unexplored periphery. Then a planetful of primeval Engines, swimming in a radioactive ocean.

"This is rich territory," Feeder said to Talker. "Galactic should send a Contact party here."

"They probably will, after we get back," Talker said.

They were good friends, above and beyond the all-enveloping friendship of the Crew. It wasn't only because they were the youngest Crew members, although that had something to do with it. They both had the same kind of functions and that made for a certain rapport. Talker translated languages; Feeder transformed foods. Also, they looked somewhat alike. Talker was a central core with radiating filaments; Feeder was a central core with radiating tentacles.

Talker thought that Feeder was the next most aware being on the Ship. He was never really able to understand how some of the others carried on the processes of consciousness.

More suns, more planets. Engine started to overheat. Usually, Engine was used only for taking off and landing, and for fine maneuvering in a planetary group. Now he had been running continuously for weeks, both over and under the speed of light. The strain was telling on him.

Feeder, with Doctor's help, rigged a cooling system for him. It was crude, but it had to suffice. Feeder rearranged nitrogen, oxygen and hydrogen atoms to make a coolant for the system. Doctor diagnosed a long rest for Engine. He said that the gallant old fellow couldn't stand the strain for more than a week.

The search continued, with the Crew's spirits gradually dropping. They all realized that Pushers were rather rare in the Galaxy, as compared to the fertile Walls and Engines.

The Walls were getting pockmarked from interstellar dust. They complained that they would need a full beauty treatment when they got home. Talker assured them that the Company would pay for it.

Even Eye was getting bloodshot from staring into space so continuously.

They dipped over another planet. Its characteristics were flashed to Thinker, who mulled over them.

Closer, and they could make out the forms.

Pushers! Primitive Pushers!

They zoomed back into space to make plans. Feeder produced twenty-three different kinds of intoxicants for a celebration.

The Ship wasn't fit to function for three days.

"EVERYONE ready now?" Talker asked, a bit fuzzily. He had a hangover that burned all along his nerve ends. What a drunk he had thrown! He had a vague recollection of embracing Engine, inviting him to share his tree when they got back home.

He shuddered at the idea.

The rest of the Crew were pretty shaky, too. The Walls were letting air leak into space; they were just too wobbly to seal their edges properly. Doctor had passed out.

But the worst off was Feeder. Since his system could adapt to any type of fuel except atomic, he had been sampling every batch he made, whether it was an unbalanced iodine, pure oxygen or a supercharged ester. He was really miserable. His tentacles, usually a healthy aqua, were shot through with orange streaks. His system was working furiously, purging itself of everything, and Feeder was suffering the effects of the purge.

The only sober ones were Thinker and Engine. Thinker didn't drink, which was unusual for a spacer, though typical of Thinker, and Engine couldn't.

They listened while Thinker reeled off some astounding facts. From Eye's pictures of the planet's surface, Thinker had detected the presence of metallic construction. He put forth the alarming suggestion that these Pushers had constructed a mechanical civilization.

"That's impossible," three of the Walls said flatly, and most of the Crew were inclined to agree with them. All the metal they had ever seen had been buried in the ground or lying around in worthless oxidized chunks.

"Do you mean that they make things out of metal?" Talker demanded, "Out of just plain dead metal? What could they make?"

"They couldn't make anything," Feeder said positively. "It would break down constantly. I mean metal doesn't *know* when it's weakening."

But it seemed to be true. Eye magnified his pictures, and everyone could see that the Pushers had made vast shelters, vehicles, and other articles from inanimate material.

The reason for this was not readily apparent, but it wasn't a good sign. However, the really hard part was over. The Pusher planet had been found. All that remained was the relatively easy job of convincing a native Pusher, which shouldn't be too hard. Talker knew that cooperation was the keystone of the Galaxy, even among primitive peoples.

The Crew decided not to land in a populated region. Of course, there was no reason not to expect a friendly greeting, but it was the job of a Contact Team to get in touch with them as a race. All they wanted was an individual.

Accordingly, they picked out a sparsely populated land-mass, drifting in while that side of the planet was dark.

They were able to locate a solitary Pusher almost at once.

EYE adapted his vision to see in the dark, and they followed the Pusher's movements. He lay down after a while, beside a small fire. Thinker told them that this was a well-known resting habit of Pushers.

Just before dawn, the Walls opened, and Feeder, Talker and Doctor came out.

Feeder dashed forward and tapped the creature on the shoulder. Talker followed with a communication tendril.

The Pusher opened his seeing organs, blinked them, and made a movement with his eating organ. Then he leaped to his feet and started to run.

The three Crew members were astounded. The Pusher hadn't even waited to find out what the three of them wanted!

Talker extended a filament rapidly, and caught the Pusher, fifty feet away, by a limb. The Pusher fell.

"Treat him gently," Feeder said. "He might be startled by our appearance." He twitched his tendrils at the idea of a Pusher—one of the strangest sights in the Galaxy, with his multiple organs—being startled at someone else's appearance.

Feeder and Doctor scurried to the fallen Pusher, picked him up and carried him back to the Ship.

The Walls sealed again. They released the Pusher and prepared to talk.

As soon as he was free, the Pusher sprang to his limbs and ran at the place where the Walls had sealed. He pounded against them frantically, his eating organ open and vibrating.

"Stop that," the Wall said. He bulged, and the Pusher tumbled to the floor. Instantly, he jumped up and started to run forward.

"Stop him," Talker said. "He might hurt himself."

One of the Accumulators woke up enough to roll into the Pusher's path. The Pusher fell, got up again, and ran on.

Talker had his filaments in the front of the Ship also, and he caught the Pusher in the bow. The Pusher started to tear at his tendrils, and Talker let go hastily.

"Plug him into the communication system!" Feeder shouted. "Maybe we can reason with him!"

Talker advanced a filament: toward the Pusher's head, waving it in the universal sign of communication. But the Pusher continued his amazing behavior, jumping out of the way. He had a piece of metal in his hand and he was waving it frantically.

"What do you think he's going to do with that?" Feeder asked. The Pusher started to attack the side of the Ship, pounding at one of the Walls. The Wall stiffened instinctively and the metal snapped.

"Leave him alone," Talker said. "Give him a chance to calm down."

TALKER consulted with Thinker, but they couldn't decide what to do about the Pusher. He wouldn't accept communication. Every time Talker extended a filament, the Pusher showed all the signs of violent panic. Temporarily, it was an impasse.

Thinker vetoed the plan of finding another Pusher on the planet. He considered this Pusher's behavior typical; nothing would be gained by approaching another. Also, a planet was supposed to be contacted only by a Contact Team.

If they couldn't communicate with this Pusher, they never would with another on the planet.

"I think I know what the trouble is," Eye said. He crawled up on an Accumulator. "These Pushers have evolved a mechanical civilization. Consider for a minute how they went about it. They developed the use of their fingers, like Doctor, to shape metal. They utilized their seeing organs, like myself. And probably countless other organs." He paused for effect.

"These Pushers have become unspecialized!"

"They argued over it for several hours. The Walls maintained that no intelligent creature could be unspecialized. It was unknown in the Galaxy. But the evidence was before them—The Pusher cities, their vehicles ...This Pusher, exemplifying the rest, seemed capable of a multitude of things.

He was able to do everything except Push!

Thinker supplied a partial explanation. "This is not a primitive planet. It is relatively old and should have been in the Cooperation thousands of years ago. Since it was not, the Pushers upon it were robbed of their birthright. Their ability, their specialty, was to Push, but there was nothing to Push. Naturally, they have developed a deviant culture.

"Exactly what this culture is, we can only guess. But on the basis of the evidence, there is reason to believe that these Pushers are—uncooperative."

Thinker had a habit of uttering the most shattering statement in the quietest possible way.

"It is entirely possible," Thinker went on inexorably, "that these Pushers will have nothing to do with us. In which case, our chances are approximately 283 to one against finding another Pusher planet."

"We can't be sure he won't cooperate," Talker said, "until we get him into communication." He found it almost impossible to believe that any intelligent creature would refuse to cooperate willingly.

"But how?" Feeder asked. They decided upon a course of action. Doctor walked slowly up to the Pusher, who backed away from him. In the meantime, Talker extended a filament outside the Ship, around, and in again, behind the Pusher.

The Pusher backed against a Wall—and Talker shoved the filament through the Pusher's head, into the communication socket in the center of his brain.

The Pusher collapsed.

WHEN he came to, Feeder and Doctor had to hold the Pusher's limbs, or he would have ripped out the communication line. Talker exercised his skill in learning the Pusher's language.

It wasn't too hard. All Pusher languages were of the same family, and this was no exception. Talker was able to catch enough surface thoughts to form a pattern.

He tried to communicate with the Pusher.

The Pusher was silent.

"I think he needs food," Feeder said. They remembered that it had been almost two days since they had taken the Pusher on board. Feeder worked up some standard Pusher food and offered it.

"My God! A steak!" the Pusher said.

The Crew cheered along Talker's communication circuits. The Pusher had said his first words!

Talker examined the words and searched his memory. He knew about two hundred Pusher languages and many more simple variations. He found that this Pusher was speaking a cross of two Pusher tongues.

After the Pusher had eaten, he looked around. Talker caught his thoughts and broadcast them to the Crew.

The Pusher had a queer way of looking at the Ship. He saw it as a riot of colors. The walls undulated. In front of him was something resembling a gigantic spider, colored black and green, with his web running all over the Ship and into the heads of all the creatures. He saw Eye as a strange, naked little animal, something between a skinned rabbit and an egg yolk—whatever those things were.

Talker was fascinated by the new perspective the Pusher's mind gave him. He had never seen things that way before. But now that the Pusher was pointing it out, Eye *was* a pretty funny-looking creature.

They settled down to communication.

"What in hell are you things?" the Pusher asked, much calmer now than he had been during the two days. "Why did you grab me? Have I gone nuts?"

"No," Talker said, "you are not psychotic. We are a galactic trading ship. We were blown off our course by a storm and our Pusher was killed."

"Well, what does that have to do with me?"

"We would like you to join our crew," Talker said, "to be our new Pusher."

THE Pusher thought it over after the situation was explained to him. Talker could catch the feeling of conflict in the Pusher's thoughts. He hadn't decided whether to accept this as a real situation or not. Finally, the Pusher decided that he wasn't crazy.

"Look, boys," he said, "I don't know what you are or how this makes sense. I have to get out of here. I'm on a furlough, and if I don't get back soon, the U. S. Army's going to be very interested."

Talker asked the Pusher to give him more information about "army," and he fed it to Thinker.

"These Pushers engage in personal combat," was Thinker's conclusion.

"But *why*?" Talker asked. Sadly he admitted to himself that Thinker might have been right; the Pusher didn't show many signs of willingness to cooperate.

"I'd like to help you lads out," Pusher said, "but I've got a war to fight. Besides, I don't know where you get the idea that I could push anything this size. You'd need a whole division of tanks just to budge it."

"Do you approve of this war?" Talker asked, getting a suggestion from Thinker.

"Nobody likes wars—not those who have to do the dying at least."

"Then why do you fight it?"

The Pusher made a gesture with his eating organ, which Eye picked up and sent to Thinker. "It's kill or be killed. You guys know what war is, don't you?"

"We don't have any wars," Talker said.

"You're lucky," the Pusher said bitterly. "We do. Plenty of them."

"Of course," Talker said. He had the full explanation from Thinker now. "Would you like to end them?"

"Of course I would."

"Then come with us. Be our Pusher."

The Pusher stood up and walked up to an Accumulator. He sat down on it and doubled the ends of his upper limbs.

"How the hell can I stop all wars?" the Pusher demanded. "I'm just Private Dave Martinson. Even if I went to the big shots and told them—"

"You won't have to," Talker said. "All you have to do is come with us. Push us to our base. Galactic will send a Contact Team to your planet. That will end your wars."

"The hell you say," the Pusher replied. "You boys are stranded here, huh? Good enough. No monsters are going to take over Earth."

BEWILDEREDLY, Talker tried to understand the reasoning. Had he said something wrong? Was it possible that the Pusher didn't understand him?

"I thought you wanted to end wars," Talker said.

"Sure I do. But I don't want anyone *making* us stop. I'm no traitor. I'd rather fight."

"No one will make you stop. You just will stop because there will be no further need for fighting."

"Do you know why we're fighting?"

"It's obvious."

"Yeah? What's your explanation?"

"You Pushers have been separated from the main stream of the Galaxy," Talker explained. "You have your specialty—pushing—but nothing to Push. Accordingly, you have no real jobs. You play with things—metal, inanimate objects—but find no real satisfaction. Robbed of your true vocation, you fight from sheer frustration.

"Once you find your place in the galactic Cooperation—and I assure you that it is an important place—your fighting will stop. Why should you fight, which is an unnatural occupation, when you can Push? Also, your mechanical civilization will end, since there will be no need for it."

The Pusher shook his head in what Talker guessed was a gesture of confusion. "What is this pushing?"

Talker told him as best he could. Since the job was out of his scope, he had only a general idea of what a Pusher did.

"You mean to say that that is what every Earthman should be doing?"

"Of course," Talker said. "It is your great specialty."

The Pusher thought about it for several minutes. "I think you want a physicist or a mentalist or something. I could never do anything like that. I'm a junior architect. And besides—well, it's difficult to explain."

But Talker had already caught Pusher's objection. He saw a Pusher female in his thoughts. No, two, three. And he caught a feeling of loneliness, strangeness. The Pusher was filled with doubts. He was afraid.

"When we reach galactic," Talker said, hoping it was the right thing, "you can meet other Pushers. Pusher females, too. All you Pushers look alike, so you should become friends with them. As far as loneliness in the Ship goes—it just doesn't exist. You don't understand the Cooperation yet. No one is lonely in the Cooperation."

THE Pusher was still considering the idea of there being other Pushers. Talker couldn't understand why he was so startled at that. The Galaxy was filled with Pushers, Feeders, Talkers, and many other species, endlessly duplicated.

"I can't believe that anybody could end all war," Pusher said. "How do I know you're not lying? I won't go."

Talker felt as if he had been struck in the face. Thinker must have been right when he said these Pushers would be uncooperative. Was this going to be the end of Talker's career? Were he and the rest of the Crew going to spend the rest of their lives in space, because of the stupidity of a bunch of Pushers?

Even thinking this, Talker was able to feel sorry for the Pusher. It must be terrible, he thought. Doubting, uncertain, never trusting anyone. If these Pushers didn't find their place in the Galaxy, they would exterminate themselves. Their place in the Cooperation was long overdue.

"What can I do to convince you?" Talker asked.

In despair, he opened all the circuits to the Pusher. He let the Pusher see Engine's good-natured gruffness, the devil-may-care humor of the Walls; he showed him Eye's poetic attempts, and Feeder's cocky good nature. He opened his own mind and showed the Pusher a picture of his home planet, his family, the tree he was planning to buy when he got home.

The pictures told the story of all of them, from different planets, representing different ethics, united by a common bond—the galactic Cooperation.

The Pusher watched it all in silence.

After a while, he shook his head. The thought accompanying the gesture was uncertain, weak—but negative.

Talker told the Walls to open. They did, and the Pusher looked at his own planet in amazement.

"You may leave," Talker said. "Just remove the communication line and go."

"What will you do?"

"We will look for another Pusher planet."

"Where? Mars? Venus?"

"We don't know. All we can do is hope there is another in this region."

The Pusher looked at the opening, then back at the Crew. He hesitated and his face screwed up in a grimace of indecision.

"All that you showed me was true?"

No answer was necessary.

"ALL right," the Pusher said suddenly. "I'll go. I'm a damned fool, but I'll go. If this means what you say—it *must* mean what you say!"

Talker saw that the agony of the Pusher's decision had forced him out of contact with reality. He believed that he was back in a dream, where decisions are easy and unimportant.

"There's just one little trouble," Pusher said with the lightness of hysteria. "Boys, I'll be hanged if I know how to Push. You said something about faster-than-light? I can't even run the mile in an hour."

"Of course you can Push," Talker assured him, hoping he was right. He knew what a Pusher's abilities were; but this one… "Just try it."

"Sure," Pusher agreed. "I'll probably wake up out of this, anyhow."

They sealed the ship for takeoff while Pusher talked to himself.

"Funny," Pusher said. "I thought a camping trip would be a nice way to spend a furlough and all I do is get nightmares!"

Engine boosted the Ship into the air. The Walls were sealed and Eye was guiding them away from the planet.

"We're in clear space now," Talker said. Listening to Pusher, he hoped his mind hadn't cracked. "Eye and Thinker will give a direction, I'll transmit it to you, and you Push along it."

"You're crazy," Pusher mumbled. "You must have the wrong planet. I wish you nightmares would go away."

"You're in the Cooperation now," Talker said desperately. "There's the direction. Push!"

The Pusher didn't do anything for a moment. He was slowly emerging from his fantasy, realizing that he wasn't in a dream, after all. He felt the Cooperation. Eye to Thinker, Thinker to Talker, Talker to Pusher, all intercoordinated with Walls, and with each other.

"What is this?" Pusher asked. He felt the oneness of the Ship, the great warmth, the closeness achieved only in the Cooperation.

He Pushed.

Nothing happened.

"Try again," Talker begged.

PUSHER searched his mind. He found a deep well of doubt and fear. Staring into it, he saw his own tortured face.

Thinker illuminated it for him.

Pushers had lived with this doubt and fear for centuries. Pushers had fought through fear, killed through doubt.

That was where the Pusher organ was!

Martinson—specialist, Pusher—entered fully into the

Crew, merged with them, threw mental arms around the shoulders of Thinker and Talker.

Suddenly, the Ship shot forward at eight times the speed of light. It continued to accelerate.

Beside Still Waters

When people talk about getting away from it all, they are usually thinking about our great open spaces out west. But to science fiction writers, that would be practically in the heart of Times Square. When a man of the future wants solitude he picks a slab of rock floating in space four light years east of Andromeda. Here is a gentle little story about a man who sought the solitude of such a location. And who did he take along for company? None other than Charles the Robot.

MARK ROGERS was a prospector, and he went to the asteroid belt looking for radioactives and rare metals.

He searched for years, never finding much, hopping from fragment to fragment. After a time he settled on a slab of rock half a mile thick.

Rogers had been born old and he didn't age much past a point. His face was white with the pallor of space, and his hands shook a little. He called his slab of rock Martha, after no girl he had ever known.

He made a little strike, enough to equip Martha with an air pump and a shack, a few tons of dirt and some water tanks, and a robot. Then he settled back and watched the stars.

The robot he bought was a standard-model all-around worker, with built-in memory and a thirty-word vocabulary. Mark added to that, bit by bit. He was something of a tinkerer and he enjoyed adapting his environment to himself.

At first, all the robot could say was "Yes sir," and "No sir." He could state simple problems: "The air pump is laboring, sir." "The corn is budding, sir." He could perform a satisfactory salutation: "Good morning, sir."

Mark changed that. He eliminated the "sirs" from the robot's vocabulary; equality was the rule on Mark's hunk of rock. Then he dubbed the robot Charles, after a father he had never known.

As the years passed, the air pump began to labor a little as it converted the oxygen in the planetoid's rock into a breathable atmosphere. The air seeped into space, and the pump worked a little harder, supplying more.

The crops continued to grow on the tamed black dirt of the planetoid. Looking up, Mark could see the sheer blackness of the river of space, the floating points of the stars. Around him, under him, overhead, masses of rock drifted, and sometimes the starlight glinted from their black sides. Occasionally, Mark caught a glimpse of Mars or Jupiter. Once he thought he saw Earth.

Mark began to tape new responses into Charles. He added simple responses to cue words. When he said, "How does it look?" Charles would answer, "Oh, pretty good, I guess."

At first the answers were what Mark had been answering himself, in the long dialogue held over the years. But, slowly, he began to build a new personality into Charles.

Mark had always been suspicious and scornful of

women. But for some reason he didn't tape the same suspicion into Charles. Charles' outlook was quite different.

"What do you think of girls?" Mark would ask, sitting on a packing case outside the shack, after the chores were done.

"Oh, I don't know. You have to find the right one." The robot would reply dutifully, repeating what had been put on its tape.

"I never saw a good one yet," Mark would say.

"Well, that's not fair. Perhaps you didn't look long enough. There's a girl in the world for every man."

"You're a romantic!" Mark would say scornfully. The robot would pause—a built-in pause—and chuckle a carefully constructed chuckle.

"I dreamed of a girl named Martha once," Charles would say. "Maybe if I would have looked, I would have found her."

And then it would be bedtime. Or perhaps Mark would want more conversation. "What do you think of girls?" he would ask again, and the discussion would follow its same course.

Charles grew old. His limbs lost their flexibility, and some of his wiring started to corrode. Mark would spend hours keeping the robot in repair.

"You're getting rusty," he would cackle.

"You're not so young yourself," Charles would reply. He had an answer for almost everything. Nothing involved, but an answer.

It was always night on Martha, but Mark broke up his time into mornings, afternoons and evenings. Their life followed a simple routine. Breakfast, from vegetables and Mark's canned store. Then the robot would work in the fields, and the plants grew used to his touch. Mark would repair the pump, check the water supply, and straighten up the immaculate shack. Lunch, and the robot's chores were usually finished.

The two would sit on the packing case and watch the stars. They would talk until supper, and sometimes late into the endless night.

In time, Mark built more complicated conversations into Charles. He couldn't give the robot free choice, of course, but he managed a pretty close approximation of it. Slowly, Charles' personality emerged. But it was strikingly different from Mark's.

Where Mark was querulous, Charles was calm. Mark was sardonic, Charles was naive. Mark was a cynic, Charles was an idealist. Mark was often sad; Charles was forever content.

And in time, Mark forgot he had built the answers in to Charles. He accepted the robot as a friend, of about his own age. A friend of long years standing.

"The thing I don't understand," Mark would say, "is why a man like you wants to live here. I mean, it's all right for me. No one cares about me, and I never gave much of a damn about anyone. But why you?"

"Here I have a whole world," Charles would reply, "where on Earth I had to share with billions. I have the stars, bigger and brighter than on Earth. I have all space around me, close, like still waters. And I have you, Mark."

"Now, don't go getting sentimental on me—"

"I'm not. Friendship counts. Love was lost long ago,

Mark. The love of a girl named Martha, whom neither of us ever met. And that's a pity. But friendship remains, and the eternal night."

"You're a bloody poet," Mark would say, half admiringly. Charles would reply, "A poor poet."

Time passed unnoticed by the stars, and the air pump hissed and clanked and leaked. Mark was fixing it constantly, but the air of Martha became increasingly rare. Although Charles labored in the fields, the crops, deprived of sufficient air, died… Mark was tired now, and barely able to crawl around, even without the grip of gravity. He stayed in his bunk most of the time. Charles fed him as best he could, moving on rusty, creaking limbs.

"What do you think of girls?"

"I never saw a good one yet."

"Well, that's not fair."

Mark was too tired to see the end coming, and Charles wasn't interested. But the end was on its way. The air pump threatened to give out momentarily. There hadn't been any food for days.

"But why you?" Gasping in the escaping air. Strangling.

"Here I have a whole world—"

"Don't get sentimental—"

"And the love of a girl named Martha."

From his bunk Mark saw the stars for the last time. Big, bigger than ever, endlessly floating in the still waters of space.

"The stars…" Mark said.

"Yes?"

"The sun?"

" —Shall shine as now."

"A bloody poet."

"A poor poet."

"And girls?"

"I dreamed of a girl named Martha once. And maybe if—"

"What do you think of girls? And stars? And Earth?" And it was bedtime, this time forever.

Charles stood beside the body of his friend. He felt for a pulse once, and allowed the withered hand to fall. He walked to a corner of the shack and turned off the tired air pump.

The tape that Mark had prepared had a few cracked inches left to run. "I hope he finds his Martha," the robot croaked, and then the tape broke.

His rusted limbs would not bend, and he stood frozen, staring back at the naked stars. Then he bowed his head.

"The Lord is my shepherd," Charles said. "I shall not want. He maketh me to lie down in green pastures; he leadeth me…"

Restricted Area

When Robert Sheckley's highly polished first stories began appearing back in 1952, perceptive readers said to themselves that here was comer, a "big" talent that would one day become a top name in the field. And they weren't disappointed—because today when we look at the growing shelf of Sheckley fiction (which includes such wonderful collections at Untouched Hands *and such stunning novels as* Immortality, Inc.), *we can see just how far he has gone. We'd like to suggest that one reason for his phenomenal success is his distinctive, almost Puckish sense of humor, particularly evident in "Restricted Area." So watch out—this one has a long fuse, it's crackling, and it's set to go off when you least expect it.*

"NICE looking place, isn't it, Captain?" Simmons asked with elaborate casualness, looking through the port. "Rather a paradise." He yawned.

"You can't go out yet," Captain Kilpepper said, noting the biologist's immediate disappointed expression.

"But Captain—"

"No." Kilpepper looked out the port at the rolling meadow of grass. Sprinkled with red flowers, it appeared as luscious as it had two days ago when they had landed. To the right of the meadow was a brown forest shot through with yellow and orange blossoms. To the left was a row of hills, colored in contrasting shades of blue-green. A waterfall tumbled down one of the hills.

Trees, flowers, all that sort of thing. The place was undeniably pretty, and it was for that very reason that Kilpepper distrusted it. Experience with two wives and five new ships had taught him that a lovely exterior can conceal almost anything. And fifteen years in space had added lines to his forehead and gray to his hair, but hadn't given him any reason for altering his conviction.

"Here are the reports, sir," Mate Manella said, handing him a sheaf of papers. Manella had a petulant expression on his broad, rugged face. Behind the door, Kilpepper could hear shuffling feet and whispering voices. He knew it was the crew, assembled to hear what he would say this time.

They wanted outside, but bad.

Kilpepper skimmed the reports. They were the same as the last four groups. Atmosphere breathable and free of dangerous microorganisms, bacteria count nil, radargraph all clear. Some form of animal life in the nearby forest, but no energy manifestations. Detection of a large metallic mass, possibly an iron-rich mountain, several miles south. Noted for further investigation.

"That's fine," Kilpepper said unhappily. The reports vaguely annoyed him. He knew from past experience that there was usually something wrong with every planet. It paid to find it at the start, before costly accidents resulted.

"Can we go out, sir?" Manella asked, his short body stiffly erect. Kilpepper could almost feel the crewmen behind the door holding their breath.

"I don't know," Kilpepper said. He scratched his head, trying to think of some good reason for refusing again. There *must* be something wrong.

"All right," he said at last. "Post a full guard for the time being. Let four men out. No one goes beyond twenty-five feet of the ship." He had to let them go. After sixteen months in the hot, cramped spaceship, he'd have a mutiny on his hands if he didn't.

"Yes sir!" Mate Manella said, and dashed out the door.

"I suppose that means the scientific team can go out," Simmons said, his hands jammed in his pockets.

"Sure," Kilpepper said warily. "I'll go with you. After all, this expedition is expendable."

The air of the unnamed planet was fragrant after the musty, recirculated air of the ship. The breeze from the mountains was light and steady and refreshing.

Captain Kilpepper sniffed appreciatively, arms folded across his chest. The four crewmen were walking around, stretching their legs and breathing in great lungfuls of fresh air. The scientific team was standing together, wondering where to begin. Simmons bent down and plucked a spear of grass.

"Funny looking stuff," he said, holding it up to the sunlight.

"Why?" Captain Kilpepper asked, walking over.

"Look at it." The thin biologist held it higher. "Perfectly smooth. Doesn't show any sign of cell formation. Let me see—" He bent over a red blossom.

"Hey! We got visitors!" A crewman named Flynn was

the first to spot the natives. They came out of the forest and trotted across the meadow to the ship.

Captain Kilpepper glanced at the ship. The gunners were ready and alert. He touched his sidearm for reassurance, and waited.

"Oh, brother," Aramic murmured. As the ship's linguist, he eyed the advancing natives with intense professional interest. The rest of the men just stared.

In the lead was a creature with a neck at least eight feet long, like a giraffe, and thick, stubby legs, like a hippopotamus. It had a cheerful expression on its face. Its hide was purple, sprinkled with large white dots.

Next in line came five little beasts with pure white fur. They were about the size of terriers, and they had an owlishly solemn expression. A fat, red little creature with a green tail at least sixteen feet long brought up the rear.

They stopped in front of the men and bowed. There was a long moment of silence, then everyone burst into laughter.

The laughter seemed to be a signal. The five little ones leaped to the back of the hippo-giraffe. They scrambled for a moment, then climbed on each other's shoulders. In a moment they were balanced, five high, like a team of acrobats.

The men applauded wildly.

The fat animal immediately started balancing on his tail.

"Bravo!" shouted Simmons.

The five furry animals jumped off the giraffe's back and started to dance around the pig.

"Hurray!" Morrison, the bacteriologist, called.

The hippo-giraffe turned a clumsy somersault, landed on one ear, scrambled to his feet and bowed deeply.

Captain Kilpepper frowned and rubbed one hand against another. He was trying to figure out some reason for this behavior.

The natives burst into song. The melody was strange, but recognizable as a tune. They harmonized for a few seconds, then bowed and began to roll on the grass.

The crewmen were still applauding. Aramic had taken out his notebook and was jotting down the sounds.

"All right," Kilpepper said. "Crew, back inside."

They gave him reproachful looks.

"Let some of the other men have a chance," the captain said. Regretfully, the men filed back inside.

"I suppose you want to examine them some more," Kilpepper said to the scientists.

"We sure do," Simmons stated. "Never saw anything like it."

Kilpepper nodded and went back into the ship. Four more crewmen filed past him.

"Morena!" Kilpepper shouted. The mate came bounding into the bridge. "I want you to find that metal mass. Take a man and keep in radio contact with the ship at all times."

"Yes sir," Morena said, grinning broadly. "Friendly, aren't they, sir?"

"Yes," Kilpepper said.

"Nice little world," the mate said.

"Yes."

Mate Morena went off to collect his equipment.

Captain Kilpepper sat down and tried to figure out

what was wrong with the planet.

Kilpepper spent most of the next day filling out progress reports. In the late afternoon he put down his pencil and went out for a walk.

"Have you got a moment, Captain?" Simmons asked. "There's something I'd like to show you in the forest." Kilpepper grumbled out of habit, but followed the biologist. He had been curious about the forest himself.

On the way, they were accompanied by three natives. These particular three looked like dogs, except for their coloring—red and white, like peppermint candy.

"Now then," Simmons said with ill-concealed eagerness, once they were in the forest. "Look around. What do you see that strikes you as odd?"

Kilpepper looked. The trees were thick-trunked and spaced wide apart. So wide apart, in fact, that it was possible to see the next clearing through them.

"Well," he said, "you couldn't get lost here."

"It's not that," Simmons said. "Come on, look again."

Kilpepper smiled. Simmons had brought him here because he made a better audience than any of his preoccupied colleagues.

Behind them, the three natives leaped and played.

"There's no underbrush," Kilpepper stated, after walking a few yards further. There were vines twisting up the sides of the trees, covered with multi-colored flowers. Glancing around, Kilpepper saw a bird dart down, flutter around the head of one of the peppermint-colored dogs, and flyaway again.

The bird was colored gold and silver.

"Don't you see anything wrong yet?" Simmons asked impatiently.

"Only the color scheme," Kilpepper said. "Is there something else?"

"Look at the trees."

The boughs were laden with fruit. It hung in clumps, all on the lower branches, of a bewildering variety of colors, sizes and shapes. There were things that looked like grapes, and things that looked like bananas, and things that looked like watermelons, and—

"Lots of different species, I guess," Kilpepper hazarded, not sure what it was Simmons wanted him to see.

"Different species! Look, man. There are as many as ten different kinds of fruit growing on one branch!"

Examining closer, Kilpepper saw it was true. Each tree had an amazing multiplicity of fruit.

"And that's just impossible," Simmons said. "It's not my field, of course, but I can state with fair certainty that each fruit is a separate and distinct entity. They're not stages of each other."

"How do you account for it?" Kilpepper asked.

"I don't have to," the biologist grinned. "But some poor botanist is going to have his hands full."

They turned and started to walk back. "What were you here for?" Kilpepper asked.

"Me? I was doing a little anthropological work on the side. Wanted to find out where our friends lived. No luck. There are no paths, implements, clearings, anything. Not even caves."

Kilpepper didn't think it unusual that a biologist should be making a quick anthropological survey. It was impossible to represent all the sciences on an expedition of this sort. Survival was the first consideration—biology and bacteriology. Then language. After that, any botanical, ecological, psychological, sociological or any other knowledge was appreciated.

Eight or nine birds had joined the animals—or natives—around the ship when they got back. The birds were brilliantly colored also: polka dots, stripes, piebalds. There wasn't a dun or gray in the lot.

Mate Morena and Crewman Flynn trudged through an outcropping of the forest. They stopped at the foot of a little hill.

"Do we have to climb it?" Flynn asked, sighing. The large camera on his back was weighing him down.

"The little hand says we gotta." Morena pointed to his dial. The indicator showed the presence of metallic mass just over the rise.

"Spaceships ought to carry cars," Flynn said, leaning forward to balance himself against the gentle slope of the hill.

"Yeh, or camels."

Above them red and gold birds dipped and sailed, cheeping merrily. The breeze fanned the tall grass, and hummed melodiously through the leaves and branches of the nearby forest. Behind them, two of the natives followed. They were horse-shaped, except for their hides of green and white dots.

"Like a bloody circus," Flynn observed, as one of the horses capered a circle around him.

"Yeh," Morena said. They reached the top of the hill and started down. Then Flynn stopped.

"Look at that!"

At the base of the hill, rising slim and erect, was a metal pillar. They followed it up with their eyes. It climbed and climbed—and its top was lost in the clouds.

They hurried down and examined it. Closer, the pillar was more massy than they had thought. Almost twenty feet through, Morena estimated. At a guess he placed the metal as an alloy of steel, by its gray-blue color. But what steel, he asked himself, could support a shaft that size?

"How high would you say those clouds are?" Morena asked.

Flynn craned his neck. "Lord, they must be half a mile up. Maybe a mile." The pillar had been hidden from the ship by the clouds, and by its gray-blue color, which blended, into the background.

"I don't believe it," Morena said. "I wonder what the compression strain on this thing is." They stared in awe at the tremendous shaft.

"Well," Flynn said, "I'd better get some pictures." He unloaded his camera and snapped three shots of the shaft from twenty feet, then a shot with Morena for size comparison. For the next three pictures he sighted up the shaft.

"What do you figure it is?" Morena asked.

"Let the big brains figure it out," Flynn said. "It ought to drive them nuts." He strapped the camera back together. "Now I suppose we have to walk all the way back." He looked at the brown and green horses. "Wonder if I could hitch a ride."

"Go ahead and break your stupid neck," Morena said.

"Here, boy, come on here," Flynn called. One of the

horses came over and knelt beside him. Flynn climbed on his back gingerly. Once he was astride he grinned at Morena.

"Just don't smash that camera," Morena said. "It's government property."

"Nice boy," Flynn said to the horse. "Good fellow." The horse got to his feet—and smiled.

"See you back in camp," Flynn said, guiding the horse toward the hill.

"Hold it a second," Morena said. He looked glumly at Flynn, then beckoned to the other horse. "Come on, boy." The horse knelt and he climbed on.

They rode in circles for a few moments, experimenting. The horses could be guided by a touch. Their broad backs were amazingly comfortable. One of the red and gold birds came down and perched on Flynn's shoulder.

"Hey, hey, this is the life," Flynn said, patting the glossy hide of his mount. "Race you back to camp, Mate."

"You're on," Morena said. But their horses would move no faster than a slow walk, in spite of all their urging.

At the ship, Kilpepper was squatting in the grass, watching Aramic at work. The linguist was a patient man. His sisters had always remarked on his patience. His colleagues had praised him for it, and his students, during his years of teaching, had appreciated it. Now, the backlog of sixteen years of self-containment was being called to the front.

"We'll try it again," Aramic said in his calmest voice.

He flipped through the pages of *Language Approach for Alien Grade Two Intelligences*—a text written by himself—and found the diagram he wanted. He opened to the page and pointed.

The animal beside him looked like an inconceivable cross between a chipmunk and a giant panda. It cocked one eye at the diagram, the other eye wandering ludicrously around its socket.

"Planet," Aramic said, pointing. "Planet."

"Excuse me, Skipper," Simmons said. "I'd like to set up this X-ray gadget here."

"Certainly," Kilpepper said, moving to let the biologist drag the machine into place.

"Planet," Aramic said again.

"Elam vessel holam cram," the chipmunk-panda said pleasantly.

Damn it, they had a language. The sounds they made were certainly representational. It was just a question of finding a common meeting ground. Had they mastered simple abstractions? Aramic put down his book and pointed to the chipmunk-panda.

"Animal," he said, and waited.

"Get him to hold still," Simmons said, focusing the X-ray. "That's good. Now a few more."

"Animal," Aramic repeated hopefully.

"Eeful beeful box," the animal said. "Hoful toful lox, ramadan, Samduran, eeful beeful box."

Patience, Aramic reminded himself. Positive attitude. Be cheerful. Faint heart never.

He picked up another of his manuals. This one was called *Language Approach to Alien Grade One Intelligences*.

He found what he wanted and put it down again.

Smiling, he held up a finger.

"One," he said.

The animal leaned forward and sniffed his finger.

Smiling grimly, Aramic held up another finger. "Two." A third. "Three."

"Hoogelex," the animal said suddenly.

A diphthong? Their word for one? "One," he said again, waving the same finger.

"Vereserevef," the animal replied, beaming.

Could that be an alternate one? "One," he said again.

The animal burst into song.

"Sevef hevef ulud cram, aragan, biligan, homus dram—"

It stopped and looked at the *Language Approach* manual, fluttering in the air, and at the back of the linguist who, with remarkable patience, had refrained from throttling him.

After Morena and Flynn returned, Kilpepper puzzled over their report. He had the photographs rushed through and studied them with care.

The shaft was round and smooth, and obviously manufactured. Any race that could put up a thing like that could give them trouble. Big trouble.

But who had put the shaft up? Not the happy, stupid animals around the ship, certainly.

"You say the top is hidden in the clouds?" Kilpepper asked.

"Yes sir," Morena said. "That damn thing must be all of a mile high."

"Go back," Kilpepper said. "Take a radarscope. Take infrared equipment. Get me a picture of the top of that shaft. I want to know how high it goes and what's on top of it. Quick."

Flynn and Morena left the bridge.

Kilpepper looked at the still wet photographs for a minute longer, then put them down. He wandered into the ship's lab, vague worries nagging at him. The planet didn't make sense, and that bothered him. Kilpepper had discovered the hard way that there's a pattern to everything. If you can't find it in time, that's just too bad for you.

Morrison, the bacteriologist, was a small, sad man. Right now he looked like an extension of the microscope he was peering into.

"Find anything?" Kilpepper asked.

"I've found the absence of something," Morrison said, looking up and blinking. "I've found the absence of a hell of a lot of something."

"What's that?" Kilpepper asked.

"I've run tests on the flowers," Morrison said, "and I've run tests on the earth, and tests on water samples. Nothing definitive yet, but brace yourself."

"I'm braced. What is it?"

"There isn't an ounce of bacteria on this planet!"

"Oh?" Kilpepper said, because he couldn't think of anything else to say. He didn't consider it a particularly shocking announcement. But the bacteriologist was acting as if he had announced that the subsoil of the planet was one hundred percent pure green cheese.

"That's it. The water in the stream is purer than distilled alcohol. The dirt on this planet is cleaner than a boiled scalpel. The only bacteria are the ones we brought. And they're being killed off."

"How?"

"The air of this place has about three disinfecting agents I've detected, and probably a dozen more I haven't. Same with the dirt and water. This place is sterile!"

"Well, now," Kilpepper said. He couldn't appreciate the full force of the statement. He was still worried about the steel shaft. "What does that mean?"

"I'm glad you asked me that," Morrison said. "Yes, I'm really glad you asked me. It means simply that this place doesn't exist."

"Oh, come now."

"I mean it. There can't be life without microorganisms. One whole section of the life cycle is missing here."

"Unfortunately, it does exist," Kilpepper pointed out gently. "Have you any other theories?"

"Yes, but I want to finish these tests first. But I'll tell you one thing, and maybe you can work it out for yourself."

"Go on."

"I haven't been able to detect a piece of rock on this planet. That's not strictly my field, of course—but we're all jacks-of-all-trades on this expedition. Anyhow, I'm interested in geology. There's no loose rock or stone anywhere around. The smallest stone is about seven tons, I'd estimate."

"What does that mean?"

"Ah! You were wondering also?" Morrison smiled. "Excuse me. I want to complete these tests before supper."

Just before sunset, the X-rays of the animals were finished. Kilpepper had another surprise. Morrison had told him that the planet couldn't exist. Then Simmons insisted the animals couldn't exist.

"Just look at these pictures," he said to Kilpepper. "Look. Do you see any organs?"

"I don't know much about X-rays…"

"You don't have to. Just look." The X-ray showed a few bones and one or two organs. There were traces of a nervous system on some of the pictures but, mostly, the animals seemed homogeneous throughout.

"Not enough internal structure to keep a tapeworm going," Simmons said. "This simplification is impossible. There's nothing corresponding to lungs or heart. No bloodstream. No brain. Damn little nervous system. What organs they have just don't make sense."

"And your conclusion—"

"That these animals don't exist," Simmons said, in high good humor. He liked the idea. It would be fun to do a paper on a non-existent animal.

Aramic passed them, swearing softly.

"Any luck on that lingo?" Simmons asked him.

"No!" Aramic shouted, then blushed. "Sorry. I tested them right down to intelligence grade C3BB. That's amoeba class. No response."

"Perhaps they're just completely brainless," Kilpepper suggested.

"No. The ability to do tricks shows a certain level of intelligence. They have a language of sorts, also, and a definite response pattern. But they won't pay any attention. All they do is sing songs."

"I think we all need supper," Kilpepper said. "And

perhaps a slug or two of the old standby."

The old standby was much in evidence at supper. After a fifth or two had been consumed, the scientists mellowed sufficiently to consider some possibilities. They put together their facts.

Item, the natives—or animals—showed no sign of internal organs, no reproductive or excretive equipment. There seemed to be at least three dozen species, not counting birds, and more appearing every day.

The same with the plants.

Item, the planet was amazingly sterile, and acted to keep itself so.

Item, the natives had a language but evidently couldn't impart it to others. Nor could they learn another language.

Item, there were no small rocks or stone around.

Item, there was a tremendous steel shaft, rising to a height of at least half a mile, exact height to be determined when the new pictures were developed. Although there was no sign of a machine culture, the shaft was obviously the product of one. Someone must have built it and put it there.

"Throw it all together and what have you got?" Kilpepper asked.

"I have a theory," Morrison said. "It's a beautiful theory. Would you care to hear it?"

Everyone said yes except Aramic, who was still brooding over his inability to learn the native language.

"The way I see it, this planet is man-made. It must be. No race would evolve without bacteria. It was made by a super race, the race who put that steel spire there.

They built it for these animals."

"Why?" Kilpepper asked.

"This is the beautiful part," Morrison said dreamily. "Pure altruism. Look at the natives. Happy, playful. Completely devoid of violence, rid of all nasty habits. Don't they deserve a world to themselves? A world where they can romp and play in an eternal summer?"

"That *is* beautiful," Kilpepper said, stifling a grin. "But—"

"These people are here as a reminder," Morrison continued. "A message to all passing races that men can live in peace."

"There's only one flaw in that," Simmons said. "The animals could never have evolved naturally. You saw the X-rays."

"That's true..." The dreamer struggled briefly with the biologist, and the dreamer lost. "Perhaps they're robots."

"That's the explanation I favor," Simmons said. "The race that built the steel spire built these animals also. They're servants, slaves. Why, they might even think *we're* their masters."

"Where would the real masters have gone?" Morrison asked.

"How the hell should I know?" Simmons said.

"And where would these masters live?" Kilpepper asked. "We haven't spotted anything that looks like a habitation."

"They're so far advanced they don't need machines or houses. They live directly with nature."

"Then why do they need servants?" Morrison asked

mercilessly. "And why did they build the spire?"

That evening the new pictures of the steel pillar were completed and the scientists examined them eagerly. The top of the pillar was almost a mile high, hidden in thick clouds. There was a projection on either side of the top, jutting out at right angles to a distance of eighty-five feet.

"Looks like it might be a watchtower," Simmons said.

"What could they watch that high up?" Morrison asked. "All they'd see would be clouds."

"Perhaps they like looking at clouds," Simmons said.

"I'm going to bed," Kilpepper stated, in utter disgust.

When Kilpepper woke up the next morning, something didn't feel right. He dressed and went outside. There seemed to be something intangible in the wind. Or was it just his nerves?

Kilpepper shook his head. He had faith in his premonitions. They usually meant that, unconsciously, he had completed some process in reasoning.

Everything seemed to be in order around the ship. The animals were outside, wandering lazily around.

Kilpepper glared at them and walked around the ship. The scientists were back at work trying to solve the mysteries of the planet. Aramic was trying to learn the language from a mournful-eyed green and silver beast. The beast seemed unusually apathetic this morning. It barely muttered its songs, and paid no attention to Aramic.

Kilpepper thought of Circe. Could the animals be people, changed into beasts by some wicked sorcerer?

He rejected the fanciful idea, and walked on.

The crew hadn't noticed anything different. They had headed, en masse, for the waterfall, to get in some swimming. Kilpepper assigned two men to make a microscopic inspection of the steel shaft.

That worried him more than anything else. It didn't seem to bother the other scientists, but Kilpepper figured that was natural. Every cobbler to his last. A linguist would be bound to attach primary importance to the language of the people, while a botanist would think the key to the planet lay in the multi-fruit bearing trees.

And what did he think? Captain Kilpepper examined his ideas. What he needed, he decided, was a field theory. Something that would unify all the observed phenomena.

What theory would do that? Why weren't there any germs? Why weren't there any rocks?

Why, why, why. Kilpepper felt sure that the explanation was relatively simple. He could almost see it—but not quite.

He sat down in the shade, leaning against the ship, and tried to think.

Around midday Aramic, the linguist, walked over. He threw his books, one by one, against the side of the ship.

"Temper," Kilpepper said.

"I give up," Aramic said. "Those beasts won't pay any attention now. They're barely talking. And they've stopped doing tricks."

Kilpepper got to his feet and walked over to the animals. Sure enough, they didn't seem at all lively. They crept around as though they were in the last stages of malnutrition.

Simmons was standing beside them, jotting down notes on a little pad.

"What's wrong with your little friends?" Kilpepper asked.

"I don't know," Simmons said. "Perhaps they were so excited they didn't sleep last night."

The giraffe-like animal sat down suddenly. Slowly he rolled over on his side and lay still.

"That's strange," Simmons said. "First time I saw one of them do that." He bent over the fallen animal and searched for a heart beat. After a few seconds he straightened.

"No sign of life," he said.

Two of the smaller ones with glossy black fur toppled over.

"Oh lord," Simmons said, hurrying over to them. "What's happening now?"

"I'm afraid I know," Morrison said, coming out of the ship, his face ashen. "Germs."

"What are you talking about?"

"Captain, I feel like a murderer. I think we've killed these poor beasts. You remember, I told you there was no sign of any microorganism on this planet? Think of how many we've introduced! Bacteria streaming off our bodies onto these hosts. Hosts with no resistance, remember."

"I thought you said the air had several disinfecting agents?" Kilpepper asked.

"Evidently they didn't work fast enough." Morrison bent over and examined one of the little animals. "I'm sure of it."

The rest of the animals around the ship were falling now, and lying quite still. Captain Kilpepper looked around anxiously.

One of the crewmen dashed up, panting. He was still wet from his swim by the waterfall.

"Sir," he gasped. "Over by the falls—the animals—"

"I know," he said. "Get all the men down here."

"That's not all, sir," the man said. "The waterfall—you know, the waterfall—"

"Well, spit it out, man."

"It's stopped, sir. It's stopped running."

"Get those men down here!" The crewman sprinted back to the falls. Kilpepper looked around, not sure what he was looking for. The brown forest was quiet. Too quiet.

He almost had the answer….

Kilpepper realized that the gentle, steady breeze that had been blowing ever since they landed, had stopped.

"What in hell is going on here?" Simmons said uneasily. They started backing toward the ship.

"Is the sun getting darker?" Morrison whispered. They weren't sure. It was mid-afternoon, but the sun did seem less bright.

The crewmen hurried back from the waterfall, glistening wet. At Kilpepper's order they piled back into the ship. The scientists remained standing, looking over the silent land.

"What could we have done?" Aramic asked. He shuddered at the sight of the fallen animals.

The men who had been examining the shaft came running down the hill, bounding through the long grass as though the devil himself were after them.

"What now?" Kilpepper asked.

"It's that damned shaft, sir!" Morena said. "It's turning!" The shaft—that mile-high mass of incredibly strong metal—was being turned!

"What are we going to do?" Simmons asked.

"Get back in the ship," Kilpepper muttered. He could feel the answer taking shape now. There was just one more bit of evidence he needed. One thing more—

The animals sprang to their feet! The red and silver birds started flying again, winging high into the air. The hippo-giraffe reared to his feet, snorted, and raced off. The rest of the animals followed him. From the forest an avalanche of strange beasts poured onto the meadow.

At full speed they headed west, away from the ship.

"Get back in the ship!" Kilpepper shouted suddenly. That did it. He knew now, and he only hoped he could get the ship into deep space in time.

"Hurry the hell up! Get those engines going," he shouted to the gawking crewmen.

"But we've still got equipment scattered around," Simmons said. "I don't see any need for this—"

"Man the guns!" Captain Kilpepper roared, pushing the scientists toward the bay of the ship.

Suddenly there were long shadows in the west.

"Captain. We haven't completed our investigation yet—"

"You'll be lucky if you live through this," Kilpepper said, as they entered the bay. "Haven't you put it together yet? Close that bay! Get everything tight!"

"You mean the turning shaft?" Simmons said, stumbling over Morrison in the corridor of the ship. "All right, I suppose there's some super race—"

"That turning shaft is a key in the side of the planet," Kilpepper said, racing toward the bridge. "It winds the place up. The whole world is like that. Animals, rivers, wind—everything runs down."

He punched a quick orbit on the ship's tape.

"Strap down," he said. "Figure it out. A place where all kinds of wonderful food hangs from the trees. Where there's no bacteria to hurt you, not even a sharp rock to stub your toes. A place filled with marvelous, amusing, gentle animals. Where everything's designed to delight you.

"A playground!"

The scientists stared at him.

"The shaft is a key. The place ran down while we made our unauthorized visit. Now someone's winding the planet up again."

Outside the port the shadows were stretching for thousands of feet across the green meadow.

"Hang on," Kilpepper said as he punched the takeoff stud. "Unlike the toy animals, I don't want to meet the children who play here. And I especially don't want to meet their parents."

Watchbird

Strange how often the Millenium has been at hand. The idea is peace on Earth, see, and the way to do it is by figuring out angles.

WHEN Gelsen entered, he saw that the rest of the watchbird manufacturers were already present. There were six of them, not counting himself, and the room was blue with expensive cigar smoke.

"Hi, Charlie," one of them called as he came in.

The rest broke off conversation long enough to wave a casual greeting at him. As a watchbird manufacturer, he was a member manufacturer of salvation, he reminded himself wryly. Very exclusive. You must have a certified government contract if you want to save the human race.

"The government representative isn't here yet," one of the men told him. "He's due any minute."

"We're getting the green light," another said.

"Fine." Gelsen found a chair near the door and looked around the room. It was like a convention, or a Boy Scout rally. The six men made up for their lack of numbers by sheer volume. The president of Southern Consolidated was talking at the top of his lungs about watchbird's enormous durability. The two presidents he was talking at were grinning, nodding, one trying to interrupt with the results of a test he had run on watchbird's resourcefulness, the other talking about the new recharging apparatus.

The other three men were in their own little group, delivering what sounded like a panegyric to watchbird.

Gelsen noticed that all of them stood straight and tall, like the saviors they felt they were. He didn't find it funny. Up to a few days ago he had felt that way himself. He had considered himself a pot-bellied, slightly balding saint.

HE sighed and lighted a cigarette. At the beginning of the project, he had been as enthusiastic as the others. He remembered saying to Macintyre, his chief engineer, "Mac, a new day is coming. Watchbird is the Answer." And Macintyre had nodded very profoundly—another watchbird convert.

How wonderful it had seemed then! A simple, reliable answer to one of mankind's greatest problems, all wrapped and packaged in a pound of incorruptible metal, crystal and plastics.

Perhaps that was the very reason he was doubting it now. Gelsen suspected that you don't solve human problems so easily. There had to be a catch somewhere.

After all, murder was an old problem, and watchbird too new a solution.

"Gentlemen—" They had been talking so heatedly that they hadn't noticed the government representative entering. Now the room became quiet at once.

"Gentlemen," the plump government man said, "the President, with the consent of Congress, has acted to form a watchbird division for every city and town in the country."

The men burst into a spontaneous shout of triumph. They were going to have their chance to save the world after all, Gelsen thought, and worriedly asked himself what was wrong with that.

He listened carefully as the government man outlined the distribution scheme. The country was to be divided into seven areas, each to be supplied and serviced by one manufacturer. This meant monopoly, of course, but a necessary one. Like the telephone service, it was in the public's best interests. You couldn't have competition in watchbird service. Watchbird was for everyone.

"The President hopes," the representative continued that full watchbird service will be installed in the shortest possible time. You will have top priorities on strategic metals, manpower, and so forth."

"Speaking for myself," the president of Southern Consolidated said, "I expect to have the first batch of watchbirds distributed within the week. Production is all set up."

THE rest of the men were equally ready. The factories had been prepared to roll out the watchbirds for months now. The final standardized equipment had been agreed upon, and only the Presidential go-ahead had been lacking.

"Fine," the representative said. "If that is all, I think we can—is there a question?"

"Yes, sir," Gelsen said. "I want to know if the present model is the one we are going to manufacture."

"Of course," the representative said. "It's the most advanced."

"I have an objection." Gelsen stood up. His colleagues were glaring coldly at him. Obviously he was delaying the advent of the golden age.

"What is your objection?" the representative asked.

"First, let me say that I am one hundred percent in favor of a machine to stop murder. It's been needed for a long time. I object only to the watchbird's learning circuits. They serve, in effect, to animate the machine and give it a pseudo-consciousness. I can't approve of that."

"But, Mr. Gelsen, you yourself testified that the watchbird would not be completely efficient unless such circuits were introduced. Without them, the watchbirds could stop only an estimated seventy percent of murders."

"I know that," Gelsen said, feeling extremely uncomfortable. "I believe there might be a moral danger in allowing a machine to make decisions that are rightfully Man's," he declared doggedly.

"Oh, come now, Gelsen," one of the corporation presidents said. "It's nothing of the sort. The watchbird will only reinforce the decisions made by honest men from the beginning of time."

"I think that is true," the representative agreed. "But I can understand how Mr. Gelsen feels. It is sad that we must put a human problem into the hands of a machine, sadder still that we must have a machine enforce our laws. But I ask you to remember, Mr. Gelsen, that there is no other possible way of stopping a murderer *before he strikes.* It would be unfair to the many innocent people killed every year if we were to restrict watchbird on philosophical grounds. Don't you agree that I'm right?"

"Yes, I suppose I do," Gelsen said unhappily. He had told himself all that a thousand times, but something still bothered him. Perhaps he would talk it over with Macintyre.

As the conference broke up, a thought struck him. He grinned.

A lot of policemen were going to be out of work!

"NOW what do you think of that?" Officer Celtrics demanded. "Fifteen years in Homicide and a machine is replacing me." He wiped a large red hand across his forehead and leaned against the captain's desk. "Ain't science marvelous?"

Two other policemen, late of Homicide, nodded glumly.

"Don't worry about it," the captain said. "We'll find a home for you in Larceny, Celtrics. You'll like it here."

"I just can't get over it," Celtrics complained. "A lousy little piece of tin and glass is going to solve all the crimes."

"Not quite," the captain said. "The watchbirds are supposed to prevent the crimes before they happen."

"Then how'll they be crimes?" one of the policemen asked. "I mean they can't hang you for murder until you commit one, can they?"

"That's not the idea," the captain said. "The watchbirds are supposed to stop a man before he commits a murder."

"Then no one arrests him?" Celtrics asked.

"I don't know how they're going to work that out," the captain admitted.

The men were silent for a while. The captain yawned

and examined his watch.

"The thing I don't understand," Celtrics said, still leaning on the captain's desk, "is just how do they do it? How did it start, Captain?"

THE captain studied Celtrics face for possible irony; after all, watchbird had been in the papers for months. But then he remembered that Celtrics, like his sidekicks, rarely bothered to turn past the sports pages.

"Well," the captain said, trying to remember what he had read in the Sunday supplements, "these scientists were working on criminology. They were studying murderers, to find out what made them tick. So they found that murderers throw out a different sort of brain wave from ordinary people. And their glands act funny, too. All this happens when they're about to commit a murder. So these scientists worked out a special machine to flash red or something when these brain waves turned on."

"Scientists," Celtrics said bitterly.

"Well, after the scientists had this machine, they didn't know what to do with it. It was too big to move around, and murderers didn't drop in often enough to make it flash. So they built it into a smaller unit and tried it out in a few police stations. I think they tried one upstate. But it didn't work so good. You couldn't get to the crime in time. That's why they built the watchbirds."

"I don't think they'll stop no criminals," one of the policemen insisted.

"They sure will. I read the test results. They can smell him out before he commits a crime. And when they reach him, they give him a powerful shock or something. It'll stop him."

"You closing up Homicide, Captain?" Celtrics asked.

"Nope," the captain said. "I'm leaving a skeleton crew in until we see how these birds do."

"Hah," Celtrics said. "Skeleton crew. That's funny."

"Sure," the captain said. "Anyhow, I'm going to leave some men on. It seems the birds don't stop all murders."

"Why not?"

"Some murderers don't have these brain waves," the captain answered, trying to remember what the newspaper article had said. "Or their glands don't work or something."

"Which ones don't they stop?" Celtrics asked, with professional curiosity.

"I don't know. But I hear they got the damned things fixed so they're going to stop all of them soon."

"How they working that?"

"They learn. The watchbirds, I mean. Just like people."

"You kidding me?"

"Nope."

"Well," Celtrics said, "I think I'll just keep old Betsy oiled, just in case. You can't trust these scientists."

"Right."

"Birds!" Celtrics scoffed.

OVER the town, the watchbird soared in a long, lazy curve. Its aluminum hide glistened in the morning sun, and dots of light danced on its stiff wings. Silently it flew.

Silently, but with all senses functioning. Built-in

kinesthetics told the watch bird where it was, and held it in a long search curve. Its eyes and ears operated as one unit, searching, seeking.

And then something happened! The watchbird's electronically fast reflexes picked up the edge of a sensation. A correlation center tested it, matching it with electrical and chemical data in its memory files. A relay tripped.

Down the watchbird spiraled, coming in on the increasingly strong sensation. It smelled the outpouring of certain glands, tasted a deviant brain wave.

Fully alerted and armed, it spun and banked in the bright morning sunlight.

Dinelli was so intent he didn't see the watchbird coming. He had his gun poised, and his eyes pleaded with the big grocer.

"Don't come no closer."

"You lousy little punk," the grocer said, and took another step forward. "Rob me? I'll break every bone in your puny body."

The grocer, too stupid or too courageous to understand the threat of the gun, advanced on the little thief.

"All right," Dinelli said, in a thorough state of panic. "All right, sucker, take—"

A bolt of electricity knocked him on his back. The gun went off, smashing a breakfast food display.

"What in hell?" the grocer asked, staring at the stunned thief. And then he saw a flash of silver wings. "Well, I'm really damned. Those watchbirds work!"

He stared until the wings disappeared in the sky. Then he telephoned the police.

The watchbird returned to his search curve. His thinking center correlated the new facts he had learned about murder. Several of these he hadn't known before.

This new information was simultaneously flashed to all the other watchbirds and their information was flashed back to him.

New information, methods, definitions were constantly passing between them.

NOW that the watchbirds were rolling off the assembly line in a steady stream, Gelsen allowed himself to relax. A loud contented hum filled his plant. Orders were being filled on time, with top priorities given to the biggest cities in his area, and working down to the smallest towns.

"All smooth, Chief," Macintyre said, coming in the door. He had just completed a routine inspection.

"Fine. Have a seat."

The big engineer sat down and lighted a cigarette.

"We've been working on this for some time," Gelsen said, when he couldn't think of anything else.

"We sure have," Macintyre agreed. He leaned back and inhaled deeply. He had been one of the consulting engineers on the original watchbird. That was six years back. He had been working for Gelsen ever since, and the men had become good friends.

"The thing I wanted to ask you was this—" Gelsen paused. He couldn't think how to phrase what he wanted. Instead he asked, "What do you think of the watchbirds, Mac?"

"Who, me?" The engineer grinned nervously. He had been eating, drinking and sleeping watchbird ever since its inception. He had never found it necessary to have an attitude. "Why, I think it's great."

"I don't mean that," Gelsen said. He realized that what he wanted was to have someone understand his point of view. "I mean do you figure there might be some danger in machine thinking?"

"I don't think so, Chief. Why do you ask?"

"Look, I'm no scientist or engineer. I've just handled cost and production and let you boys worry about how. But as a layman, watchbird is starting to frighten me."

"No reason for that."

"I don't like the idea of the learning circuits."

"But why not?" Then Macintyre grinned again. "I know. You're like a lot of people, Chief—afraid your machines are going to wake up and say, 'What are we doing here? Let's go out and rule the world.' Is that it?"

"Maybe something like that," Gelsen admitted.

"No chance of it," Macintyre said. "The watchbirds are complex, I'll admit, but an M. I. T. calculator is a whole lot more complex. And it hasn't got consciousness."

"No. But the watchbirds can *learn*."

"Sure. So can all the new calculators. Do you think they'll team up with the watchbirds?"

GELSEN felt annoyed at Macintyre, and even more annoyed at himself for being ridiculous. "It's a fact that the watch birds can put their learning into action. No one is monitoring them."

"So that's the trouble," Macintyre said.

"I've been thinking of getting out of watchbird." Gelsen hadn't realized it until that moment.

"Look, Chief," Macintyre said. "Will you take an engineer's word on this?"

"Let's hear it."

"The watchbirds are no more dangerous than an automobile, an IBM calculator or a thermometer. They have no more consciousness or volition than those things. The watchbirds are built to respond to certain stimuli, and to carry out certain operations when they receive that stimuli."

"And the learning circuits?"

"You have to have those," Macintyre said patiently, as though explaining the whole thing to a ten-year-old. "The purpose of the watchbird is to frustrate all murder-attempts, right? Well, only certain murderers give out these stimuli. In order to stop all of them, the watchbird has to search out new definitions of murder and correlate them with what it already knows."

"I think it's inhuman," Gelsen said.

"That's the best thing about it. The watchbirds are unemotional. Their reasoning is non-anthropomorphic. You can't bribe them or drug them. You shouldn't fear them, either."

The intercom on Gelsen's desk buzzed. He ignored it.

"I know all this," Gelsen said. "But, still, sometimes I feel like the man who invented dynamite. He thought it would only be used for blowing up tree stumps."

"*You* didn't invent watchbird."

"I still feel morally responsible because I manufacture them."

The intercom buzzed again, and Gelsen irritably punched a button.

"The reports are in on the first week of watchbird operation," his secretary told him.

"How do they look?"

"Wonderful, sir."

"Send them in in fifteen minutes." Gelsen switched the intercom off and turned back to Macintyre, who was cleaning his fingernails with a wooden match. "Don't you think that this represents a trend in human thinking? The mechanical god? The electronic father?"

"Chief," Macintyre said, "I think you should study watchbird more closely. Do you know what's built into the circuits?"

"Only generally."

"First, there is a purpose. Which is to stop living organisms from committing murder. Two, murder may be defined as an act of violence, consisting of breaking, mangling, maltreating or otherwise stopping the functions of a living organism by a living organism. Three, most murderers are detectable by certain chemical and electrical changes."

Macintyre paused to light another cigarette. "Those conditions take care of the routine functions. Then, for the learning circuits, there are two more conditions. Four, there are some living organisms who commit murder without the signs mentioned in three. Five, these can be detected by data applicable to condition two."

"I see," Gelsen said.

"You realize how foolproof it is?"

"I suppose so." Gelsen hesitated a moment. "I guess that's all."

"Right," the engineer said, and left.

Gelsen thought for a few moments. There *couldn't* be anything wrong with the watchbirds.

"Send in the reports," he said into the intercom.

HIGH above the lighted buildings of the city, the watchbird soared. It was dark, but in the distance the watchbird could see another, and another beyond that. For this was a large city.

To prevent murder...

There was more to watch for now. New information had crossed the invisible network that connected all watchbirds. New data, new ways of detecting the violence of murder.

There! The edge of a sensation! Two watchbirds dipped simultaneously. One had received the scent a fraction of a second before the other. He continued down while the other resumed monitoring.

Condition four, there are some living organisms who commit murder without the signs mentioned in condition three.

Through his new information, the watchbird knew by extrapolation that this organism was bent on murder, even though the characteristic chemical and electrical smells were absent.

The watchbird, all senses acute, closed in on the organism. He found what he wanted, and dived.

Roger Greco leaned against a building, his hands in his pockets. In his left hand was the cool butt of a .45. Greco waited patiently.

He wasn't thinking of anything, in particular, just relaxing against a building, waiting for a man. Greco didn't know why the man was to be killed. He didn't care. Greco's lack of curiosity was part of his value. The other part was his skill.

One bullet, neatly placed in the head of a man he didn't know. It didn't excite him or sicken him. It was a job, just like anything else. You killed a man. So?

As Greco's victim stepped out of a building, Greco lifted the .45 out of his pocket. He released the safety and braced the gun with his right hand. He still wasn't thinking of anything as he took aim…

And was knocked off his feet.

Greco thought he had been shot. He struggled up again, looked around, and sighted foggily on his victim.

Again he was knocked down.

This time he lay on the ground, trying to draw a bead. He never thought of stopping, for Greco was a craftsman.

With the next blow, everything went black. Permanently, because the watchbird's duty was to protect the object of violence —*at whatever cost to the murderer.*

The victim walked to his car. He hadn't noticed anything unusual. Everything had happened in silence.

GELSEN was feeling pretty good. The watchbirds had been operating perfectly. Crimes of violence had been cut in half, and cut again. Dark alleys were no longer mouths of horror. Parks and playgrounds were not places to shun after dusk.

Of course, there were still robberies. Petty thievery flourished, and embezzlement, larceny, forgery and a hundred other crimes.

But that wasn't so important. You could regain lost money—never a lost life.

Gelsen was ready to admit that he had been wrong about the watchbirds. They *were* doing a job that humans had been unable to accomplish.

The first hint of something wrong came that morning.

Macintyre came into his office. He stood silently in front of Gelsen's desk, looking annoyed and a little embarrassed.

"What's the matter, Mac?" Gelsen asked.

"One of the watchbirds went to work on a slaughterhouse man. Knocked him out."

Gelsen thought about it for a moment. Yes, the watchbirds would do that. With their new learning circuits, they had probably defined the killing of animals as murder.

"Tell the packers to mechanize their slaughtering," Gelsen said. "I never liked that business myself."

"All right," Macintyre said. He pursed his lips, then shrugged his shoulders and left.

Gelsen stood beside his desk, thinking. Couldn't the watchbirds differentiate between a murderer and a man engaged in a legitimate profession? No, evidently not. To them, murder was murder. No exceptions. He frowned. That might take a little ironing out in the circuits.

But not too much, he decided hastily. Just make them a little more discriminating.

He sat down again and buried himself in paperwork, trying to avoid the edge of an old fear.

THEY strapped the prisoner into the chair and fitted the electrode to his leg.

"Oh, oh," he moaned, only half-conscious now of

what they were doing.

They fitted the helmet over his shaved head and tightened the last straps. He continued to moan softly.

And then the watchbird swept in. How he had come, no one knew. Prisons are large and strong, with many locked doors, but the watchbird was there—

To stop a murder.

"Get that thing out of here!" the warden shouted, and reached for the switch. The watchbird knocked him down.

"Stop that!" a guard screamed, and grabbed for the switch himself. He was knocked to the floor beside the warden.

"This isn't murder, you idiot," another guard said. He drew his gun to shoot down the glittering, wheeling metal bird.

Anticipating, the watchbird smashed him back against the wall.

There was silence in the room. After a while, the man in the helmet started to giggle. Then he stopped.

The watchbird stood on guard, fluttering in mid-air—

Making sure no murder was done.

New data flashed along the watchbird network. Unmonitored, independent, the thousands of watchbirds received and acted upon it.

The breaking, mangling or otherwise stopping the functions of a living organism by a living organism. New acts to stop.

"Damn you, git going!" Farmer Ollister shouted, and raised his whip again. The horse balked, and the wagon rattled and shook as he edged sideways.

"You lousy hunk of pigmeal, git going!" the farmer yelled and he raised the whip again.

It never fell. An alert watchbird, sensing violence, had knocked him out of his seat.

A living organism? What is a living organism? The watchbirds extended their definitions as they became aware of more facts. And, of course, this gave them more work.

The deer was just visible at the edge of the woods. The hunter raised his rifle, and took careful aim.

He didn't have time to shoot.

WITH his free hand, Gelsen mopped perspiration from his face. "All right," he said into the telephone. He listened to the stream of vituperation from the other end, then placed the receiver gently in its cradle.

"What was that one?" Macintyre asked. He was unshaven, tie loose, shirt unbuttoned.

"Another fisherman," Gelsen said. "It seems the watchbirds won't let him fish even though his family is starving. What are we going to do about it, he wants to know."

"How many hundred is that?"

"I don't know. I haven't opened the mail."

"Well, I figured out where the trouble is," Macintyre said gloomily, with the air of a man who knows just how he blew up the Earth—after it was too late.

"Let's hear it."

"Everybody took it for granted that we wanted all murder stopped. We figured the watchbirds would think as we do. We ought to have qualified the conditions."

"I've got an idea," Gelsen said, "that we'd have to know just why and what murder is, before we could qualify the conditions properly. And if we knew that, we wouldn't need the watchbirds."

"Oh, I don't know about that. They just have to be told that some things which look like murder are not murder."

"But why should they stop fisherman?" Gelsen asked.

"Why shouldn't they? Fish and animals are living organisms. We just don't think that killing them is murder."

The telephone rang. Gelsen glared at it and punched the intercom. "I told you no more calls, no matter what."

"This is from Washington," his secretary said. "I thought you'd—"

"Sorry." Gelsen picked up the telephone. "Yes. Certainly is a mess… Have they? All right, I certainly will." He put down the telephone.

"Short and sweet," he told Macintyre. "We're to shut down temporarily."

"That won't be so easy," Macintyre said. "The watchbirds operate independent of any central control, you know. They come back once a week for a repair checkup. We'll have to turn them off then, one by one."

"Well, let's get to it. Monroe over on the Coast has shut down about a quarter of his birds."

"I think I can dope out a restricting circuit," Macintyre said.

"Fine," Gelsen replied bitterly; "You make me very happy."

THE watchbirds were learning rapidly, expanding and adding to their knowledge. Loosely defined abstractions were extended, acted upon and re-extended.

To stop murder…

Metal and electrons reason well, but not in a human fashion.

A living organism? *Any* living organism!

The watchbirds set themselves the task of protecting all living things.

The fly buzzed around the room, lighting on a table top, pausing a moment, then darting to a windowsill.

The old man stalked it, a rolled newspaper in his hand.

Murderer!

The watchbirds swept down and saved the fly in the nick of time.

The old man writhed on the floor a minute and then was silent. He had been given only a mild shock, but it had been enough for his fluttery, cranky heart.

His victim had been saved, though, and this was the important thing. Save the victim and give the aggressor his just desserts.

GELSEN demanded angrily. "Why aren't they being turned off!"

The assistant control engineer gestured. In a corner of the repair room lay the senior control engineer. He was just regaining consciousness.

"He tried to turn one of them off," the assistant engineer said. Both his hands were knotted together. He was making a visible effort not to shake.

"That's ridiculous. They haven't got any sense of self-preservation."

"Then turn them off yourself. Besides, I don't think any more are going to come."

What could have happened? Gelsen began to piece it together. The watchbirds still hadn't decided on the limits of a living organism. When some of them were turned off in the Monroe plant, the rest must have correlated the data.

So they had been forced to assume that they were living organisms, as well.

No one had ever told them otherwise. Certainly they carried on most of the functions of living organisms.

Then the old fears hit him. Gelsen trembled and hurried out of the repair room. He wanted to find Macintyre in a hurry.

THE nurse handed the surgeon the sponge.

"Scalpel."

She placed it in his hand. He started to make the first incision. And then he was aware of a disturbance.

"Who let that thing in?"

"I don't know," the nurse said, her voice muffled by the mask.

"Get it out of here."

The nurse waved her arms at the bright winged thing, but it fluttered over her head.

The surgeon proceeded with the incision—as long as he was able.

The watchbird drove him away and stood guard.

"Telephone the watchbird company!" the surgeon ordered. "Get them to turn the thing off."

The watchbird was preventing violence to a living organism.

The surgeon stood by helplessly while his patient died.

FLUTTERING high above the network of highways, the watchbird watched and waited. It had been constantly working for weeks now, without rest or repair. Rest and repair were impossible, because the watchbird couldn't allow itself—a living organism—to be murdered. And that was what happened when watchbirds returned to the factory.

There was a built-in order to return, after the lapse of a certain time period. But the watchbird had a stronger order to obey—preservation of life, including its own.

The definitions of murder were almost infinitely extended now, impossible to cope with. But the watchbird didn't consider that. It responded to its stimuli, whenever they came and whatever their source.

There was a new definition of living organism in its memory files. It had come as a result of the watchbird discovery that watchbirds were living organisms. And it had enormous ramifications.

The stimuli came! For the hundredth time that day, the bird wheeled and banked, dropping swiftly down to stop murder.

Jackson yawned and pulled his car to a shoulder of the road. He didn't notice the glittering dot in the sky. There was no reason for him to. Jackson wasn't contemplating murder, by any human definition.

This was a good spot for a nap, he decided. He had been driving for seven straight hours and his eyes were starting to fog. He reached out to turn off the ignition key—

And was knocked back against the side of the car.

"What in hell's wrong with you?" he asked

indignantly. "All I want to do is—" He reached for the key again, and again he was smacked back.

Jackson knew better than to try a third time. He had been listening to the radio and he knew what the watchbirds did to stubborn violators.

"You mechanical jerk," he said to the waiting metal bird. "A car's not alive. I'm not trying to kill it."

But the watchbird only knew that a certain operation resulted in stopping an organism. The car was certainly a functioning organism. Wasn't it of metal, as were the watchbirds? Didn't it run?

MACINTYRE said, "Without repairs they'll run down." He shoved a pile of specification sheets out of his way.

"How soon?" Gelsen asked.

"Six months to a year. Say a year, barring accidents."

"A year," Gelsen said. "In the meantime, everything is stopping dead. Do you know the latest?"

"What?"

"The watchbirds have decided that the Earth is a living organism. They won't allow farmers to break ground for plowing. And, of course, everything else is a living organism—rabbits, beetles, flies, wolves, mosquitoes, lions, crocodiles, crows, and smaller forms of life such as bacteria."

"I know," Macintyre said.

"And you tell me they'll wear out in six months or a year. What happens *now*? What are we going to eat in six months?"

The engineer rubbed his chin. "We'll have to do

something quick and fast. Ecological balance is gone to hell."

"Fast isn't the word. Instantaneously would be better." Gelsen lighted his thirty-fifth cigarette for the day. "At least I have the bitter satisfaction of saying 'I told you so.' Although I'm just as responsible as the rest of the machine-worshipping fools."

Macintyre wasn't listening. He was thinking about watchbirds. "Like the rabbit plague in Australia."

"The death rate is mounting," Gelsen said. "Famine. Floods. Can't cut down trees. Doctors can't—what was that you said about Australia?"

"The rabbits," Macintyre repeated. "Hardly any left in Australia now."

"Why? How was it done?"

"Oh, found some kind of germ that attacked only rabbits. I think it was propagated by mosquitos—"

"Work on that," Gelsen said. "You might have something. I want you to get on the telephone, ask for an emergency hookup with the engineers of the other companies. Hurry it up. Together you may be able to dope out something."

"Right," Macintyre said. He grabbed a handful of blank paper and hurried to the telephone.

"WHAT did I tell you?" Officer Celtrics said. He grinned at the captain. "Didn't I tell you scientists were nuts?"

"I didn't say you were wrong, did I?" the captain asked.

"No, but you weren't *sure*."

"Well, I'm sure now. You'd better get going. There's

plenty of work for you."

"I know." Celtrics drew his revolver from its holster, checked it and put it back. "Are all the boys back, Captain?"

"All?" the captain laughed humorlessly. "Homicide has increased by fifty percent. There's more murder now than there's ever been."

"Sure," Celtrics said. "The watchbirds are too busy guarding cars and slugging spiders." He started toward the door, then turned for a parting shot.

"Take my word, Captain. Machines are *stupid*."

The captain nodded.

THOUSANDS of watchbirds, trying to stop countless millions of murders—a hopeless task. But the watchbirds didn't hope. Without consciousness, they experienced no sense of accomplishment, no fear of failure. Patiently they went about their jobs, obeying each stimulus as it came.

They couldn't be everywhere at the same time, but it wasn't necessary to be. People learned quickly what the watchbirds didn't like and refrained from doing it. It just wasn't safe. With their high speed and superfast senses, the watchbirds got around quickly.

And now they meant business. In their original directives there had been a provision made for killing a murderer, if all other means failed.

Why spare a murderer?

It backfired. The watchbirds extracted the fact that murder and crimes of violence had increased geometrically since they had begun operation. This was true, because their new definitions increased the possibilities of murder. But to the watchbirds, the rise showed that the first methods had failed.

Simple logic. If A doesn't work, try B. The watchbirds shocked to kill.

Slaughterhouses in Chicago stopped and cattle starved to death in their pens, because farmers in the Midwest couldn't cut hay or harvest grain.

No one had told the watchbirds that all life depends on carefully balanced murders. Starvation didn't concern the watchbirds, since it was an act of omission.

Their interest lay only in acts of commission.

Hunters sat home, glaring at the silver dots in the sky, longing to shoot them down. But for the most part, they didn't try. The watchbirds were quick to sense the murder intent and to punish it.

Fishing boats swung idle at their moorings in San Pedro and Gloucester. Fish were living organisms.

Farmers cursed and spat and died, trying to harvest the crop. Grain was alive and thus worthy of protection. Potatoes were as important to the watchbird as any other living organism. The death of a blade of grass was equal to the assassination of a President—

To the watchbirds.

And, of course, certain machines were living. This followed, since the watchbirds were machines and living.

God help you if you maltreated your radio. Turning it off meant killing it. Obviously—its voice was silenced, the red glow of its tubes faded, it grew cold.

The watchbirds tried to guard their other charges. Wolves were slaughtered, trying to kill rabbits. Rabbits were electrocuted, trying to eat vegetables. Creepers were burned out in the act of strangling trees.

A butterfly was executed, caught in the act of outraging a rose.

This control was spasmodic, because of the fewness of the watchbirds. A billion watchbirds couldn't have carried out the ambitious project set by the thousands.

The effect was of a murderous force, ten thousand bolts of irrational lightning raging around the country, striking a thousand times a day.

Lightning which anticipated your moves and punished your intentions.

"GENTLEMEN, *please*," the government representative begged. "We must hurry."

The seven manufacturers stopped talking.

"Before we begin this meeting formally," the president of Monroe said, "I want to say something. We do not feel ourselves responsible for this unhappy state of affairs. It was a government project; the government must accept the responsibility, both moral and financial."

Gelsen shrugged his shoulders. It was hard to believe that these men, just a few weeks ago, had been willing to accept the glory of saving the world. Now they wanted to shrug off the responsibility when the salvation went amiss.

"I'm positive that that need not concern us now," the representative assured him. "We must hurry. You engineers have done a very excellent job. I am so proud of the cooperation you have shown in this emergency. You are hereby empowered to put the outlined plan into action."

"Wait a minute," Gelsen said.

"There is no time."

"The plan's no good."

"Don't you think it will work?"

"Of course it will work. But I'm afraid the cure will be worse than the disease."

The manufacturers looked as though they would have enjoyed throttling Gelsen. He didn't hesitate.

"Haven't we learned yet?" he asked. "Don't you see that you can't cure human problems by mechanization?"

"Mr. Gelsen," the president of Monroe said, "I would enjoy hearing you philosophize, but, unfortunately, people are being killed. Many crops are being totally ruined. There is widespread famine in some sections of the country already. The watchbirds must be stopped at once!"

"Murder must be stopped, too. I remember all of us agreeing upon that. But this is not the way!"

"What would you suggest?" the representative asked.

GELSEN took a deep breath. What he was about to say took all the courage he had.

"Let the watchbirds run down by themselves," Gelsen suggested.

There was a near-riot. The government representative broke it up.

"Let's take our lesson," Gelsen urged, "admit that we were wrong trying to cure human problems by mechanical means. Start again. Use machines, yes, but not as judges and teachers and fathers."

"Ridiculous," the representative said coldly. "Mr. Gelsen, you are overwrought. I suggest you control yourself." He cleared his throat. "All of you are ordered by the President to carry out the plan you have submitted." He looked sharply at Gelsen. "Not to do so will be treason."

"I'll cooperate to the best of my ability," Gelsen said.

"Good. Those assembly lines must be rolling within the week."

Gelsen walked out of the room alone. Now he was confused again. Had he been right or was he just another visionary? Certainly, he hadn't explained himself with much clarity.

Did he know what he meant?

Gelsen cursed under his breath. He wondered why he couldn't ever be sure of anything. Weren't there any values he could hold on to?

He hurried to the airport and to his plant.

THE watchbird was operating erratically now. Many of its delicate parts were out of line, worn by almost continuous operation. But gallantly it responded when the stimuli came.

A spider was attacking a fly. The watchbird swooped down to the rescue.

Simultaneously, it became aware of something overhead. The watchbird wheeled to meet it.

There was a sharp crackle and a power bolt whizzed by the watchbird's wing. Angrily, it spat a shock wave.

The attacker was heavily insulated. Again it spat at the watchbird. This time, a bolt smashed through a wing. The watchbird darted away, but the attacker went after it in a burst of speed, throwing out more crackling power.

The watchbird fell, but managed to send out its message. Urgent! A new menace to living organisms and this was the deadliest yet!

Other watchbirds around the country integrated the message. Their thinking centers searched for an answer.

"WELL, Chief, they bagged fifty today," Macintyre said, coming into Gelsen's office.

"Fine," Gelsen said, not looking at the engineer.

"Not so fine." Macintyre sat down. "Lord, I'm tired! It was seventy-two yesterday."

"I know." On Gelsen's desk were several dozen lawsuits, which he was sending to the government with a prayer.

"They'll pick up again, though," Macintyre said confidently. "The Hawks are especially built to hunt down watchbirds. They're stronger, faster, and they've got better armor. We really rolled them out in a hurry, huh?"

"We sure did."

"The watchbirds are pretty good, too," Macintyre had to admit. "They're learning to take cover. They're trying a lot of stunts. You know, each one that goes down tells the others something."

Gelsen didn't answer.

"But anything the watchbirds can do, the Hawks can do better," Macintyre said with a cheerful expression on his face. "The Hawks have special learning circuits for hunting. They're more flexible than the watchbirds. They learn faster."

Gelsen gloomily stood up, stretched for several seconds, gave out a low yawn, and walked to the window. The sky was blank. Looking out, he realized that his uncertainties were over. Right or wrong, he had made up his mind.

"Tell me," he said, still watching the sky, "what will the Hawks hunt after they get all the watchbirds?"

"Huh?" Macintyre said. "Why—"

"Just to be on the safe side, you'd better design something to hunt down the Hawks. Just in case, I mean."

"You think—"

"All I know is that the Hawks are self-controlled. So were the watchbirds. Remote control would have been too slow, the argument went on. The idea was to get the watchbirds and get them fast. That meant no restricting circuits."

"We can dope something out," Macintyre said uncertainly.

"You've got an aggressive machine up in the air now. A murder machine. Before that it was an anti-murder machine. Your next gadget will have to be even more self-sufficient, won't it?"

Macintyre didn't answer.

"I don't hold you responsible," Gelsen said. "It's me. It's everyone."

In the air outside was a swift-moving dot.

"That's what comes," said Gelsen, "of giving a machine the job that was supposed to be our own responsibility."

OVERHEAD, a Hawk was zeroing in on a watchbird.

The armored murder machine had learned a lot in a few days. Its sole function was to kill. At present it was impelled toward a certain type of living organism, metallic like itself.

But the Hawk had just discovered that there were other types of living organisms, too—

Which had to be murdered.

Keep Your Shape

Only a race as incredibly elastic as the Grom could have a single rule of war…

PID the Pilot slowed the ship almost to a standstill, and peered anxiously at the green planet below.

Even without instruments, there was no mistaking it. Third from its sun, it was the only planet in this system capable of sustaining life. Peacefully it swam beneath its gauze of clouds.

It looked very innocent. And yet, twenty previous Grom expeditions had set out to prepare this planet for invasion—and vanished utterly, without a word.

Pid hesitated only a moment, before starting irrevocably down. There was no point in hovering and worrying, he and his two crewmen were as ready now as they would ever be… Their compact Displacers were stored in body pouches, inactive but ready.

Pid wanted to say something to his crew, but wasn't sure how to put it.

The crew waited. Ilg the Radioman had sent the final message to the Grom planet. Ger the Detector read sixteen dials at once, and reported, "No sign of alien activity." His body surfaces flowed carelessly.

NOTICING the flow, Pid knew what to say to his crew. Ever since they had left Grom, shape-discipline had been disgustingly lax. The Invasion Chief had warned him; but still, he had to do something about it. It was his duty, since lower castes such as Radiomen and Detectors were notoriously prone to Shapelessness.

"A lot of hopes are resting on this expedition," he began slowly. "We're a long way from home now."

Ger the Detector nodded. Ilg the Radioman flowed out of his prescribed shape and molded himself comfortably to a wall.

"However," Pid said sternly, "distance is no excuse for promiscuous Shapelessness."

Ilg flowed hastily back into proper Radioman's shape.

"Exotic forms will undoubtedly be called for," Pid went on. "And for that we have a special dispensation. But remember—any shape not assumed strictly in the line of duty is a foul, lawless device of The Shapeless One!"

Ger's body surfaces abruptly stopped flowing.

"That's all." Pid said, and flowed into his controls. The ship started down, so smoothly coordinated that Pid felt a glow of pride.

They were good workers, he decided. He just couldn't expect them to be as shape-conscious as a high-caste Pilot. Even the Invasion Chief had told him that.

"Pid," the Invasion Chief had said at their last interview, "we need this planet desperately."

"Yes, sir," Pid had said, standing at full attention, never quivering from Optimum Pilot's Shape.

"One of you," the Chief said heavily, "must get through and set up a Displacer near an atomic power source. The army will be standing by at this end, ready to step through."

"We'll do it, sir," Pid said.

"This expedition has to succeed," the Chief said, and his features blurred momentarily from sheer fatigue. "In strictest confidence, there's considerable unrest on Grom. The Miner caste is on strike, for instance. They want a new digging shape. Say the old one is inefficient."

Pid looked properly indignant. The Mining Shape had been set down by the Ancients fifty thousand years ago, together with the rest of the basic shapes. And now these upstarts wanted to change it!

"That's not all," the chief told him. "We've uncovered a new Cult of Shapelessness. Picked up almost eight thousand Grom, and I don't know how many more we missed."

Pid knew that Shapelessness was a lure of The Shapeless One, the greatest evil that the Grom mind could conceive of. But why, he wondered, did so many Grom fall for His lures?

THE Chief guessed his question. "Pid," he said, "I suppose it's difficult for you to understand. Do you enjoy Piloting?"

"Yes, sir," Pid said simply. *Enjoy* Piloting! It was his entire life! Without a ship, he was nothing.

"Not all Grom feel that way," the Chief said. "I don't understand it either. All my ancestors have been Invasion Chiefs, back to the beginning of time. So of course *I* want to be an Invasion Chief. It's only natural, as well as lawful. But the lower castes don't feel that way." The Chief shook his body sadly. "I've told you this for a reason. We Grom need more room. This unrest is caused purely by crowding. All our psychologists say so. Another planet to expand into will cure everything. So we're counting on you, Pid."

"Yes, sir," Pid said, with a glow of pride.

The Chief rose to end the interview. Then he changed his mind and sat down again.

"You'll have to watch your crew," he said. "They're loyal, no doubt, but low-caste. And you know the lower castes."

Pid did indeed.

"Ger, your Detector, is suspected of harboring Alterationist tendencies. He was once fined for assuming a quasi-Hunter shape. Ilg has never had any definite charge brought against him. But I hear that he remains immobile for suspiciously long periods of time. Possibly, he fancies himself a Thinker."

"But, sir," Pid protested. "If they are even slightly tainted with Alterationism or Shapelessness, why send them on this expedition?"

The Chief hesitated before answering. "There are

plenty of Grom I could trust," he said slowly. "But those two have certain qualities of resourcefulness and imagination that will be needed on this expedition." He sighed. "I really don't understand why those qualities are usually linked with Shapelessness."

"Yes, sir," Pid said.

"Just watch them."

"Yes, sir," Pid said again, and saluted, realizing that the interview was at an end. In his body pouch he felt the dormant Displacer, ready to transform the enemy's power source into a bridge across space for the Grom hordes.

"Good luck," the chief said. "I'm sure you'll need it."

THE ship dropped silently toward the surface of the enemy planet. Ger the Detector analyzed the clouds below, and fed data into the Camouflage Unit. The Unit went to work. Soon the ship looked, to all outward appearances, like a cirrus formation.

Pid allowed the ship to drift slowly toward the surface of the mystery planet. He was in Optimum Pilot's Shape now, the most efficient of the four shapes allotted to the Pilot caste. Blind, deaf and dumb, an extension of his controls, all his attention was directed toward matching the velocities of the high-flying clouds, staying among them, becoming a part of them.

Ger remained rigidly in one of the two shapes allotted to Detectors. He fed data into the Camouflage Unit, and the descending ship slowly altered into an altocumulus.

There was no sign of activity from the enemy planet.

Ilg located an atomic power source, and fed the data to Pid. The Pilot altered course. He had reached the lowest level of clouds, barely a mile above the surface of the planet. Now his ship looked like a fat, fleecy cumulus.

And still there was no sign of alarm. The unknown fate that had overtaken, twenty previous expeditions still had not showed itself.

Dusk crept across the face of the planet as Pid maneuvered near the atomic power installation. He avoided the surrounding homes and hovered over a clump of woods.

Darkness fell, and the green planet's lone moon was veiled in clouds.

One cloud floated lower.

And landed.

"Quick, everyone out!" Pid shouted, detaching himself from the ship's controls. He assumed the Pilot's Shape best suited for running, and raced out the hatch. Ger and Ilg hurried after him. They stopped fifty yards from the ship, and waited.

Inside the ship a little-used circuit closed. There was a silent shudder, and the ship began to melt. Plastic dissolved, metal crumpled. Soon the ship was a great pile of junk, and still the process went on. Big fragments broke into smaller fragments, and split, and split again.

Pid felt suddenly helpless, watching his ship scuttle itself. He was a Pilot, of the Pilot caste. His father had been a Pilot, and his father before him, stretching back to the hazy past when the Grom had first constructed ships. He had spent his entire childhood around ships, his entire manhood flying them.

Now, shipless, he was naked in an alien world.

IN a few minutes there was only a mound of dust to show where the ship had been. The night wind scattered it through the forest. And then there was nothing at all.

They waited. Nothing happened. The wind sighed and the trees creaked. Squirrels chirped, and birds stirred in their nests. An acorn fell to the ground.

Pid heaved a sigh of relief and sat down. The twenty-first Grom expedition had landed safely.

There was nothing to be done until morning, so Pid began to make plans. They had landed as close to the atomic power installation as they dared. Now they would have to get closer. Somehow, one of them had to get very near the reactor room, in order to activate the Displacer.

Difficult. But Pid felt certain of success. After all, the Grom were strong on ingenuity.

Strong on ingenuity, he thought bitterly, but terribly short of radioactives. That was another reason why this expedition was so important. There was little radioactive fuel left, on any of the Grom worlds. Ages ago, the Grom had spent their store of radioactives in spreading throughout their neighboring worlds, occupying the ones that they could live on.

Now, colonization barely kept up with the mounting birthrate. New worlds were constantly needed.

This particular world, discovered in a scouting expedition, was needed. It suited the Grom perfectly. But it was too far away. They didn't have enough fuel to mount a conquering space fleet.

Luckily, there was another way. A better way.

Over the centuries, the Grom scientists had developed the Displacer. A triumph of Identity Engineering, the Displacer allowed mass to be moved instantaneously between any two linked points.

One end was set up at Grom's sole atomic energy plant. The other end had to be placed in proximity to another atomic power source, and activated. Diverted power then flowed through both ends, was modified, and modified again.

Then, through the miracle of Identity Engineering, the Grom could *step* through from planet to planet; or pour through in a great, overwhelming wave.

It was quite simple.

But twenty expeditions had failed to set up the Earth-end Displacer.

What had happened to them was not known.

For no Grom ship had ever returned to tell.

BEFORE dawn they crept through the woods,

taking on the coloration of the plants around them. Their Displacers pulsed feebly, sensing the nearness of atomic energy.

A tiny, four-legged creature darted in front of them. Instantly, Ger grew four legs and a long, streamlined body and gave chase.

"Ger! Come back here!" Pid howled at the Detector, throwing caution to the winds.

Ger overtook the animal and knocked it down. He tried to bite it, but he had neglected to grow teeth. The animal jumped free, and vanished into the underbrush. Ger thrust out a set of teeth and bunched his muscles for another leap.

"Ger!"

Reluctantly, the Detector turned away. He loped silently back to Pid.

"I was hungry," he said.

"You were not," Pid said sternly.

"Was," Ger mumbled, writhing with embarrassment.

Pid remembered what the Chief had told him. Ger certainly did have Hunter tendencies. He would have to watch him more closely.

"We'll have no more of that," Pid said. "Remember—the lure of Exotic Shapes is not sanctioned. Be content with the shape you were born to."

Ger nodded, and melted back into the underbrush. They moved on.

At the extreme edge of the woods they could observe the atomic energy installation. Pid disguised himself as a clump of shrubbery, and Ger formed himself into an old log. Ilg, after a moment's thought, became a young oak.

The installation was in the form of a long, low building, surrounded by a metal fence. There was a gate, and guards in front of it.

The first job, Pid thought, was to get past that gate. He began to consider ways and means.

From the fragmentary reports of the survey parties, Pid knew that, in some ways, this race of Men were like the Grom. They had pets, as the Grom did, and homes and children, and a culture. The inhabitants were skilled mechanically, as were the Grom.

But there were terrific differences, also. The Men were of fixed and immutable form, like stones or trees. And to compensate, their planet boasted a fantastic array of species, types and kinds. This was completely unlike Grom, which had only eight distinct forms of animal life.

And evidently, the Men were skilled at detecting invaders, Pid thought. He wished he knew how the other expeditions had failed. It would make his job much easier.

A MAN lurched past them on two incredibly stiff legs. Rigidity was evident in his every move. Without looking, he hurried past.

"I know," Ger said, after the creature had moved away. "I'll disguise myself as a Man, walk through the gate to the reactor room, and activate my Displacer."

"You can't speak their language," Pid pointed out.

"I won't speak at all. I'll ignore them. Look." Quickly Ger shaped himself into a Man.

"That's not bad," Pid said.

Ger tried a few practice steps, copying the bumpy walk of the Man.

"But I'm afraid it won't work," Pid said.

"It's perfectly logical," Ger pointed out.

"I know. Therefore the other expeditions must have tried it. And none of them came back."

There was no arguing that. Ger flowed back into the shape of a log. "What, then?" he asked.

"Let me think," Pid said.

Another creature lurched past, on four legs instead of two. Pid recognized it as a Dog, a pet of Man. He watched it carefully.

The Dog ambled to the gate, head down, in no particular hurry. It walked through, unchallenged, and lay down in the grass.

"Hmm," Pid said.

They watched. One of the Men walked past, and touched the Dog on the head. The Dog stuck out its tongue and rolled over on its side.

"I can do that," Ger said excitedly. He started to flow into the shape of a Dog.

"No, wait," Pid said. "We'll spend the rest of the day thinking it over. This is too important to rush into."

Ger subsided sulkily.

"Come on, let's move back," Pid said. He and Ger

started into the woods. Then he remembered Ilg.

"Ilg?" he called softly.

There was no answer.

"Ilg!"

"What? Oh, yes," an oak tree said, and melted into a bush. "Sorry. What were you saying?"

"We're moving back," Pid said.

"Were you, by any chance, Thinking?"

"Oh, no," Ilg assured him. "Just resting."

Pid let it go at that. There was too much else to worry about.

THEY discussed it for the rest of the day, hidden in the deepest part of the woods. The only alternatives seemed to be Man or Dog. A Tree couldn't walk past the gates, since that was not in the nature of trees. Nor could anything else, and escape notice.

Going as a Man seemed too risky. They decided that Ger would sally out in the morning as a Dog.

"Now get some sleep," Pid said.

Obediently his two crewmen flattened out, going immediately Shapeless. But Pid had a more difficult time.

Everything looked too easy. Why wasn't the atomic installation better guarded? Certainly the Men must have learned something from the expeditions they had captured in the past. Or had they killed them without asking any questions?

You couldn't tell what an alien would do.

Was that open gate a trap?

Wearily he flowed into a comfortable position on the lumpy ground. Then he pulled himself together hastily.

He had gone Shapeless!

Comfort was not in the line of duty, he reminded himself, and firmly took a Pilot's Shape.

But a Pilot's Shape wasn't constructed for sleeping on damp, bumpy ground. Pid spent a restless night, thinking of ships, and wishing he were flying one.

He awoke in the morning tired and ill tempered. He nudged Ger.

"Let's get this over with," he said.

Ger flowed gaily to his feet.

"Come on, Ilg," Pid said angrily, looking around. "Wake up."

There was no reply.

"Ilg!" he called.

Still there was no reply.

"Help me look for him," Pid said to Ger. "He must be around here somewhere."

Together they tested every bush, tree, log and shrub in the vicinity. But none of them was Ilg.

Pid began to feel a cold panic run through him. What could have happened to the Radioman?

"Perhaps he decided to go through the gate on his own," Ger suggested.

Pid considered the possibility. It seemed unlikely. Ilg had never shown much initiative. He had always been content to follow orders.

They waited. But midday came, and there was still

no sign of Ilg.

"We can't wait any longer," Pid said, and they started through the woods. Pid wondered if Ilg had tried to get through the gates on his own. Those quiet types often concealed a foolhardy streak.

But there was nothing to show that Ilg had been successful. He would have to assume that the Radioman was dead, or captured by the Men.

That left two of them to activate a Displacer.

And he still didn't know what had happened to the other expeditions.

AT the edge of the woods, Ger turned himself into a facsimile of a Dog. Pid inspected him carefully.

"A little less tail," he said.

Ger shortened his tail.

"More ears."

Ger lengthened his ears.

"Now even them up."

They became even.

Pid inspected the finished product. As far as he could tell, Ger was perfect, from the tip of his tail to his wet, black nose.

"Good luck," Pid said.

"Thanks." Cautiously Ger moved out of the woods, walking in the lurching style of Dogs and Men. At the gate the guard called to him. Pid held his breath.

Ger walked past the Man, ignoring him. The Man started to walk over. Ger broke into a run.

Pid shaped a pair of strong legs for himself, ready to dash if Ger was caught.

But the guard turned back to his gate. Ger stopped running immediately, and strolled quietly toward the main door of the building.

Pid dissolved his legs with a sigh of relief… and then tensed again.

The main door was closed!

Pid hoped the Radioman wouldn't try to open it. That was not in the nature of Dogs.

As he watched, another Dog came running toward Ger. Ger backed away from him. The Dog approached and sniffed. Ger sniffed back.

Then both of them ran around the building.

That was clever, Pid thought. There was bound to be a door in the rear.

He glanced up at the afternoon sun. As soon as the Displacer was activated, the Grom armies would begin to pour through. By the time the Men recovered from the shock, a million or more Grom troops would be here, weapons and all. With more following.

The day passed slowly, and nothing happened.

Nervously Pid watched the front of the plant. It shouldn't be taking so long, if Ger were successful.

Late into the night he waited. Men walked in and out of the installation, and Dogs barked around the gates. But Ger did not appear.

Ger had failed. Ilg was gone. Only he was left.

And *still* he didn't know what had happened.

By morning, Pid was in complete despair. He knew that the twenty-first Grom expedition to this planet was near the point of complete failure. Now it was all up to him.

He saw that workers were arriving in great number, rushing through the gates. He decided to take advantage of the apparent confusion, and started to shape himself into a Man.

A Dog walked past the woods where he was hiding.

"Hello," the Dog said.

It was Ger!

"What happened?" Pid asked, with a sigh of relief. "Why were you so long? Couldn't you get in?"

"I don't know," Ger said, wagging his tail. "I didn't try."

Pid was speechless.

"I went hunting," Ger said complacently. "This form is ideal for Hunting, you know. I went out the rear gate with another Dog."

"But the expedition—your duty—"

"I changed my mind," Ger told him. "You know, Pilot, I never wanted to be a Detector."

"But you were *born* a Detector!"

"That's true," Ger said. "But it doesn't help. I always wanted to be a Hunter."

Pid shook his entire body in annoyance. "You can't," he said, very slowly, as one would explain to a Gromling. "The Hunter shape is forbidden to you."

"Not here it isn't," Ger said, still wagging his tail.

"Let's have no more of this," Pid said angrily. "Get

into that installation and set up your Displacer. I'll try to overlook this heresy."

"No," Ger said. "I don't want the Grom here. They'd ruin it for the rest of us."

"He's right," a nearby oak tree said.

"Ilg!" Pid gasped. "Where are you?"

BRANCHES stirred. "I'm right here," Ilg said. "I've been Thinking."

"But—your caste—"

"Pilot," Ger said sadly, "why don't you wake up? Most of the people on Grom are miserable. Only custom makes us take the caste-shape of our ancestors."

"Pilot," Ilg said, "all Grom are born Shapeless!"

"And being born Shapeless, all Grom should have Freedom of Shape," Ger said.

"Exactly," Ilg said. "But he'll never understand. Now excuse me. I want to Think." And the oak tree was silent.

Pid laughed humorlessly. "The Men will kill you off," he said. "Just as they killed off all the other expeditions."

"No one from Grom has been killed," Ger told him. "The other expeditions are right here."

"Alive?"

"Certainly. The Men don't even know we exist. That Dog I was Hunting with is a Grom from the twelfth expedition. There are hundreds of us here, Pilot. We like it."

Pid tried to absorb it all. He had always known that the lower castes were lax in caste-consciousness. But this was preposterous!

This planet's secret menace was freedom!

"Join us, Pilot," Ger said. "We've got a paradise here. Do you know how many species there are on this planet? An uncountable number! There's a shape to suit every need!"

Pid ignored them. Traitors!

He'd do the job all by himself.

So Men were unaware of the presence of the Grom. Getting near the reactor might not be so difficult after all. The others had failed in their duty because they were of the lower castes, weak and irresponsible. Even the Pilots among them must have been secretly sympathetic to the Cult of Shapelessness the Chief had mentioned, or the alien planet could never have swayed them.

What shape to assume for his attempt?

Pid considered.

A Dog might be best. Evidently Dogs could wander pretty much where they wished. If something went wrong, Pid could change his shape to meet the occasion.

"The Supreme Council will take care of all of you," he snarled, and shaped himself into a small brown Dog. "I'm going to set up the Displacer myself."

He studied himself for a moment, bared his teeth at Ger, and loped toward the gate.

HE loped for about ten feet and stopped in utter horror.

The smells rushed at him from all directions. Smells in a profusion and variety he had never dreamed existed. Smells that were harsh, sweet, sharp, heavy, mysterious, overpowering. Smells that terrified. Alien and repulsive and inescapable, the odors of Earth struck him like a blow.

He curled his lips and held his breath. He ran on for a few steps, and had to breathe again. He almost choked.

He tried to remold his Dog-nostrils to be less sensitive. It didn't work. It wouldn't, so long as he kept the Dog-shape. An attempt to modify his metabolism didn't work either.

All this in the space of two or three seconds. He was rooted in his tracks, fighting the smells, wondering what to do.

Then the noises hit him.

They were a constant and staggering roar, through which every tiniest whisper of sound stood out clearly and distinct. Sounds upon sounds— more noise than he had ever heard before at one time in his life. The woods behind him had suddenly become a madhouse.

Utterly confused, he lost control and became Shapeless.

He half-ran, half-flowed into a nearby bush. There he re-shaped, obliterating the offending Dog ears and nostrils with vicious strokes of his thoughts.

The Dog-shape was out. Absolutely. Such

appalling sharpness of senses might be fine for a Hunter such as Ger—he probably gloried in them. But another moment of such impressions would have driven Pid the Pilot mad.

What now? He lay in the bush and thought about it, while gradually his mind threw off the last effects of the dizzying sensory assault.

He looked at the gate. The Men standing there evidently hadn't noticed his fiasco. They were looking in another direction. ...a Man?

Well, it was worth a try.

STUDYING the Men at the gate, Pid carefully shaped himself into a facsimile—synthesis, actually, embodying one characteristic of that, another of this.

He emerged from the side of the bush opposite the gate, on his hands and knees. He sniffed the air, noting that the smells the Man-nostrils picked up weren't unpleasant at all. In fact, some of them were decidedly otherwise. It had just been the acuity of the Dog-nostrils, the number of smells they had detected and the near-brilliance with which they had done so, that had shocked him.

Also, the sounds weren't half so devastating. Only relatively close sounds stood out. All else was an undetailed whispering.

Evidently, Pid thought, it had been a long time since Men had been Hunters.

He tested his legs, standing up and taking a few clumsy steps. *Thud* of foot on ground. Drag the other leg forward in a heavy arc. *Thud.* Rocking from side to side, he marched back and forth behind the bush. His arms flapped as he sought balance. His head wobbled on its neck, until he remembered to hold it up. Head up, eyes down, he missed seeing a small rock. His heel turned on it. He sat down, hard.

The ankle hurt. Pid curled his Man-lips and crawled back into the bush.

The Man-shape was too unspeakably clumsy. It was offensive to plod one step at a time. Body held rigidly upright. Arms wobbling. There had been a deluge of sense-impressions in the Dog-shape; there was dull, stiff, half-alive inadequacy to the Man-shape.

Besides, it was dangerous, now that Pid thought it over, as well as distasteful. He couldn't control it properly. It wouldn't look right. Someone might question him. There was too much about Men he didn't—couldn't—know. The planting of the Displacer was too important a thing for him to fumble again. Only luck had kept him from being seen during the sensory onslaught.

The Displacer in his body pouch pulsed and tugged, urging him to be on his way toward the distant reactor room.

Grimly, Pid let out the last breath he had taken with his Man-lungs, and dissolved the lungs.

What shape to takes?

Again he studied the gate, the Men standing beside it, the building beyond in which was the all-important reactor.

A small shape was needed. A fast one. An unobtrusive one.

He lay and thought.

The bush rustled above him. A small brown shape had fluttered down to light on a twig. It hopped to another twig; twittering. Then it fluttered off in a flash, and was gone.

That, Pid thought, was it.

A SPARROW that was not a Sparrow rose from the bush a few moments later. An observer would have seen it circle the bush, diving, hedgehopping, even looping, as if practicing all maneuvers possible to Sparrows.

Pid tensed his shoulder muscles, inclined his wings. He slipped off to the right, approached the bush at what seemed breakneck speed, though he knew this was only because of his small size. At the last second he lifted his tail. Not quite quickly enough. He swooped up and over the top of the bush, but his legs brushed the top leaves, his beak went down, and he stumbled in air for a few feet back-forward.

He blinked beady eyes as if at a challenge. Back toward the bush at a fine clip, again up and over. This time cleanly.

He chose a tree. Zoomed into its network of branches, wove a web of flight, working his way around and around the trunk, over and under branches that flashed before him, through crotches with no more than a feather's-breath to spare.

At last he rested on a low branch, and found himself chirping in delight.

The tree extruded a feeler from the branch he sat on, and touched his wings and tail.

"Interesting," said the tree. "I'll have to try that shape some time."

Ilg.

"Traitor," hissed Pid, growing a mouth in his chest to hiss it, and then he did something that caused Ilg to exclaim in outrage.

Pid flew out of the woods. Over the underbrush and across the open space toward the gate.

This body would do the trick!

This body would do anything!

He rose, in a matter of a few Sparrow heartbeats, to an altitude of a hundred feet. From here the gate, the Men, the building were small, sharp shapes against a green-brown mat. Pid found that he could see not only with unaccustomed clarity, but with a range of vision that astonished him. To right and to left he could see far into the hazy blue of the sky, and the higher he rose the farther he could see.

He rose higher.

The Displacer pulsed, reminding him of the job he had to do.

HE stiffened his wings and glided, regretfully putting aside his desires to experiment with this wonderful shape, at least for the present. After he planted the Displacer, he would go off by himself for a while and do it just a little more—somewhere where Ilg and Ger would not see him—before the Grom Army arrived and the invasion began.

He felt a tiny twinge of guilt, as he circled. It was Evil to want to keep this alien flying shape any longer than was absolutely necessary to the performance of his duty. It was a device of the Shapeless One—

But what had Ilg said? *All Grom are born Shapeless.* It was true. Grom children were amorphous, until old enough to be instructed in the caste-shape of their ancestors.

Maybe it wasn't *too* great a sin to alter your Shape, then—just once in a long while. After all, one must be fully aware of the nature of Evil in order to meaningfully reject it.

He had fallen lower in circling. The Displacer pulse had strengthened. For some reason it irritated him. He drove higher on strong wings, circled again. Air rushed past him—a smooth, whispering flow, pierced by his beak, streaming invisibly past his sharp eyes, moving along his body in tiny turbulences that moved his feathers against his skin.

It occurred to him—or rather struck him with considerable force—that he was satisfying a longing of his Pilot Caste that went far deeper than Piloting.

He drove powerfully with his wings, felt tonus across his back, shot forward and up. He thought of the controls of his ship. He imagined flowing into them, becoming part of them, as he had so often done—and for the first time in his life the thought failed to excite him.

No machine could compare with this!

What he would give to have wings of his own!

...Get from my sight, Shapeless One!

The Displacer must be planted, activated. All Grom depended on him.

He eyed the building, far below. He would pass over it. The Displacer would tell him which window to enter—which window was so near the reactor that he could do his job before the Men even knew he was about.

He started to drop lower, and the Hawk struck.

IT had been above him. His first inkling of danger was the sharp pain of talons in his back, and the stunning blow of a beak across his head.

Dazed, he let his back go Shapeless. His body-substance flowed from the grasp of the talons. He dropped a dozen feet and resumed Sparrow-shape, hearing an astonished squawk from the attacker.

He banked, and looked up. The Hawk was eyeing him.

Talons spread again. The sharp beak gaped. The Hawk swooped.

Pid had to fight as a Bird, naturally. He was four hundred feet above the ground.

So he became an impossibly deadly Bird.

He grew to twice the size of the Hawk. He grew a foot-long beak with a double razor's edge. He grew talons like six-inch scimitars. His eyes gleamed a red challenge.

The Hawk broke flight, squalling in alarm. Frantically, tail down and widespread, it thundered its wings and came to a dead stop six feet from Pid.

Looking thoughtfully at Pid, it allowed itself to plummet. It fell a hundred feet, spread its wings, stretched its neck and flew off so hastily that its wings became blurs.

Pid saw no reason to pursue it.

Then, after a moment, he did.

He glided, keeping the Hawk in sight, thoughts racing, feeling the newness, the power, the wonder of Freedom of Shape.

Freedom…

He did not want to give it up.

The bird-shape was wondrous. He would experiment with it. Later, he might tire of it for a time and assume another—a crawling or running shape, or even a swimming one. The possibilities for excitement, for adventure, for fulfillment and simple sensual pleasure were endless!

Freedom of Shape was—obviously, now that you thought on it—the Grom birthright. And the caste-system was artificial—obviously. A device for political and priestly benefit—obviously.

Go away, Shapeless One… this does not concern you.

He rose to a thousand feet, two thousand, three. The Displacer's pulse grew feebler and finally vanished.

At four thousand feet he released it and watched it spin downward, vanish into a cloud.

Then he set out after the Hawk, which was now only a very small dot on the horizon. He would find out how the Hawk had broken flight as it had—skidded on air—how he wanted to do that too! There were so many things he wanted to learn about flying. In a week, he thought, he should be able to duplicate all the skill that millenia had evolved into Birds. Then his new life would really begin.

He became a torpedo-shape with huge wings, and sped after the Hawk.

The Hour of Battle

As one of the Guardian ships protecting Earth, the crew had a problem to solve. Just how do you protect a race from an enemy who can take over a man's mind without seeming effort or warning?

"That hand didn't move, did it?" Edwardson asked, standing at the port, looking at the stars.

"No," Morse said. He had been staring fixedly at the Attison Detector for over an hour. Now he blinked three times rapidly, and looked again. "Not a millimeter."

"I don't think it moved either," Cassel added, from behind the gunfire panel. And that was that. The slender black hand of the indicator rested unwaveringly on zero. The ship's guns were ready, their black mouths open to the stars. A steady hum filled the room. It came from the Attison Detector, and the sound was reassuring. It reinforced the fact that the Detector was attached to all the other Detectors, forming a gigantic network around Earth.

"Why in hell don't they come?" Edwardson asked, still looking at the stars. "Why don't they hit?"

"Aah, shut up," Morse said. He had a tired, glum

look. High on his right temple was an old radiation burn, a sunburst of pink scar tissue. From a distance it looked like a decoration.

"I just wish they'd come," Edwardson said. He returned from the port to his chair, bending to clear the low metal ceiling. "Don't you wish they'd come?" Edwardson had the narrow, timid face of a mouse; but a highly intelligent mouse. One that cats did well to avoid.

"Don't you?" he repeated.

The other men didn't answer. They had settled back to their dreams, staring hypnotically at the Detector face.

"They've had enough time," Edwardson said, half to himself.

Cassel yawned and licked his lips. "Anyone want to play some gin?" he asked, stroking his beard. The beard was a memento of his undergraduate days. Cassel maintained he could store almost fifteen minutes worth of oxygen in its follicles. He had never stepped into space unhelmeted to prove it.

Morse looked away, and Edwardson automatically watched, the indicator. This routine had been drilled into them, branded into their subconscious. They would as soon have cut their throats as leave the indicator unguarded.

"Do you think they'll come soon?" Edwardson asked, his brown rodent's eyes on the indicator. The men didn't answer him. After two months together in space their conversational powers were exhausted. They weren't interested in Cassel's undergraduate days, or in Morse's conquests.

They were bored to death even with their own thoughts and dreams, bored with the attack they expected momentarily.

"Just one thing *I'd* like to know," Edwardson said, sliding with ease into an old conversational gambit. "How far can they do it?"

They had talked for weeks about the enemy's telepathic range, but they always returned to it.

As professional soldiers, they couldn't help but speculate on the enemy and his weapons. It was their shoptalk.

"Well," Morse said wearily, "Our Detector network covers the system out beyond Mars' orbit."

"Where we sit," Cassel said, watching the indicators now that the others were talking.

"They might not even know we have a detection unit working," Morse said, as he had said a thousand times.

"Oh, stop," Edwardson said, his thin face twisted in scorn. "They're telepathic. They must have read every bit of stuff in Everset's mind."

"Everset didn't know we had a detection unit," Morse said, his eyes returning to the dial. "He was captured before we had it."

"Look," Edwardson said, "They ask him, 'Boy, what would you do if you knew a telepathic race was coming to take over Earth? How would you guard the planet?'"

"Idle speculation," Cassel said. "Maybe Everset

didn't think of this."

"He thinks like a man, doesn't he? Everyone agreed on this defense. Everset would, too."

"Sillogistic," Cassel murmured. "Very shaky."

"I sure wish he hadn't been captured," Edwardson said.

"It could have been worse," Morse put in, his face sadder than ever. "What if they'd captured *both* of them?"

"I wish they'd come," Edwardson said.

Richard Everset and C. R. Jones had gone on the first interstellar flight. They had found an inhabited planet in the region of Vega. The rest was standard procedure.

A flip of the coin had decided it. Everset went down in the scouter, maintaining radio contact with Jones, in the ship.

The recording of that contact was preserved for all Earth to hear…

"Just met the natives," Everset said. "Funny looking bunch. Give you the physical description later."

"Are they trying to talk to you?" Jones asked, guiding the ship in a slow spiral over the planet.

"No. Hold it. Well I'm damned! They're telepathic! How do you like that?"

"Great," Jones said. "Go on."

"Hold it. Say, Jonesy, I don't know as I like these boys. They haven't got nice minds. Brother!"

"What is it?" Jones asked, lifting the ship a little higher.

"Minds! These bastards are power-crazy. Seems they've hit all the systems around here, looking for someone to—"

"Yeh?"

"I've got that a bit wrong," Everset said pleasantly. "They are not so bad."

Jones had a quick mind, suspicious nature and good reflexes. He set the accelerator for all the G's he could take, lay down on the floor and said, "Tell me more."

"Come on down," Everset said, in violation of every law of spaceflight. "These guys are all right. As a matter of fact, they're the most marvelous—"

That was where the recording ended, because Jones was pinned to the floor by twenty G's acceleration as he boosted the ship to the level needed for the C--jump.

He broke three ribs getting home, but he got there.

A telepathic species was on the march. What was Earth going to do about it?

A lot of speculation necessarily clothed the bare bones of Jones' information. Evidently the species could take over a mind with ease. With Everset, it seemed that they had insinuated their thoughts into his, delicately altering his previous convictions. They had possessed him with remarkable ease.

How about Jones? Why hadn't they taken him? Was distance a factor? Or hadn't they been prepared for the suddenness of his departure?

One thing was certain. Everything Everset knew, the enemy knew. That meant they knew where Earth was, and how defenseless the planet was to their form of attack.

It could be expected that they were on their way.

Something was needed to nullify their tremendous advantage. But what sort of something? What armor is there against thought? How do you dodge a wavelength?

Pouch-eyed scientists gravely consulted their periodic tables.

And how do you know when a man has been possessed? Although the enemy was clumsy with Everset, would they continue to be clumsy? Wouldn't they learn?

Psychologists tore their hair and bewailed the absence of an absolute scale for humanity.

Of course, something had to be done at once. The answer, from a technological planet, was a technological one. Build a space fleet and equip it with some sort of a detection-fire network.

This was done in record time. The Attison Detector was developed, a cross between radar and the electroencephalograph. Any alteration from the typical-human brain wave pattern of the occupants of a Detector-equipped ship would boost the indicator around the dial. Even a bad dream or a case of indigestion would jar it.

It seemed probable that any attempt to take over a human mind would disturb something. There had to be a point of interaction, somewhere.

That was what the Attison Detector was supposed to detect. Maybe it would.

The spaceships, three men to a ship, dotted space between Earth and Mars, forming a gigantic sphere with Earth in the center.

Tens of thousands of men crouched behind gunfire panels, watching the dials on the Attison Detector.

The unmoving dials.

"Do you think I could fire a couple of bursts?" Edwardson asked, his fingers on the gunfire button. "Just to limber the guns?"

"Those guns don't need limbering," Cassel said, stroking his beard. "Besides, you'd throw the whole fleet into a panic."

"Cassel," Morse said, very quietly. "Get your hand off your beard."

"Why should I?" Cassel asked.

"Because," Morse answered, almost in a whisper, "I am about to ram it right down your fat throat."

Cassel grinned and tightened his fists. "Pleasure," he said. "I'm tired of looking at that scar of yours." He stood up.

"Cut it," Edwardson said wearily. "Watch the birdie."

"No reason to, really," Morse said, leaning back. "There's an alarm bell attached." But he looked at the dial.

"What if the bell doesn't work?" Edwardson asked.

"What if the dial is jammed? How would you like something cold slithering into your mind?"

"The dial'll work," Cassel said. His eyes shifted from Edwardson's face to the motionless indicator.

"I think I'll sack in," Edwardson said.

"Stick around," Cassel said, "Play you some gin."

"All right." Edwardson found and shuffled the greasy cards, while Morse took a turn glaring at the dial.

"I sure wish they'd come," he said.

"Cut," Edwardson said, handing the pack to Cassel.

"I wonder what our friends look like," Morse said, watching the dial.

"Probably remarkably like us," Edwardson said, dealing the cards. Cassel picked them up one by one, slowly, as if he hoped something interesting would be under them.

"They should have given us another man," Cassel said. "We could play bridge."

"I don't play bridge," Edwardson said.

"You could learn."

""Why didn't we send a task force?" Morse asked, "Why didn't we bomb their planet?"

"Don't be dumb," Edwardson said. "We'd lose any ship we sent. Probably get them back at us, possessed and firing."

"Knock with nine," Cassel said.

"I don't give a good damn if you knock with a thousand," Edwardson said gaily. "How much do I owe you now?"

"Three million five hundred and eight thousand and ten dollar's."

"I sure wish they'd come," Morse said.

"Want me to write a check?"

"Take your time. Take until next week:"

"Someone should reason with the bastards," Morse said, looking out the port. Cassel immediately looked at the dial.

"I just thought of something," Edwardson said.

"Yeh?"

"I bet it feels horrible to have your mind grabbed," Edwardson said. "I bet it's awful."

"You'll know when it happens," Cassel said.

"Did Everset?"

"Probably. He just couldn't do anything about it."

"My mind feels fine," Cassel said. "But the first one of you guys starts acting queer—watch out."

They all laughed.

"Well," Edwardson said, "I'd sure like a chance to reason with them. This is stupid."

"Why not?" Cassel asked.

"You mean go out and meet *them?"*

"Sure," Cassel said. "We're doing no good sitting here."

"I should think we could do something," Edwardson said slowly. "After all, they're not invincible. They're reasoning beings."

Morse punched a course on the ship's tape, then looked up.

"You think we should contact the command? Tell

them what we're doing?"

"No!" Cassel said, and Edwardson nodded in agreement. "Red tape. We'll just go out and see what we can do. If they won't talk, we'll blast 'em out of space."

"Look!"

Out of the port they could see the red flare of a reaction engine; the next ship in their sector, speeding forward.

"They must have got the same idea," Edwardson said.

"Let's get there first," Cassel said. Morse shoved the accelerator in and they were thrown back in their seats.

"That dial hasn't moved yet, has it?" Edwardson asked, over the clamor of the Detector alarm bell.

"Not a move out of it," Cassel said, looking at the dial with its indicator slammed all the way over to the highest notch.

We Are Alone

They came not as conqueror or pilferers, but seekers of companionable intelligences...

HAD THE LANDING been on Earth, or any of the planets of Sol system, Magglio would have guided the ship down with studied, offhand ease. But since they were out in the big, unknown galaxy, somewhere around Altair, he gripped the throttle in a bonecrushing embrace, ready to pour on the power if anything happened. Anything—what?

Perspiration poured down his thin, tight face as he remembered the spaceman's legends he had laughed at. Mirage-planets, where landing distances are dangerously deceptive; living planets, planets of death. It didn't ease his mind any to know that none of these wonders had ever been discovered, since theirs was the first ship to venture into interstellar space. Such might be there—and that was enough.

Salzman, the navigator, was trying the impossible stunt of reading six dials with one eye, while focusing the other on the red planet rushing up to meet them. He had a hand on the auxiliary power control, in case something happened to the main drive—or to

Magglio. If he had had a third eye, it would have been watching Oliver, the engineer.

Oliver was manning the big atomic cannon, in case of attack. He had it centered on the planet, all safeties off, and his finger was dangerously taut on the instigator switch. He had partially convinced himself during the last few days, that an alien space armada was waiting for them, hovering just out of sight around the curve of the planet. Should he fire, just in hopes of scaring them off?

As they came nearer, Salzman could make out the rolling contour of the land: the reel of the planet resolved itself into a forest of pink, red and purple. Scattered through the forest were black dots, which grew into towns and villages as they screamed down through the thickening atmosphere. He noted their positions automatically; he was still too busy reading dials for them to register properly on his consciousness.

Magglio had perspiration in his right eye, but he didn't dare release a control to wipe it, or even to blink. The surface of the planet was looming beneath them, stretched as far as he could see. Perhaps it would split into a gigantic mouth, like the kidders on Pluto-base always said. Or perhaps—he tightened at the controls, waiting for something to happen.

The ship screamed through the atmosphere as it decelerated—

—but on the whole it was an uneventful landing.

Magglio regained control of himself, found an open patch and set the ship down in an elegant skid. Oliver talked himself out of his fears long enough to switch the cannon over to safety. Shakily, Salzman raised his hand and looked at the imprint of the throttle across his palm. It was all right, no hordes of attackers, no monsters—yet; no seventy-foot dragons or green-eyed ghouls. Only the red forest, a trifle singed where the ship ploughed across the treetops, but still peaceful.

After a moment's silence they began pounding each other on the back, shouting from sheer release of anxiety. Salzman picked up little Magglio, grinned in his face, and tossed him to Oliver. The engineer grunted when he caught him, looked puzzled for a moment, then decided his dignity was shot for the rest of the trip anyhow, and tossed him back to Salzman.

"Easy, you apes," Magglio said, regaining his feet and smoothing back his hair, "or I'll turn you over to the Ufangies."

SALZMAN mussed the pilot's hair again, grinning. He knew all about the Ufangies. They were a tribe of orange and black flying reptiles with fins for underwater work who subsisted solely on human eyeballs.

They were also an interesting example of legend making, a part of the complex 'natural' history of space. The first men on Mars had been disappointed at not finding any intelligent life, so they spun yarns about Visties and Serbens, and scared grown men with tales of what was lurking on the Jovian moons. The Jovian explorers didn't find any intelligence either—monsterous or human—so they added the eyeball-eating Ufangies, and pushed them to Saturn.

Now that the solar system was Earth's backyard—albeit a wild and lonely one—the horrors had supposedly fled to deep space. They might, the stories ran, be lurking anywhere, ready to pounce upon the unwary spaceman.

Salzman wondered just how much Magglio believed in the things; he knew that the pilot wore a little charm on his wrist specifically designed to ward off aliens. Or, for that matter, how much Oliver believed in the hordes of attackers waiting to blast their ship.

Or how much he himself believed in them. Salzman realized that he wasn't immune, even though he knew that, in essence, all the stories said the same thing—there *is* intelligent life out there, just a bit farther than we've gone. That, he knew, was Earth's hope. *Any* sort of intelligence, just so that we're not alone in the immensity of space.

They had landed early in the morning, and by the time they were organized for land reconnaissance it was noon. Salzman and Oliver finished the last of the atmosphere tests, while Magglio read a comic book he had smuggled on board.

"It's O.K.," Salzman said, squeezing into the operating chamber. "Breathable, without enough deviation from Earth-normal to matter. Anyone show up?"

Magglio shook his head. He had been watching the front vision plate for any sign of curious natives.

"Then we'll visit them. Full armor, sidearms, breather and radio."

"Who you gonna talk to on the radio?" Magglio asked, then immediately said, "Oh, no!"

"Yes," Salzman replied, smiling pleasantly as he unpacked a blaster. "You'll cover us."

"No," Magglio said. "I wanna explore. I'm a hero too, see?"

"No," Salzman said, and that ended it. "I'll take you out tomorrow, if everything goes right. But now—full security."

* * *

Salzman and Oliver moved out through the hatch and climbed down the ladder curving around the side of the ship. Oliver was first; he put his foot down gingerly, half expecting the earth to open up under it, even though the ship was resting solidly enough.

When they were both on the ground they waved to Magglio, and moved toward the forest. They were breathing the air of the planet, but aside from their faces, they were completely enclosed in light, radiation-proof armor.

"Let me lead," Salzman said to Oliver. The engineer was fingering his sidearm nervously as they approached the forest. Following the rough direction he had noticed from the air, Salzman started toward the nearest town.

In the forest both men were prepared for any eventuality. Oliver kept his hand on the butt of his blaster, preparing himself for savages to come swarming out from behind the trees. Salzman, with more imagination, was ready for things to come dropping out of the sky, thrusting through the ground, materializing suddenly out of thin air, and a dozen other possibilities, simultaneously or one by one.

The wind rustled the red branches; nothing happened.

THE TOWN turned out to be a small village, and a silent one. Its wide, stone-paved streets were bare. Not an animal showed itself, not a bird flew overhead. Weapons ready, the two men explored one of the houses. It was built of white stone and pink woods, and showed a high degree of craftsmanship. Within there were chairs and couches, tables and stands…

"They must be humans!" Oliver cried, when the shape of the furniture struck him. He started to sit down, then leaped up. "Might be booby trapped," he muttered eyeing the chair accusingly.

"It would be more logical to booby trap the doorway," Salzman commented. He lowered himself into the chair. Oliver released his breath when it didn't explode.

"Built for something about our size," he said. Suddenly, irrationally, he felt like Goldilocks, sitting in the little bear's chair—the one that fitted just right. He laughed out loud, but didn't bother explaining to Oliver. The literal-minded engineer would think he had cracked up.

They walked to the next room, separated by an arched doorway, and stopped short. On the walls were paintings—with human subjects!

"Oh brother!" Oliver shouted. "They *are* human! Humans!" He slapped Salzman on the back so hard he almost stumbled into a wall.

"But where in hell are they?" Salzman asked, moving quickly from painting to painting. The subjects were blondes, brunettes and redheads, male and female. They seemed entirely human, except for a pale, ethereal look that could have been the artist's technique.

They hurried on through the house, barely noting the other rooms. Urns, garments, vases, writing instruments, all would be of interest later. Right now they wanted to find people.

In the rear of the house they found a kitchen, with food still hot. The wood fire beneath the pots was smouldering feebly. "Someone sure left in a hurry," Salzman said.

Quickly they searched five more houses, and found them about the same. Some of the others were less orderly. Clothes were strewn around, sandals left in the middle of rooms. In two houses food had been spilled over the floor.

"They left in a *hell* of a hurry," Oliver said finally, as they stood in the street.

"That's for sure," Salzman said. He pushed back his hood and scratched his blond, balding head. He wasn't sure what to do next. His orders from the Foundation had been general. To survey the planets of a number of G-76 suns, in a specific sector, looking for Earth-type planets. If he found an inhabited one, to make contact with the natives if possible, and if they could be approached peacefully.

He wasn't sure if this constituted unpeaceful behavior or not. Oliver trailed behind him as he walked slowly up the street, wondering why the inhabitants could have fled.

"I suppose they fled because of us," Oliver said, paralleling his trend of thought.

"Probably. These people are civilized, but not necessarily sophisticated. Who knows what they thought when they saw this ball of fire appear in the skies? The devil descending to the earth, perhaps."

"That's by *our* standards," Oliver objected, "how do we know they have superstitions of that sort?"

"We don't. But they're similar to us in development, which argues a like nervous system. Like inventions argue a like mentality. I know that's dubious, but I'll keep it for a working hypothesis until I find something better."

"I wonder why they didn't leave a rear-guard," Oliver mused. "Or arrange an ambush of some sort. Just leaving their homes that way… Well, now what?"

"We track them," Salzman said, coming to a decision. "We show them what we look like. We make peaceful gestures, and try to get them to talk."

Oliver nodded, and they started to the other end of the village.

THE UNDERBRUSH was trampled and torn, showing the direction in which the exodus had gone. They had no trouble following it; it was big enough to have been made by a bulldozer. On the way, Salzman called Magglio and brought him up to date.

"If you capture a small blonde," Magglio told them, his voice crackly in the earphones, "throw her over your shoulder and bring her back to me. But if they're a tribe of twenty-foot Serbens, remember, I warned you!"

"Right," Salzman said cheerfully, and signed off.

As they moved through the forest, something kept nagging at Salzman's mind, bothering him. He looked around at the big, silent red trees, the slightly waving branches. Nothing wrong there. But the feeling continued, just beyond recognition. He glanced at Oliver. The big engineer was plodding along beside him, kicking up dirt with his boots. He couldn't quite put his finger on it—and then he had it.

"Notice something funny?" he asked Oliver.

"What?" Oliver said, feeling automatically for his blaster.

"No animals. No birds. No nothing."

"Perhaps they haven't evolved," Oliver said, after due thought.

"They must have," Salzman told him. "The humans and plants can't be the only things on this planet. Nature was never *that* selective."

"They're hiding, then. Timid, like people."

Salzman nodded, but that didn't seem to cover it. The forest was too quiet; it seemed to be waiting for something to happen. His imagination started to play tricks on him again, weaving fantastic but plausible reasons for everything. Perhaps the forest is one big entity, he thought, and the animals and humans are symbiotes. Nuts, he told himself. Why did they build villages then?

They walked on, sweating copiously inside their plastic armor, following the spoor of the villagers. In an hour they were out of one part of the forest, following the trail across a narrow valley. It tightened, climbing between stubby mountains, heading steadily up. Both men were winded, but they pushed on. Finally they rounded a bend in the trail and found themselves facing a blockade. It was made of piled branches and rocks, and stood about twelve feet high. On either side of it were smooth towering boulders.

"We could blast it down," Oliver said.

"Hmm." Salzman touched the nearest boulder wall, then glanced at the sun. It was low on the horizon, and long shadows were stretching across the red land.

"Too late." He flicked on his radio. "Magglio?"

"Yeah?"

"Haul out the scouter and bring us in. No blondes today." He signed off and turned to Oliver. "We'll try another village tomorrow. I don't think it'll be too hard to find s*omeone*."

* * *

Five days later, Salzman decided he had been too optimistic. With the scouter rocket-plane they covered every village and town in a fifty-mile radius—a total of twelve. In each, it was the same. Deserted streets, empty houses—with still-burning fires to show that the natives had detected them minutes before they arrived. By air they caught tantalizing glimpses of human shapes diving into concealment in the red forest. When they landed even the glimpse was gone.

On the fourth day they returned to the first village. It showed unmistakable signs of having been reinhabitated while they were away. But again, the natives had managed to find out just when they were coming, and to get out perhaps half an hour before the Earthmen arrived.

The remaining hours of the fourth day were spent in the village, looking for some sign of electrical equipment. It seemed that the natives had some system of keeping informed on their exact movements, almost down to the minute. But the only mechanical device in the village was a wheel. Smoke signals and drums were obviously out. Magglio suggested carrier pigeons, but they still hadn't seen any birds.

Before sunrise on the fifth day they took the scouter to the far side of the continent. Oliver estimated they covered four thousand miles in something like five and a half hours. They roared down to a village full-jet, decelerating so rapidly in the last few hundred feet that they were almost plastered against the scouter's walls. All in all, from the time they appeared as a dot in the sky to the time they landed in the middle of the village, not more than three minutes could have elapsed.

But the natives had had their usual fifteen-minute-plus head start.

THEY DIDN'T stop to figure out how, this time. In line with a plan they had arranged the night before, Salzman and Oliver set out after the trail of the fleeing natives. Magglio took the scouter up again and circled around, trying to spot the bunch.

"They're about a mile and a half ahead," Magglio's voice said, sharp in the earphones. "Bear a little more right—that's good!"

Salzman grunted as he climbed the mountain slope. He paused on a ledge and gave Oliver a hand up. The weeks in free-fall hadn't been very good for their muscles, he thought. In the sky he could see the little scouter Magglio was piloting, hovering overhead. Stretched beneath them was red forest, broken here and there by ragged mountains.

"They're still going in a straight line," Magglio told them. A couple hundred of them, heading toward another section of forest."

The two men moved on. It seemed to Salzman that two grown men should be able to move faster than an entire village—with old men and women, and children. But they seemed unable to overtake the natives, or even come close.

"Hey chief," Magglio radioed. "I spotted a way you can cut them off. Take a right at the next cut—"

Another hour passed as they labored through the winding shortcut. Magglio's ship hovered overhead, careful not to give away their position. The sun beat down on the plastic as they scrambled over rocks and between trees.

"This is a hell of a note," Oliver grumbled. He had

run out of swear words, having called the natives everything he could think of—except human beings. "I could have stayed in Montana and done this. My lord, we push a tin can across sixteen light years of space, just to find someone not from Earth to talk to. We just went to be friends, and this suspicious bunch of—"

"Hey chief," Magglio called. "They must have spotted you! They're bearing away again, relative to your position!"

"Spotted us!" Salzman shouted into the earphone. "Again? How could they?"

"I don't know," Magglio's voice said in his ears. "I can swear not a person has left the main bunch."

"You sure there aren't a few of them you can't see?" Salzman asked, sitting down on the ground.

"Sure as sure," Magglio told him. "The forest is thin around here. I could spot a cat. As far as I… Chief, are you and Oliver sitting down?"

"Yes, why?"

"Because the whole bunch of them sat down a moment ago!" Magglio said.

Salzman jumped to his feet, pulled Oliver up, and started again on a run.

"They just got up again," Magglio told them. "They're running—now they've stopped—they're sitting again."

Salzman had sat down again.

"That ties it," he said to Oliver in a quiet voice. "Either they've got scanners built into every tree—or they're telepathic!"

Magglio picked them up in the scouter and brought them back to the ship. Oliver sat quietly, looking as though his best friend had kicked him in the teeth. Salzman was cursing steadily, beating one fist into his thigh. It was all he could do to keep from hitting Oliver or Magglio. To come so far, and find a pack of telepathic rabbits masquerading as human beings!

By the time they reached the ship he had regained his calm completely. He was determined to keep it from now on, no matter what happened. The trees could start running away, he felt, and he wouldn't be surprised any more.

AFTER SUPPER that evening the three men stretched out on the purple grass around the ship. They had discarded the plastic armor, since there was nothing to arm against, but kept their blasters as a safety measure.

"I noticed something else," Magglio told them. "I saw what looked like animals—they bolted like mad too, whenever you came inside of about a mile or two of them. Also a few birds. Not a living thing stayed less than a mile away."

"Everything's probably telepathic on this planet," Salzman said. "It ties in. But if they're telepathic—if they can read our minds—then why do they run? They know we're just here to establish communication." He paused. "Have you been thinking about their women?" he accused Magglio.

"Who me?" Magglio was highly indignant. "Not on

your life. I been thinking about my girlfriend at home; I'm faithful, see?"

"If they can read our minds," Salzman went on, more to himself than to the others, "then they know we want to be friends. We're not here to colonize, we're not going to rob them—since we can't carry five pounds extra weight on the ship. We're here, damn it, to bridge the gap between the stars. To *talk*. What's wrong with them?"

"Maybe they just want to be left alone," Oliver offered.

"Then why run? Why not ignore us? No, I think they must be afraid of something."

"Monsters," Magglio said.

"I thought of that—but not if they can read our minds. We're not angels, but our intentions are good." Salzman remained deep in thought, his head bent forward on his chest.

"Tomorrow," he said at last, "we're rounding up a native. I hadn't thought of the telepathy angle before, but I think this'll work." Briefly, he told them what they were to do.

"Now go to bed," he finished shortly.

*

In his bunk, Salzman tried to fit the pieces together. It was no use. But he was sure he could clear it up tomorrow. Once they could talk to the natives. Intelligent life! That was the important thing. He had been excited by the idea since childhood; otherwise he wouldn't be out in space, spending his manhood in a metal spheroid.

Sleep wouldn't come at once. Salzman rolled and tossed for an hour or more, trying to get comfortable. Finally he dozed off fitfully, thinking of Serbens and Visties. Magglio's Ufangies and Oliver's hordes of aliens.

He was in the forest. Only it had altered. Instead of the soft reds, pinks and purples of the day, everything was a bloody crimson. Blood dripped from the leaves, and the roots and branches oozed blood. He was being chased, by a horrible mangled thing that screamed and moaned and crashed through the underbrush after him, now racing upright on two legs, now down on all fours like a dog, and constantly coming closer, until—he awoke, cursing.

"What's up?" Oliver asked, from the next bunk.

"Nightmare," Salzman answered. "Overexcited, I guess." It annoyed him. It was his first dream in years, and his first nightmare since child hood. Were Magglio's monster stories getting him down, he wondered?

Finally sleep came again.

THE NEXT morning was as hot as the previous ones. The men piled into the scouter quickly.

"Think pleasant thoughts," Magglio reminded them mockingly, as he poured on the jets. "Think about having a pint of beer with the chief's daughter. If they've got a chief, and if he's got beer and a daughter."

"No wonder they're running, if they're reading *your* thoughts," Oliver said. Magglio grinned and winked.

Salzman watched the red forest pass beneath them, they sped toward the area he had selected. He wondered what he would say when they rounded a native up. What right had they, to force these people out of their homes, run them through the woods like foxes, track them down and make them talk?

What right, he asked himself—plenty of right! They had crossed sixteen light years of space to make contact with intelligent life. All Earth was waiting to hear the results of their mission. They had given their lives to the job, as a labor of love. What right—why, the right of intelligence—to make contact with other intelligences, to exchange information to better both races.

And the silly fools ran like stampeded cattle, he thought bitterly. Wasn't there a brave man among them?

"Here we are," Magglio said as they shot over a village. "And there they are."

"Let's round them up," Salzman said tightly.

The scouter dipped over the treetops, then swung low over the natives. They were running in blind panic, and Salzman could see that the men were racing ahead of the women and children, in a hysterical effort to escape.

"Land Oliver in front of them." Salzman said. The scouter passed the crowd, and, a few hundred yards further, Oliver parachuted out.

Immediately the natives reversed, and started in the

opposite direction.

"Now me on the flank" Salzman said. He parachuted out. Spilling air out of his chute he landed in a clear space. Quickly he chucked the harness and started forward.

"I'm landing on the other side," Magglio said over the earphones. "We've got them on three sides, and they've got a sheer wall to their backs." This was the maneuver they had planned at night. The scouter dipped and swung, herding the natives like sheep. Salzman ran, tearing his way through the underbrush, toward the crowd. He could hear them, panting and moaning, only a few hundred yards ahead.

As he ran he cleared his sidearm—just in case.

Suddenly he came to an abrupt halt.

"Oliver—Magglio—over to me!" he called over the radio, "One of them's coming!"

The native staggered toward Salzman, slipping and falling, and picking himself up again. He didn't resemble any of the portraits—not now. As he got closer, Salzman could see that the man's face was twisted and contorted; his body was jerking uncontrollably, in a series of nerve and muscle spasms that threatened to tear his bones apart. His skin was pallid and splotched in spots, cancerous looking. He resembled a corpse more than a living creature.

Magglio and Oliver came up abruptly, then stopped, a few paces behind Salzman.

Salzman felt something *itch* his mind, as the native

came up to ten feet of him. Then, when it stopped, Salzman felt a thought.

"Go away."

"Why?" Salzman asked out loud.

"You are killing our minds. Take anything, but go away."

"We come as friends," Salzman said soothingly. "We mean no harm, we did not mean to break any of your taboos. If you are sick we have medicine on our ship—we can cure—"

The native slumped to his knees. *"You are making our minds crazy."*

"Good Lord!" Oliver gasped. "Could we have brought some disease?"

"No," the native thought at them. *"It is your thoughts. They are powerful, evil thoughts—too horrible to stand. Your minds have—diseases—which we catch, if we come into contact—"*

"Thoughts?" Salzman echoed. He looked back at Oliver and Magglio. Was it possible that one of them had a pathological mind? Could he have it? Quickly he discounted the possibility. They had been screened too carefully for sanity and stability before leaving Earth. Nothing like that could have slipped by.

The native was losing strength, but he caught the thought.

"No," he said. *"All your thoughts. The thoughts behind."*

Behind. Now what could that mean, Salzman wondered, staring at the panting native on the ground.

"You are monsters," the native's weakening thought said. *"You have hideous things in your minds. Things which*

eat eyeballs—horrible terrors—and other things."

"Space legends!" Oliver gasped. "You've got us all wrong, friend. Those are only—"

"No!" the native thought angrily. *"Not those. The things behind! The horrors in the night. Those secret things that you do not yourselves think about, for they would drive you insane too, and kill you. The blood-red forest"*

Salzman had guessed it a few seconds back, but he didn't want to believe it. Now he had no choice. "He means our subconscious minds," he said heavily.

"Yes," the native said. *"That is the right thought. The things you cannot let yourselves think about, for they would make you sick. But we—we* must *think them, when you are near."*

He tried to tell them something else, but his weakening control snapped. For a moment there was nothing—and then a babbling lunacy of thoughts, driving the Earthmen back by their sheer intensity. There were all Magglio's monsters, screaming and gibbering, coming out of that mad mind. The Ufangies were there, orange and black and scaly, and Oliver's hordes of invaders swept on, hacking their way through the bleeding forest that Salzman had dreamed of, led by a faceless thing that screamed its hate for all living creatures. And behind them, from deeper in the Earthmen's minds, were tremendous, slimy creatures compounded of all the insecurities and fears that infect young boys growing up in Earth's superstition-infested darknesses. The things that crawl out of the black mouths of alleys were there, and the horrors that grin from open closet doors at night, when the family is asleep. And behind that, from the deep in babies' memories, leering blindly—

The Earthmen ran, sobbing and tripping blindly, and madness pursued them all the way to the scouter. Magglio shoved the little ship viciously into the air, with Oliver still climbing through the doorway. Salzman managed to drag him the rest of the way in, as they roared up into the clean air.

FOR A WHILE it didn't seem as though Oliver was going to come around. He wouldn't talk or move, but just stared blankly into space. Lacking knowledge of psychiatry, Salzman tried a home remedy. He threw a pan of water in the engineer's face, then knocked him flat on his back. It was crude shock-therapy, but it worked.

"You O.K.?" Salzman asked.

"They couldn't let us get near them," Oliver said dully, "they couldn't stand our monsterous, horrible thoughts—the ones we don't dare think out loud." He pulled himself to his feet, holding Salzman's arm for support. "Even the animals couldn't stand it."

"Forget it," Salzman said steadily. "It isn't our fault."

"Just think," Oliver went on in the same dull voice. "The glimpse we got of our subconscious was enough to jar our sanity, they got it full force."

"Forget it."

"I feel so dirty!"

"Shut up!" Magglio screamed.

The engineer looked blank for a moment, then tried to smile. Magglio whistled tunelessly as they prepared for takeoff. “Shall we try another G-type sun, chief? Another planet?”

“I wonder if we should,” Salzman said.

If you've enjoyed this book, you will not want to miss these terrific titles...

ARMCHAIR SCI-FI, FANTASY, & HORROR DOUBLE NOVELS, $12.95 each

D-1 **THE GALAXY RAIDERS** by William P. McGivern
SPACE STATION #1 by Frank Belknap Long

D-2 **THE PROGRAMMED PEOPLE** by Jack Sharkey
SLAVES OF THE CRYSTAL BRAIN by William Carter Sawtelle

D-3 **YOU'RE ALL ALONE** by Fritz Leiber
THE LIQUID MAN by Bernard C. Gilford

D-4 **CITADEL OF THE STAR LORDS** by Edmund Hamilton
VOYAGE TO ETERNITY by Milton Lesser

D-5 **IRON MEN OF VENUS** by Don Wilcox
THE MAN WITH ABSOLUTE MOTION by Noel Loomis

D-6 **WHO SOWS THE WIND...** by Rog Phillips
THE PUZZLE PLANET by Robert A. W. Lowndes

D-7 **PLANET OF DREAD** by Murray Leinster
TWICE UPON A TIME by Charles L. Fontenay

D-8 **THE TERROR OUT OF SPACE** by Dwight V. Swain
QUEST OF THE GOLDEN APE by Ivar Jorgensen and Adam Chase

D-9 **SECRET OF MARRACOTT DEEP** by Henry Slesar
PAWN OF THE BLACK FLEET by Mark Clifton.

D-10 **BEYOND THE RINGS OF SATURN** by Robert Moore Williams
A MAN OBSESSED by Alan E. Nourse

ARMCHAIR SCIENCE FICTION CLASSICS, $12.95 each

C-1 **THE GREEN MAN**
by Harold M. Sherman

C-2 **A TRACE OF MEMORY**
By Keith Laumer

ARMCHAIR MASTERS OF SCIENCE FICTION SERIES, $16.95 each

M-1 **MASTERS OF SCIENCE FICTION, Vol. One**
Bryce Walton—"Dark of the Moon" and other tales

M-2 **MASTERS OF SCIENCE FICTION, Vol. Two**
Jerome Bixby: "One Way Street" and other tales

Made in the USA
Lexington, KY
23 March 2014